THE MONET MURDERS

The last thing Jason West,
an ambitious young FBI special agent
with the Art Crime Team,
wants—or needs—is his uncertain and
unacknowledged romantic relationship
with irascible legendary
Behavioral Analysis Unit Chief
Sam Kennedy.

And it's starting to feel like Sam is not
thrilled with the idea either.

But personal feelings must be put aside
when Sam requests Jason's help to catch a
deranged killer targeting wealthy, upscale
art collectors. A killer whose calling card is
a series of grotesque paintings
depicting the murders.

THE MONET MURDERS
Art of Murder Book II
May 2017

Copyright (c) 2017 by Josh Lanyon

Cover by Johanna Ollila
Cover and book design by Kevin Burton Smith
Edited by Keren Reed, Dianne Thies

ISBN-13: 978-1-945802-17-1
ISBN-10: 1945802170

Published in the United States of America
JustJoshin Publishing, Inc.
www.joshlanyon.com

This is a work of fiction. Any resemblance to persons living or dead is entirely coincidental.

THE
MONET
MURDERS

ART OF MURDER BOOK II

Josh Lanyon

JUST JOSHIN'
PUBLISHING INC.

To the Catalina Gang. May you always have a drink in your glass and sand in your shoes.

Chapter One

"**E**merson Harley understood that the threat was not simply to the greatest cultural and artistic achievements of all time—the fascist forces of World War Two threatened civilization itself."

The speeches were well under way when his cell phone began to vibrate.

Having arrived late, Jason stood at the back of the sizeable audience crowding into the wide entrance hall of the California History Museum of Beverly Hills, but even so, he felt the disapproval radiating from that chunk of prime real estate at the front of the room, the holdings currently occupied by the West family—*his* family. How the hell they could possibly know he was even present, let alone failing to live up to *famille* expectation was a mystery, but after thirty-three years he was used to it.

Surreptitiously, he pulled his cell out for a quick look at the caller and felt a leap of pleasure. *Sam.*

Behavioral Analysis Unit Chief Sam Kennedy and he were, well, *involved.* That was maybe the best word for it.

All the same, he nearly shelved the call. Not that he didn't look forward to talking to Sam—God knows, it was a rare enough occurrence these days—but the dedication of a museum wing to your grandfather did kind of take precedence. Should, anyway.

Some instinct made him click Accept. He smiled in apology, edging his way through the crowd of black ties and evening dresses, stepping into the Ancient Americas room with its exhibition of pre-Columbian art and ceramics.

"Hey." Jason kept his voice down, but that "hey" seemed to whisper up and down the row of stony Olmec faces. It would be hard, maybe impossible, to put a collection like this together nowadays. Not only were artifacts of enormous cultural significance disappearing into private hands at a breathtaking rate, Native American activists often—and maybe rightly—blocked the excavation of human remains and artifacts as desecration of sacred space.

"Hey," Sam said crisply. "You're about to get called out to a crime scene. Homicide."

"Okay." This was a little weird. How would Sam, posted back at Quantico, know that? And why would he bother to inform Jason?

"I can't talk." Sam was still brusque, still speaking quietly, as though afraid of being overheard. That in itself was interesting. Not like Sam had ever given a damn about what anyone thought about anything. "I wanted you to have a heads-up. I'm on scene as well."

Jason's heart gave another of those disconcerting jumps. *Finally.* Same corner of the crime fighting universe at the same time. It had been... what? Massachusetts had been June, and it was now February. Eight months. Almost a year. It felt like a year.

"Got it." Jason was equally curt. Because he did get it. These days Sam was in a different league. When they'd met, Sam had been under a cloud, his career on the line. Now his reputation was restored, and his standing was pretty much unassailable. Jason, by contrast, remained a lowly field agent with the Art Crime Team. And though the Bureau did not have an official non-frat policy, discretion was part of the job description. Right there with *Fidelity, Bravery, Integrity.*

His phone alerted him to another incoming call.

"See you here." Sam disconnected.

Jason automatically clicked the incoming call. "West."

A cool, cultured voice said, "Agent West, this is ADC Ritchie."

After an astonished beat, he said politely, "Ma'am?" Like a phone call from the Assistant Director in Charge was a usual thing.

"I'm sorry to call you out on what I know is a special evening for you and your family, but we have a situation that could benefit from your particular expertise."

Jason said blankly, "Of course."

This kind of call—not that he had so many of this kind of call—typically came from Supervisory Special Agent George Potts, his squad supervisor at the very large and very powerful Los Angeles field office.

"We have a dead foreign national on—or, more exactly, *under*—Santa Monica pier. He appears to be a buyer for the Nacht Galerie in Berlin. Gil Hickok at LAPD is requesting our support. Also..." ADC Ritchie's tone changed indefinably. "BAU Chief Sam Kennedy seems to feel your participation in this investigation would be particularly helpful."

Translation: the ADC was as bewildered as Jason. Why the hell would the BAU butt into the investigation of the homicide of a German national—let alone requisition manpower from the local field office Art Crime Team?

Except...Detective Gil Hickok didn't just head LAPD's Art Theft Detail. He was basically the art cop for most of Southern California and had been for the last twenty years. Smaller forces like Santa Monica PD didn't keep their own art experts on the payroll; they relied on LAPD's resources. LAPD's two-man Art Theft Detail was the only such full-time municipal law enforcement unit in the United States. If Gil was requesting Jason's assistance, there was a good reason—beyond the fact that a murdered buyer from one of Germany's leading art galleries would naturally be of interest to Jason.

Attention now fully engaged, Jason was eager to get on site—and that had zero to do with the fact that Sam would be there.

He heard out Ritchie, who really had little to add beyond the initial information, and said, "I'm on my way."

Clicking off, he stepped into the arched doorway, scanning the crowd. All eyes were fastened on the short, stout man behind the lectern positioned at the front of the newly constructed hall, trying to cope with the piercing bursts of mic feedback punctuating his speech.

"In March 1945, Harley was named Deputy Chief of the MFAA Section under British Monuments Man Lt. Col. Geoffrey Webb. Stationed at SHAEF headquarters at Versailles and later in Frankfurt, Harley and Webb coordinated the operations of Monuments Men in the field as well as managing submitted field reports and planning future MFAA operations. Harley traveled extensively and at great personal peril across the

American Zone of Occupation in pursuit of looted works of art and cultural objects."

Correction. Not all eyes were fastened on museum curator Edward Howie. Jason's sister Sophie was watching for him.

Sophie, tall, dark, and elegant in a jade green Vera Wang halter gown, was married to Republican Congressman Clark Vincent, also in attendance. Clark tried to be in attendance anywhere the press might be. Sophie was the middle kid, but if she suffered from middle-child syndrome, it had manifested itself in rigorous overachievement and a general bossiness of anyone in her realm. She had seventeen years on Jason and considered him her pet project.

Jason held his phone up and shook his head, his expression that blend of apology and resolve all law enforcement officers perfected for such occasions. There were inevitably a lot of them. That was another part of the job description.

Sophie, who moonlighted as the family enforcer, expressed her displeasure through her eyebrows. She paid a lot of money for those brows, and they served her well. Right now they were looking Harley-Quinnish.

Jason tried to work a bit more *abject* into his silent apology—he was, in fact, sincerely sorry to miss the dedication, but if anyone would have understood, it was Grandpa Harley, who had missed more than a few family celebrations of his own while trying to save civilization from the Nazis. Sophie shook her head in disapproval and disappointment. But there was also resignation in that gesture, and Jason took that as permission for takeoff.

He jetted.

* * * * *

It took a fucking *forever* to find a place to park.

That was something they didn't ever show on TV or the movies: the detective having to park a mile away and hike to his crime scene. But it happened.

Especially when you were last man on the scene.

Santa Monica on a Sunday night—even in February—was a busy place. The one-hundred-year-old landmark pier was bustling with fun seekers, street vendors, and performance artists—even a few die-hard fishermen, poles in hand. As Jason reached the bottom of Colorado Avenue, he could see the glittering multicolored Ferris wheel churning leisurely through the heavy purple and pewter clouds. Little cars whizzed up and down the twinkling yellow loops of the rollercoaster.

The pier deck was filled, as were the lower lots barricaded by black and whites, their blue and red LED lights flashing in the night like sinister amusement-park rides. Jason had to park south of the pier and hike back along the mostly empty beach. As he walked past parked cars and the towering silhouettes of palm trees, he could see uniformed officers and crime-scene technicians in the distance, moving around beneath the crooked black shape of the pier. Flashlight beams darted like fireflies among the pylons. Small clutches of people stood short distances from each other, watching.

He reached the perimeter of the crime scene, flashed his tin, and got a few surprised looks from the unis. That probably had more to do with his formal dress—he hadn't had a chance to do more than grab his backup piece and replace his tux with his vest—than the Bureau being on the scene.

"The party's over there," an officer informed him, holding up the yellow and black CS ribbon.

"Can't wait for the buffet," Jason muttered, ducking under the tape. His shoes sunk into the soft, pale sand with a whisper.

The neon lights of the pier and the glittering solar panels of the Ferris wheel lit the way across the beach. From the arcade overhead drifted the sound of shouts—happy shouts—music and games. He could hear the jaunty tunes of the vintage carousel and the screams of people riding the rollercoaster.

All the while, beneath the pier, came the steady *click, click, click* of cameras flashing from different angles.

This time of month the tide would be surging back in around eleven thirty, so the forensics team would have to move fast.

As Jason drew nearer, he became self-consciously aware of a tall blond figure in a blue windbreaker with gold FBI letters across his wide back.

And he somehow knew—though Sam was not looking his way, was turned away from him—that Sam was aware he was on approach.

How did that work? Extrasexual perception?

Anyway, it made a nice distraction from what was coming. Not that Jason was squeamish, but no one liked homicide scenes. It was the part that came after—the puzzle, the challenge, the race to stop the unsub from striking again—that he liked.

He reached the small circle silently observing the forensic specialists at work. Gil Hickok acknowledged him first.

He said, "Here's West," and Sam turned.

Even in the dark, where he was more shadow than flesh and bone, Sam Kennedy made an imposing figure. It was something that went beyond his height or the breadth of his shoulders or that imperious, not-quite-handsome profile. Sheer force of personality. That was probably a lot of it.

Also a lot of aftershave.

"Agent West." It was strange to hear Sam in person again after all those months of phone calls. His voice was deep and held a suggestion of his Wyoming boyhood. His expression was unreadable in the flickering light, but then Sam's expression was usually unreadable, day or night.

Jason nodded hello. They might have been meeting for the first time. Well, no, because the first time they'd met, they'd disliked each other at first sight. So compared to that, this was downright cozy.

Hickok took in Jason's black tie and patent leather kicks, drawling, "You didn't have to dress up. It's a casual-wear homicide."

Hickok—Hick to his friends—was in his late fifties. Portly, genial, and perpetually grizzled. He wore a rumpled raincoat, rain or shine, smelled like pipe tobacco, and collected corny jokes, which he delighted in sharing with bewildered suspects during interrogations. They'd worked together several times over the past year. Jason liked him.

"'You can never be overdressed or overeducated,'" he quoted.

"Says the overdressed, overeducated guy." Hick chuckled and shook hands with him.

Sam did not shake hands. Jason met his eyes, but again it was too dark to interpret that gleam. Hopefully there was nothing in his own expression either. He prided himself on his professionalism, and there was no greater test of professionalism than being able to keep your love life out of your work life.

Not that he and Sam were in love. It was hard to define what they were—and getting harder by the minute.

Hickok pointed out the homicide detectives who had caught the case. Diaz and Norquiss were already busy interviewing the clusters of potential witnesses, so Jason really was last to arrive.

"What have we got?" he asked. The real question was *what am I doing here?* But presumably that would be explained. His gaze went automatically to the victim. The combination of harsh lamplight and deep shade created a chiaroscuro effect around the sprawled figure.

The deceased was about forty. Caucasian. A large man. Not fat, but soft. Doughy. His hair was blond and chin length, his eyes blue and glazing over. His mouth was slack with surprise. The combination of dramatic lighting and that particular expression was reminiscent of some of Goya's works. People in Goya's paintings so often wore that same look of shock as horrific events overtook them.

He wore jeans, tennis shoes, and a sweatshirt that read *I Heart Santa Monica.*

Sadly, the sentiment had not been reciprocated. A dark shadow formed an aureole beneath the victim's head, but it wasn't a lot of blood. He bore no obvious signs of having been shot or stabbed or strangled or even bludgeoned.

But if it was a simple case of homicide, Sam wouldn't be here. Though he traveled more than typical BAU chiefs—or agents—even he didn't turn up at common crime scenes.

"Do you know him?" Sam asked.

"Me?" Jason glanced at him. "No."

"You've never dealt with him in a professional context?"

"I've never dealt with him in any context. Who is he?"

Hick said, "Donald Kerk. A German national, according to his passport. He was the art buyer for Nacht Galerie in Berlin."

The Nacht Galerie was known for its collection of street culture: paintings by hip young artists on the cusp of real fame, and avant-garde photography. They specialized in light installation and graphic design. Not Jason's area of expertise.

"He still has his passport?"

"And his wallet, containing his hotel room key, so robbery doesn't appear to have been a motive. Mr. Kerk wound up his visit to our fair city with what looks like an ice pick to the base of his skull."

Yeowch.

"That's not going to do much for tourism." Jason was looking at Sam. Waiting for Sam to explain what made this a matter for FBI involvement, let alone for the ACT.

Sam started to speak but paused as they were joined by Detectives Diaz and Norquiss.

Norquiss was a statuesque redhead in a black pantsuit. Her partner was big and burly, with an impressive scar down the left side of his face. He wore jeans and a corduroy blazer that was starting to strain at the shoulders.

"Oh goody. *More* feebs." Norquiss looked Jason up and down. "To what do we owe this honor?"

Diaz said, "You could have waited till the wedding was over, Agent."

Jason sighed, and Hick chuckled. "Now, now, kiddies. *I* invited the Bureau in."

"*Why?*" Norquiss demanded. "This is nothing we're not fully equipped to handle on our own."

Sam said, "There are indications Kerk's homicide is connected to a case already under BAU investigation."

"Oh, for fu—!" Diaz cut the rest of it short. He exchanged looks with Norquiss, who folded her arms in a not-too-subtle display of resistance. In most cases, local law enforcement had to invite the Bureau into an investigation, but there were exceptions to the rule. This appeared to be one of them.

"Connected how?" Jason asked.

It was Hick who answered. "Here, West. I want to get your opinion of something."

The *something* turned out to be a 6x8 inch oil painting on canvas board.

"This was propped against the right side of the body," Hick informed him.

"Like a museum exhibit label?"

"Yeah, maybe." Hick sounded surprised at this suggestion.

Jason reached for his gloves. Of course, he wasn't wearing gloves. Hadn't expected to be called out to a crime scene that night.

"Use mine." Sam peeled off his own latex gloves and handed them to Jason.

Jason pulled on the still warm plastic—an act which felt strangely intimate—and took the canvas board from Hickok, who flicked on his flashlight to better illume the painted surface.

He recognized the creative intent at once. How could he miss it? Those distinct brushstrokes. The careful and strongly horizontal representation of the sky and sea that were so typical of the artist's early efforts. The ocean and shoreline were probably supposed to represent Sainte-Adresse, although they might as easily have been Santa Catalina. Wherever it was supposed to be—and despite the distinctive signature in the lower right-hand corner—it was a lousy effort and a lousy forgery.

Not even taking into account the macabre and incongruous central figure of the corpse floating in the surf. He felt a prickling at the nape of his neck at the image of that indistinct but clearly bloodied form. Maybe the location was generic. The focus of the work—a murder scene—was not.

"It's sure as hell not Monet," Jason said.

"It's his style," Norquiss said.

"I think Monet would beg to differ."

"Maybe it's an early work," Diaz suggested.

"No. It's not even a good imitation," Jason said. "This is not genius in the making. It's fully formed ineptitude."

Hick laughed. "What did I tell you?" he asked Sam.

"You can't know for sure without running tests. I don't think it's so terrible." Norquiss sounded defensive. Maybe she was a regular at garage sales. Had she really thought they'd discovered a genuine Monet at the crime scene?

Jason said, "For the sake of argument, why would Kerk be wandering around the beach carrying a priceless painting? And if this was a robbery gone bad, why would the unsub have then left a priceless painting at the scene?"

"Maybe robbery wasn't the motive. Maybe the perp had no idea this was a priceless painting."

"That still doesn't explain why Kerk would be casually carrying around a valuable piece of art."

Norquiss retorted, "What makes no sense is that the perp would bother to stage the scene when this whole area is going to be underwater in about an hour."

She had a point. The oily black tide was already starting to swirl around the pilings. The marine air was redolent with salty decay.

"Maybe your perp isn't familiar with the tides—"

"All right, never mind all that," Sam cut in impatiently. "You don't believe that Kerk purchased this work?" The question for Jason was clearly rhetorical. Sam already knew the answer.

"No way." Jason glanced at Hick.

"Hell no," Hick said. "That's not a mistake even a rookie buyer would make. Sorry, guys," he added to Norquiss and Diaz. "However this piece figures in, there's no way an experienced art dealer purchased a forgery of this quality."

A forgery that seemed to suggest—predict—the crime that had only occurred a few hours earlier that evening.

Having been shut up once, Jason kept the thought to himself. It wasn't like Sam would have overlooked that point.

Norquiss and Diaz exchanged frustrated looks. "Then what do we have here?" Norquiss asked. "What are we looking at?"

Sam's deep voice was somber as he answered her. "Best guess? The calling card of a serial killer."

Chapter Two

The Hotel Casa del Mar had started life as a ritzy and exclusive beach club for the rich and famous in the 1920s. It was now open to all and sundry—although with rooms starting at half a grand per night, not really. Donald Kerk must have been pretty good at his job.

Or maybe he was independently wealthy.

Or just really, really liked staying on the beach.

Kerk had booked one of the Palm Terrace rooms. Elegantly furnished in shades of cream, blue, and gold intended to suggest surf and sand. Amenities included a private patio just a few steps from the pool deck, a four-poster bed with Italian-designed bed linen, a personal reading library, an Italian marble bathroom with hydrothermal tub, and complimentary access to the Audi Q7 SUV house car.

Kerk had not been driving the house car, though. He had been walking on the beach when he had been struck down.

Just enjoying the ocean view, or had he gone out to meet someone? That was the question. One of the questions.

"Want to give me a hint what we're looking for?" Jason asked.

From the other side of the dividing wall, Sam answered. "We'll know it if we find it."

Riiight. Well, so far Jason could find nothing that suggested Kerk was anything but what he seemed: an affluent businessman mixing work with a little pleasure. No sign of other paintings in the style of the canvas on the beach. No sign of any paintings at all. Which made sense. Any purchases Kerk made on this trip would almost certainly have been shipped home.

From the hall outside, he could hear Hickok on his cell phone. The words *serial killer* had a way of carrying.

Jason, still wearing the latex gloves Sam had loaned him, opened the hand-painted armoire containing Kerk's travel wardrobe and dragged out Kerk's empty suitcase. He unlatched the lid and checked the pockets as well as the bottom and top of the case.

Nothing. Not even dirty clothes. In fact, Kerk's freshly laundered underwear were sitting wrapped in tissue in a fancy hotel laundry service basket on the immaculate bed.

He made a mental note and began to go methodically through each and every item in the armoire. A couple of expensively tailored suits, a couple of dress shirts with garish prints in red and mustard. A pair of well-made shoes. That was about it.

Clearly Kerk hadn't planned on staying long or doing much that didn't involve suits and ties.

Jason checked pockets, hems, soles, heels. Nothing out of the ordinary. No drugs, no contraband, no weapons, no explosives, no counterfeit money or stolen art.

He slid the final hanger across the wooden bar. So much for that. Kerk's clothing carried a hint of his personal scent, but Jason was mostly aware of Sam's aftershave. Sandalwood and musk. He had smelled it on the beach too, despite the sea breeze. Sam was a little bit of a hygiene fanatic, which Jason had found amusing until Sam had explained in one of those late night phone calls that he had trouble getting the scent of death out of his head sometimes.

Jason shut the armoire door. Not only did he not know what they were looking for, he was uneasy about why they were in Kerk's hotel room at all. Sure, per Title 18, United States Code, Section 668, it was a federal offense to obtain by theft or fraud any object of cultural heritage from a museum. But they had already established that the painting in question was not a major artwork, let alone stolen from a museum. On their walk from the crime scene with Hickok, Sam had not volunteered why he needed to personally examine the victim's belongings. Why he could not trust Santa Monica PD to do their job.

Typical Sam. Hands-on. He didn't trust anyone to do theirs properly. *Properly* meaning like he would do it.

Jason listened to the rustling sounds of Sam—wearing his spare set of gloves—going through the stack of receipts he'd found on the small desk on the other side of the dividing wall.

Okay, maybe to do what Sam did, to achieve those legendary results, he needed this. Maybe he couldn't get enough information from photographs and reports. Maybe he required this tactile experience of the victim's environment in order to form a picture of both prey and predator.

If so, that was opposite of the way Jason liked to work. Jason found this much contact, call it familiarity, with the victim distracting. Even disturbing. He preferred to keep an emotional distance. Could do his job better if he kept an emotional distance.

But then very rarely was Jason dealing with victims of homicide. He was usually on the trail of thieves, forgers, con artists. Not that he didn't run into violent offenders. Humans were always unpredictable. He rubbed his right shoulder absently.

"Do you want me to take the bathroom?"

"That would be helpful." Sam sounded preoccupied.

Jason stepped into the shining marble bathroom and raised his brows at his reflection in the mirror over the sink. Now there was a look: black tie and bulletproof vest. The wind had whipped his hair into dark tufts like devil horns. One of his cuffs was flopping loose.

"Shit."

"Problem?" Sam appeared in the open window that divided the bathroom from the bedroom. His eyes were very blue in the bright overhead light. Jason had forgotten how blue they were.

"No. Well. I lost a cufflink."

Sam's pale brows rose. Clearly he had no response to that, but those cufflinks had been a gift from Grandfather Harley when Jason turned sixteen. Besides being Tiffany and rare, they held sentimental value for him. He had idolized the old man.

Sam left the window, and Jason began retracing his footsteps. Introducing forensic evidence into a crime scene was every bit as bad as removing evidence, and losing a freaking cufflink was a particularly idiotic thing to have happened.

As he moved quietly around the room, he couldn't help thinking that this was a very strange—and very strained—reunion. Not that he'd been expecting to fall into Sam's arms, but for the last nine minutes, he and Sam had been alone for the first time in months, and Sam seemed to have nothing to say to him. Seemed unaware he was even in the same room.

It wasn't going to violate the professional code of conduct to say, *Hey, nice to see you again, Jason!* Was it?

Especially after all those months of phone calls.

All those midnight long-distance conversations when Sam had maybe a drink too many or Jason was half falling asleep. All those playful, provocative comments about what they'd do when they finally met up again.

Well, here they were.

Jason glanced at Sam's broad back. Actually, he didn't think Sam was unaware of him so much as deliberately tuning him out. Which was probably the professional and appropriate thing to do.

Sam continued to ignore him as Jason finished retracing his movements around the room. The goddamned cufflink was nowhere to be found. He'd probably lost it on the beach, which at this point was the best case scenario. If it turned up when SMPD conducted their own search, he'd never hear the end of it.

He returned to the bathroom and proceeded to inspect under the lid of the toilet tank. Aside from a surprisingly nice Rothko-esque print over the porcelain fixture, there was nothing of interest. He checked out the sink and bathtub drains and the heating vents.

Nothing. Nada. Zilch.

A damp bath towel hung on the back of the door. There were still pools of water on the sink counter. So Kerk had washed up before his fatal stroll. Which might mean he had been planning to meet someone. Or maybe he was just a tidy, well-groomed guy. Actually, judging by the amount of personal care products, he was for sure a tidy, well-groomed guy.

"How did you find out about the Kerk homicide?" Jason asked, sifting through the tubes of toothpaste and hair gel, verifying that they did indeed contain toothpaste and hair gel.

After a moment, Sam's voice floated through the open window. "Santa Monica PD contacted LAPD's Art Theft Detail. Hickok contacted the LA field office once they realized they had a dead German national on their hands."

"Right. But—" Jason stared at his own listening reflection. Furrowed brow. Green eyes narrowed in thought. He looked a little worried. He *was* a little worried.

Because how the hell had Sam arrived so fast? It wasn't like the FBI flew around the country in private jets. Not even the BAU.

As though reading his mind, Sam said, "I was already in LA."

Jason stared at the mirrored window opening and the room beyond. It took a second to compute. "I didn't realize."

Understatement of the year.

From this angle, he could see Sam's reflection. Just a slice. Enough to see that Sam was not moving, was standing perfectly still, listening to Jason. Despite his casual tone, Sam was deliberately choosing his words, and Jason's heart began to thump with something unpleasantly like anxiety.

What the hell was going on?

Sam said in brisk reminder, like this was not a big deal, "I monitor the Roadside Ripper Taskforce."

"Right. Sure." Jason answered automatically, following Sam's lead. But of course this *was* kind of a big deal. For eight months he and Sam had been…what? Flirting? Fencing? Engaging in some kind of verbal foreplay. Foreplay, hell. Afterplay?

There was no commitment, of course. No…understanding. Per se. If there was an understanding, it was that once they managed to land in the same city at the same time, they would hook up.

Jason didn't want to ask, didn't want to look like it mattered as much as it felt like it did, but after all, if it really *wasn't* a big deal, he'd ask the normal questions. He braced himself to get the words out casually.

"When did you get in?"

"This morning."

Okay. So that wasn't too bad. Jason had been out of the office most of the day, and maybe Sam hadn't had a chance to phone.

"Are you here regularly? Monitoring the taskforce?"

Sam's reflection moved, picked up what looked like a day planner. His tone was vague as he flipped through the pages. "I've looked in a time or two."

Don't ask. Leave it alone. Don't push this. But of course he had to ask. Of course he couldn't leave it alone.

He said—and now he was the one with the artificially careless tone, "Since Kingsfield?"

Stricken, he watched Sam close his eyes and expel a long breath. That...weary, wordless admission was all he needed to know. Except Sam had no idea he was being observed. Believed Jason was still waiting for an answer. He opened his eyes, looked down at the day planner, and said without inflection, "Yes."

Jason said nothing. There was nothing he *could* say without sounding exactly like what Sam clearly feared. Unprofessional. Emotional. Immature. Something.

He felt incredibly, embarrassingly hurt. And foolish—which hurt even more than the ice-cold realization that Sam had never had any intention of pursuing their...whatever the hell it was.

But no. That couldn't be right, because Sam was the one who had come after *him* in Massachusetts. Jason had accepted no for an answer. There had been no reason for Sam to bring up the possibility of anything more between them. No reason for Sam to take him to bed one final time and promise, well, in the end nothing very serious. A date.

A date that might have led to something more. Or might not have.

Somewhere along the line, Sam had changed his mind.

Which he had a right to do.

Of course. Hell. Jason changed his mind all the time about...stuff. People. No. Maybe not people. He was actually a pretty good judge of character. But relationships. Yes. He had changed his mind a few times about pursuing relationships. No reason Sam couldn't or shouldn't do the same.

It would have been nice to know, during all those flirty phone calls. Not so flirty lately, though. Not so many calls either.

So. It was over. Before it had ever begun. Good to know.

Which was why getting involved with coworkers was always a bad idea, regardless of company policy.

He snapped out of his preoccupation as someone thumped on the front entrance, and jumped to open the heavy door for Hickok.

"Sure is quiet in here. I was starting to wonder if you two gave up and went home." He took a closer look at Jason. "Did you find something?" Hickok looked from Jason to the other room where Sam was still searching.

"Not yet." Jason rolled up his loose shirtsleeve. He was relieved that his fingers were perfectly steady, because his heart was still hopping in his chest like a cricket that had just escaped being squashed.

"Nothing?" Hickok asked.

"Not so far. We're waiting on the night manager to show up and open the room safe."

If there was anything more than cash or maybe traveler's checks in that safe, Jason would be very surprised. But then it was a night for surprises.

Sam appeared around the corner, carrying Kerk's brown leather day planner. "According to this, Kerk was at Bergamot Station, Baus Wirther & Kimmel, Stripes, Fletcher-Durrand Gallery, and 30303 Art Gallery and Lounge this week." He looked in inquiry at Jason and Hickok.

Hickok whistled. "Heavy hitters all of them." He glanced at Jason. "Aren't you guys investigating Fletcher-Durrand?"

Jason nodded. In answer to Sam's look, he said, "We're looking into customer allegations of fraud and forgery. It's early days, though, and we're talking about the oldest and still one of the most prestigious galleries in California."

"That's interesting," Sam said, "but I doubt this homicide has anything to do with fraud or forgery. Do any of these museums handle or specialize in Monet?"

"Galleries," Jason said. "And no."

Sam eyed him for a moment and then nodded as though duly noting the correction.

"What makes you think this is the work of a serial killer? What is it you're not telling us?" Hickok asked.

"Besides everything," Jason put in.

That sounded more waspish than he'd intended, and it drew another of those thoughtful looks from Sam before he answered.

"This is the third homicide of someone involved in the art world where the unsub has left a painting in the style—general style," he amended, apparently for Jason's benefit, "of Monet. A painting which seems to depict the murder."

"That painting wasn't just dry, it was cured," Hickok said. "That means it was painted days ago. Maybe a week ago."

Jason's scalp prickled with unease. He asked, "Who were the other victims?"

But he didn't hear Sam's answer.

His attention was caught by movement on the other side of the French doors leading onto the room's private patio. Wind shaking the topiaries? A ghostly hand picking at the folds of a collapsed umbrella? He looked more closely, but it still took a disbelieving second or two to recognize the outline as human. A silhouette. Someone stood on the other side of the glass, watching them.

"What the hell?" Jason brushed past Sam. He reached the French doors, unlocking and throwing them open as the figure on the patio turned, shoving through the wrought-iron gate, which clanged noisily behind him.

Jason drew his weapon. "FBI. Stop right there," he yelled.

The dark-clad figure did not stop. The gate bounced open with the force of his exit.

Jason followed, pushing through the gate, which clanged loudly again.

The figure sprinted across the terrace, past the blue oblong of the brightly lit pool, heading for the taller fence at the end of the courtyard.

Good luck with that. Did he not realize the pool terrace was a couple of stories up?

Jason called back to Sam and Hickok, who had also drawn their weapons, "He'll have to try for the elevators. We can cut him off."

He didn't wait for a reply. There wasn't time for discussion. He gave chase. In fact, it was a relief to act, to have something that required his immediate and full attention—and a relief to get away from Sam. Fueled by adrenaline, he hit the terrace running, racing across the bricks about the same time the figure in black realized his miscalculation.

He turned, keeping the lounge chairs and potted palms between himself and Jason as he traveled the length of the stone deck, making for the steps leading down to the elevators.

He—the build was definitely male—was about Jason's height. Stocky. He wore black jeans, a black hoodie, and a backpack. The amber glow of the heater lamps illuminated glimpses of pale skin and Caucasian features.

"Hold it right there," Jason ordered, leveling his weapon as he kept pace with the suspect. Unfortunately, you could not shoot someone for spying on you, or fleeing from you, or even appearing on the scene at the very moment you were getting dumped by your sort-of-boyfriend. And anyway, Jason had no desire to shoot if it was at all possible to avoid it.

He also had no desire to *be* shot. Been there and done that. The suspect did not appear to be armed. He was certainly not brandishing a weapon. That didn't mean he wasn't carrying. That didn't mean at any moment this unsub wouldn't make a fast and fatal reach.

Stay alert. Stay alive. Like the old training films used to say. Jason's heart pounded, and sweat trickled between his shoulder blades. He watched the other's hands every second.

Lights blinked on in surrounding hotel rooms. Curtains slid back, shutters flashed wide, glass doors opened.

Shit.

Stay inside, people. And for the love of God, no posting to YouTube.

Out of his peripheral, he could see Sam already in position, blocking access to the elevators. Hickok was closing in from the other side, completing the pincer movement. This was over. The suspect just didn't know it yet.

"You're not going anywhere," Jason called. "Drop the bag."

The suspect looked to the elevators and then back at Hickok.

Jason repeated, "Drop the bag. Get on the ground."

The suspect hesitated. Was he just stupid? Or *really* stupid? *Did* he have a weapon? Jason's hand tightened on the Glock's grip. Sweat prickled his hairline.

"*You.* On the ground. Facedown *on the ground.*"

"Okay! Okay!" The suspect showed his palms. A blur of white. No gloves. No weapon. "I'm with the press."

"On. The. Fucking. Ground."

The suspect complied, dropping to his knees, still protesting. "I'm with the *press.* Chris Shipka. You *know* me."

Maybe yes, maybe no. Still, Jason's tension eased a fraction. Their unsub was exhibiting the right mix of alarm and indignation you'd expect from a citizen who felt he was being unjustly accused. "Arms spread to your side. Palms up."

"Lie down and shut up." Hickok came up behind the suspect, planting a foot in his backpack and knocking him prone. "Arms outstretched."

"Watch my camera!"

"Don't move a muscle, asshole."

Shipka continued to protest as Hickok patted him down with rough efficiency.

Jason kept his pistol trained unwaveringly on Shipka. His heart was still pounding hard. But hey, compared to eight months ago? When having to pull his weapon had practically triggered an anxiety attack? Here was progress.

"He's unarmed," Hickok informed Jason. He yanked open Shipka's backpack and swore. "Unless you count this." He held up a Nikon camera in one hand and a telephoto lens in the other.

"Be careful with that! For fuck's sake," Shipka protested. "Haven't you Nazis heard of freedom of the press?"

Shit. Shit. And triple shit. Speaking of YouTube videos.

Jason slowly lowered his pistol. Sam reached them, holstering his own weapon. He took in the camera Hickok held aloft and swore. "That's just goddamned *great.* ID?"

Hickok pulled out a wallet, thumbed through the contents, and said morosely, "Christopher Shipka, age 35, lives in Van Nuys." He looked up at Jason and Sam. "He's got a press card. He works for the *Valley Voice.*"

"I *told* you." Shipka's muffled voice sounded incensed. "Can I get up now?"

"No. You sure as hell can't," Hickok snapped.

"What the hell were you doing outside that hotel room?" Jason asked.

"I followed you." Shipka raised his head to peer at Jason. "I followed you from the museum."

"*Me?*" Alarm washed through Jason. "What are you talking about? You followed—you did *what?*" He could feel both Sam and Hickok staring at him.

"I'm the one writing those stories about you," Shipka said. He sounded sort of sheepish and sort of defiant.

"Christ," Hickok said. "It's the president of your fan club."

Jason stared at Hickok and then at Shipka's pale face once more. He did look...not familiar exactly. But not unfamiliar. His features were ordinary, nondescript. Not handsome. Not unattractive. He looked like a million other guys. Just another face in the crowd.

Jason's bewilderment must have shown because Shipka said, "I've been writing articles about you for the last two years. Don't tell me you never noticed. I've covered all your big cases."

"All my..."

Sam swore. The words were soft but savage, and Jason couldn't help feeling they were directed at him as much as Shipka.

He was not unaware that he'd occasionally received some favorable mentions in the local papers. Stories of stolen paintings safely restored to their rightful owners made a nice change from car accidents and home invasions, plus Jason's family was politically connected, so yes. He knew—and his supervisors knew—that he sometimes garnered the right kind of attention for the LA field office.

He had never paid attention to the bylines of those articles. Hadn't kept his press clippings. He wasn't in this for accolades or attaboys, but he couldn't help remembering something Sam had said early in their relationship.

And in return, you'll be the guy who gets to pose in front of the cameras...

Was this unfair idea of who Jason was and what he wanted part of what had gone wrong between them? He had no idea. And he did not know what to say. Could not even look at Sam. Somehow this felt like his fault, but it wasn't like he had done anything to bring it on. He'd been doing his job. Like everybody else on this terrace.

Hickok said something under his breath and got heavily to his feet. Shipka sat up. He was looking at Jason expectantly. And Jason had no idea what to say to him either.

Sam knew what to say, though. Sam always knew what to say.

"All right, Mr. Shipka," he drawled. "You can get up now. And you can start talking. Make it good."

Chapter Three

When the alarm went off at six the next morning, Jason didn't move. He'd been awake for the last three hours, which he'd spent staring unseeingly at the dim outline of the white crossbeams overhead.

It didn't matter. It was only about a twenty-minute drive from his bungalow on Carroll Canal to the Federal Building on Wilshire, though depending on what was happening with workday traffic, that commute could take double the time. Usually Jason liked to get into the office early. Early in and late out. It wasn't just ambition. He loved his job.

Usually. Today…not so much.

Granted, he hadn't had much of a night's sleep—he hadn't made it home until after one in the morning—and then he had tossed and turned for a couple of hours. He did not feel refreshed.

He felt…numb.

Twenty-four hours earlier he'd been content with his life. Even happy.

Now?

Putting aside the thing with Sam, which he did not understand and did not want to think about, but which hurt like hell—*so much for not thinking about it*—he had apparently picked up his own press corps. It was more than embarrassing. It was a genuine problem. He could not work undercover if his face kept showing up in the newspapers, and his job required a fair bit of undercover work. Even if it didn't, having a reporter tagging along and publicly speculating on what he was working next—which was what would be happening in this morning's edition of the *Valley Voice*— was a disaster.

Sam thought it was a disaster, and he ought to know, being a guy who got plenty of unwanted attention from the press himself.

So there was that. And there was the thing with Sam that he wasn't going to let himself think about.

On the bright side, he had not experienced a panic attack when he had to draw his weapon. True, he had not been under fire. Still. Mark that one in the victory column. The very short victory column.

Was he still part of the investigation into the Kerk homicide? He didn't know. It had not been clear at the end of the evening. Sam had questioned Shipka, who had defiantly informed them that cued by his police scanner, he had deduced Jason being called away from a museum wing being dedicated to his grandfather meant he was about to join a high profile homicide investigation with ties to the Los Angeles art community.

Not a direct hit, but too close for comfort.

The only bright spot was that Shipka hadn't recognized Sam. Didn't know that Sam headed up one of the BAUs—or that would have been in the morning paper too: a serial killer on the loose in Los Angeles.

Great.

No question now of what Sam knew or didn't know about Jason's background. He'd stood there and listened, unmoved, as Shipka babbled on about Grandpa Harley being one of the original Monuments Men, and Great-Great-Great Grandpa West being *oh yeah,* that *Thomas West.* The former governor of California. And about Jason's sister being married to Congressman Clark Vincent, whose politics, by the way—not that anyone was asking—were diametrically opposed to Jason's. In short, Sam now knew everything about Jason that made him both an asset and a liability on any case he worked and, in Chris Shipka's opinion, *news.*

Basically Jason's family was everything Sam seemed to scorn. Not that it mattered, since…they weren't whatever they had been, or whatever Jason imagined they had been, twenty-four hours earlier.

Anyway, it wasn't like Jason had ever been looking for romance or a relationship. The connection with Sam—Kennedy—had been unexpected and unneeded. Yeah, the *last* thing he needed. From that perspective, this shift was not only inevitable, it was preferable.

So why did he feel so…empty? Hollow. *Bereft.* Now there was a good old-timey word to explain feeling like the world had kicked you in the guts.

"To hell with it," Jason muttered, and threw back the white duvet.

The pale, painted floorboards were cold. He padded past the French doors—offering a view of the garden and the green-blue of the canal—the picture window, the giant *trumeau* mirror leaning against the wall, the claw-foot tub beneath more windows. Master bedroom and bathroom were just one long room, which worked fine for a guy living on his own, but did not afford a lot of privacy should he ever have company again.

Which felt increasingly unlikely.

He brushed his teeth, stepped into the giant shower with its clear glass walls and white glass subway tile, and turned the taps on full. The blast of cold water made him yelp, but it woke him up too. He reached for the soap.

He'd moved into the house five months earlier. His first real home. Up until he'd purchased the tiny 1924 charmer with its blue shake siding, angled rooms, sloping ceilings, and overabundance of windows offering a premium view of the canal, he'd always lived in low-maintenance apartments and condominiums. The privacy and comfort of an actual house with a small but mature garden still felt luxurious.

He'd talked quite a bit about this house to Sam—and had looked forward to showing him around eventually.

And he really, *really* needed to stop thinking about Kennedy.

The shower helped some, and a cup of scalding black coffee helped more.

By the time Jason forced his way into the river of traffic merging onto the Santa Monica Freeway, he had managed to reach a certain state of detachment.

Realistically, the situation between himself and Kennedy was always going to end like this. So why the drama? Kennedy was a professional, and Jason was a professional.

Anyway, for all he knew, Kennedy could already be on his way back to Quantico. And if he wasn't? Well, so what if he didn't want Jason on his taskforce? The last thing Jason needed was to get swept up in another serial-killer investigation.

Thanks, but no thanks. As one of the only two ACT members on the West Coast, it wasn't like he didn't already have his hands full. Especially with Shane Donovan, his NorCal counterpart, away on vacation, treasure hunting off the coast of Vietnam.

There might not even *be* a taskforce. And if there was, it was likely Kennedy would monitor long distance as he did with the Roadside Ripper.

But really, as far as Jason could tell, there was no reason Santa Monica PD shouldn't hang on to their own dead German tourist.

He was about to change the steady stream of bad news on the radio for Grant-Lee Phillips—which was a mistake because Phillips' music inevitably reminded him of Sam—when the *way*-too-cheerful newscaster announced, "A local paper is reporting the FBI may have joined Los Angeles law enforcement in the hunt for a possible serial killer targeting wealthy art patrons in the Southland."

"No," Jason groaned. "No, you did not..." Eyes on the sudden bulwark of red brake lights materializing in front of him, he reached for the volume.

"According to Christopher Shipka, a reporter for the *Valley Voice*, agents from the FBI's Los Angeles field office as well as a leading profiler on loan from Quantico are working in conjunction with LAPD to solve the brutal slaying of German art dealer Donald Kerk."

Jason swore. Yeah, just when he thought it couldn't get much worse. Although the description of Sam—no, Kennedy—as a "leading profiler on loan" was sort of amusing. If Shipka only knew.

Well, he probably did. Or would. Soon enough. He'd been a busy guy last night after being released from custody.

The announcer continued to boom his bad news like he was reading advertising copy for a President's Day appliance sale. "Kerk's body was found yesterday evening beneath the Santa Monica pier. Though the Department of the Medical Examiner has not yet released the official cause of death, sources at LAPD reveal that Kerk is the latest victim in what is believed to be a series of homicides over the past months."

"Past months *where*?" Jason demanded. "Says who?"

But the announcer had already moved on to more death and disaster in the Southland.

The federal building on Wilshire was—Jason not being a fan of Corporate Late Modernism—about as ugly a piece of 1960s architecture as you could hope to find in the city. Dominating the fortress-like complex was the imposing white concrete, tinted glass, and metal monolith which at various times in its history housed everything from the IRS, the audit division of NASA, the US Weather Bureau, to, of course, the FBI. No lie about politics making for strange bedfellows.

Jason parked in the still mostly empty staff lot, went through the employee entrance, and took a high-speed elevator to his office on the seventeenth floor. As the floor numbers flew by, he tried again to reassure himself that Kennedy was probably already on his way back to Quantico—and that he was glad about it.

It really was for the best. Best case scenario for everyone involved, although the idea was weirdly depressing too.

The elevator doors slid silently open, revealing blue carpet, white walls, and—Jason's heart sank—BAU Chief Sam Kennedy.

For the craziest moment Jason couldn't think of anything to say.

Kennedy stared back at him. He wore a black suit paired with a crisp white shirt and a gray silk tie. It was the first time Jason had ever seen him in the traditional FBI uniform of power suit and tie, and the effect was pretty devastating. Nothing like the combo of rugged masculinity and top notch tailoring to weaken your resolve.

Even more devastating was the way Kennedy's blue eyes seemed to light for a moment as though the unexpected sight of Jason gave him plea-sure—before his expression returned to its usual impassivity.

I'll be remembering what it feels like to touch you this way every time I see you tomorrow.

No. Do not start that.

Jason nodded curtly. He was struggling with how to address Kennedy now. "Sir" stuck in his throat, and "Sam" belonged to a past that increas-ingly felt like it had occurred in an alternate universe.

"Just the man I wanted to see," Kennedy said. He was his normal, brusque self, so Jason had surely imagined that fleeting warmth in his gaze.

"Oh yeah?" Jason returned politely. He sounded as enthusiastic as he felt, but Kennedy gave no sign he noticed.

"Grab a cup of coffee, and meet me in your office. I want to go over a couple of things with you."

Now here was something troubling. If Jason's immediate boss, George Potts, or SAC Robert Wheat, or ADC Danielle Ritchie, or, frankly, any of his superiors had taken that high-handed tone with him, he wouldn't have thought twice about it. In fact, if eight months ago Kennedy had taken that high-handed tone with him—and he had, on a regular basis—Jason wouldn't have thought much about it.

Now it raised his hackles.

That was illogical and unprofessional. This hostile reaction was nothing more than hurt pride, and it made Jason impatient and angry with himself.

So he gave another one of those tight nods and went to get himself a cup of coffee he didn't want.

When he reached his office, Kennedy had removed the copy of *Monet or The Triumph of Impressionism* from Jason's bookshelf and was glancing through it. He looked up at Jason's entrance.

"This is nice." His nod seemed to indicate Jason's office rather than the book. Jason did have more artwork on his walls than agents typically bothered with. In fact, one of his favorite paintings—a fake William Wendt by Lucius Lux—hung behind his desk. The painting had been a thank-you to Jason for keeping Lux out of jail. That had been a good decision on Jason's part because over the years Lux had developed into a useful informant.

Although he'd been suspiciously silent on the topic of Fletcher-Durrand.

"Thanks."

Jason had only once known Kennedy to be ill at ease. That had been in Kingsfield when he'd come to say good-bye—the good-bye that had turned into hello to the possibility of something more. Something real. He was not ill at ease now, but he was not entirely comfortable either. He was watching Jason closely—Jason could feel his gaze even as he did his best to ignore it.

Kennedy replaced the book, taking a moment to study one of the framed photos on Jason's bookshelf, and said, "This is the grandfather who had a museum wing dedicated to him last night?"

Not much of a guess given the World War Two Naval Reserve uniform.

"That's right." Jason sipped his coffee. He stayed on the far side of his desk, resting his hip on the flattop surface rather than taking his chair. He didn't want to sit while Kennedy stood over him. Which was silly. They weren't adversaries, after all. And yet, Jason definitely felt on defense.

"And that's where you developed your passion for preserving and protecting art?" Kennedy asked.

Okay. Jason appreciated the effort at cordiality or whatever this was supposed to be, but enough was enough.

"I take it I'm off the taskforce?"

Kennedy's brows drew together. "If you mean the investigation into Kerk's death, there is no taskforce."

"I see."

Actually, he did not see.

Kennedy pulled out the hard plastic chair in front of Jason's desk and sat down, facing Jason. "I'd like to get your thoughts, though." He opened a manila file and slid a photo across the desk.

Jason set down his coffee cup and picked up the photo. He studied it.

Female, African-American, mid-to-late fifties, and—judging by the clothes and oversize jewelry she wore in the photograph—both arty and affluent.

He looked in inquiry to Kennedy.

"Gemini Earnst. Art critic."

"Ah. Okay. I know the name. I've never dealt with her."

"Well, you missed your chance. Three months ago her body was found floating in the fountain in the Stuyvesant Town Oval. Someone jabbed a tool, likely an ice pick, into the base of her skull."

"Ouch," Jason said automatically. Why the idea of an ice pick was more disturbing than an ordinary knife, he couldn't say, but it definitely sent a chill down his spine. "Was a fake Monet found at the scene?"

Kennedy's gaze was one of tacit approval. "No. At least, not initially. The painting showed up three days later. It was still tacky."

"Still tacky?" Proof of the distracting effect Kennedy had on him, it took Jason a second or two to realize Kennedy was referring to the oils not being cured rather than the gaucheness of leaving bad art at a crime scene.

Kennedy seemed to be waiting for more. Jason said, "So the unsub decided to try to stage the scene *after* the fact?"

"Correct."

"Which means..." Jason thought it over while Kennedy waited. "Unlike Kerk, Earnst's death wasn't planned in advance?"

"Among other things? Yeah. Maybe. Earnst's may have been a crime of opportunity. Or the offender was still evolving, still formulating his ritual. Earnst may have been our unsub's first victim, though I'm not convinced of that."

If anyone would know, it was Kennedy. He'd spent nearly eighteen years hunting monsters. He'd literally written the book on them.

"Last night you mentioned three homicides." And thirty seconds later Jason had been chasing down Chris Shipka. Which reminded him of the radio news report he'd heard on his way into the office. He was not looking forward to sharing *that* bit of information with Kennedy.

"Our second known victim." Kennedy slid another photo across the desk.

Jason picked up the photo, examined it. The image was of a man in his early forties. Multiracial and strikingly attractive with pale, pale blue eyes and bronze dreadlocks.

Jason shook his head. "I don't know him."

On the surface there did not appear to be a lot connecting these three victims. Different gender, different race, different age, even different nationality.

"Wilson Lapham."

"Never heard of him."

"What about the Lapham Foundation?"

Jason considered. "Nope."

"Bettina and John Lapham are wealthy art collectors. Wilson was their oldest son. He taught art and supposedly dabbled with painting on the weekends. That's the only art connection we've found so far."

The word 'dabbled' sounded weird on Kennedy's tongue. But then he was not a man with much patience for dabblers in any arena.

"An art teacher, an art critic, and an art buyer?"

"Correct."

"Is there anything else that connects them?"

"We've uncovered nothing so far."

Jason nodded. He thought over Kennedy's previous statement. "You said *we*."

"The special agent I've assigned to this case is a friend of yours. Jonnie Gould."

Jonnie. Right. She'd resigned from the Bureau following her marriage to a fellow agent, but after Chris had been posted to Quantico, Kennedy had made Jonnie an offer it seemed she couldn't refuse. You could take the girl out of the Bureau, but you couldn't take the Bureau out of the girl.

Jason stared down again at the photo of Wilson Lapham. "You said his parents collect art? How big is this Lapham Foundation?"

"I don't know if it's of national importance, but apparently it's a big deal in New England. Lapham was found six weeks ago, floating in the ornamental lake on his parents' Connecticut estate. Same MO. An ice pick or similar weapon forcibly penetrating the brain tissue beneath the base of the skull. A painting which seemed to depict the crime scene was found beside the lake."

Kennedy slid another couple of photographs his way. One showed the crime scene, and one seemed to show a painting depicting the crime scene. Jason studied both images, paying close attention to the portrait of the crime scene. Despite the bogus signature and ersatz brushstrokes, this was not Monet. But it was not a generic lake either. The painting captured the same fountain of four herons spouting water from their long bills as graced the photograph of the Laphams' real-life water feature.

Kennedy commented, "This time the painting was completely cured."

Jason absorbed that. "Premeditation. Obviously. Also access. The unsub was familiar with both the victim's schedule and environment."

"Yes. Good."

Don't patronize me, Jason thought bitterly. He could feel Kennedy willing him to look up and meet his gaze. Jason continued to study the photos. One thing you learned in the Bureau was how to hide your feelings.

After a moment Kennedy said, "My question for you is why Monet?"

And my question for you is why me? Not like there weren't ACT members closer to home. The entire operation was based out of DC, so it wasn't as if Kennedy couldn't consult with agents every bit as—or more—experienced in art and art-related crimes as Jason.

"You want a disquisition on Impressionism in general or Claude Monet in particular?" Jason asked.

"Disquisition," Kennedy said thoughtfully. "I might have to look that one up."

Yeah. Not really. Despite the occasional drawl and cowboy-up attitude, Kennedy held a Masters in Criminal Psychology.

"Did the Laphams collect Monet? Was Earnst an expert on Monet? I can tell you that the Nacht Galerie doesn't specialize in 19th century art. You won't find Monet in any of their collections. They're all about street culture and the avant-garde."

"Go on."

"Go on?" Jason uttered a short, slightly exasperated laugh. "I'd be guessing. Maybe you're looking for a Monet wannabe. Maybe the unsub is hostile to the revival in figurative painting as exemplified by Neo Rauch and the New Leipzig school. Maybe the Laphams made fun of one of his paintings. Maybe Earnst wrote a bad review of his last exhibit."

"That sounds a little too much like bad TV."

Did Kennedy watch TV? Not that Jason had ever noticed.

"In this case, maybe *The X-Files*. What I'm saying is I find it difficult to believe Monet plays a significant role in your investigation."

"Would those paintings merit an exhibition or a showing?"

"God, no. They're bad. As in dreadful." Jason made the mistake of glancing up. Kennedy was still watching him, and their gazes collided, steadied, locked on. The intensity of that hard blue stare felt almost physical. It made Jason's chest ache.

And it made him angry because why was he feeling so much when Kennedy clearly felt nothing? Didn't even seem to remember that there might be anything to feel.

"By the way," Jason said. "Chris Shipka and the *Valley Voice* are reporting that agents from this office as well as a leading profiler on loan from Quantico are working in conjunction with LAPD to catch a serial killer targeting Southern California art patrons."

"Oh, for God's sake." Kennedy sounded mostly disgusted. "I should have dropped that idiot off the terrace last night."

"Just like old times," Jason muttered.

To his surprise, Kennedy laughed. He shuffled his photos back into his file folder. "Speaking of old times, I'd like you to accompany me to the galleries Kerk visited during the past week."

"Wait. What? *Why?*" That time Jason didn't bother to hide his consternation. Spending a day or two driving around town—stuck in the close confines of a car—with Sam Kennedy? No thanks.

Kennedy said coolly, "Because I think it will be helpful, Agent West."

Jason stood. Kennedy rose too, which did nothing to ease Jason's feeling of being cornered.

"I don't— I'm not— I've got a full caseload. I'm the only ACT agent on the West Coast right now, and I'm already spearheading the investigation into Fletcher-Durrand. That's a *major* case. We may be filing charges. It's…big."

"I appreciate that," Kennedy said smoothly. "But I think you'll agree stopping a serial killer is also big."

"That's not my"—at the last second he managed to switch *job* for— "area of expertise."

"I'm well aware of your abilities," Kennedy said, still infuriatingly cool and calm. "Your background and your contacts within the art world are exactly what I require at this time. And we both know you're a fully trained and experienced field agent able to step in and assist other units when and if needed."

He didn't bother—maybe he was being tactful—to remind Jason that the Art Crime Team was still largely viewed as nonessential, even superfluous, by many who believed those resources could be better used elsewhere. Members of the ACT were subject to being reassigned to other squads and units as deemed necessary. And without warning—let alone debate.

So it was really just stubbornness—possibly tinged with bravado—when Jason said, "No. No fucking way."

For a split second Kennedy looked startled. Then his eyes narrowed, his expression hardening. "Excuse me?"

Jason had just enough control not to say what he was thinking, which was *I'm not working with you again.* "My case is at a critical juncture. I'm not jeopardizing it because you think your investigation takes precedence."

That at least was safely familiar territory and something they'd argued numerous times during those late night phone calls.

If you could save a dozen people or one masterpiece, which would it be?

Jason always came back to *which masterpiece and who are the people?* Which amused Kennedy, although his answer had been a categorical *people over paintings.*

Okay, what about sculpture? Jason had countered.

That debate, and similar arguments, had been friendly and philosophical. This felt like a declaration of war.

Kennedy's pale brows rose—and that derisive half smile was pure déjà vu. He said almost gently, "No? Well, I suggest you have a word with Supervisory Special Agent George Potts."

"You're damned right I will."

Kennedy didn't bother to respond. He opened Jason's office door, stepped into the hall, and closed the door quietly, with great finality, behind him.

Chapter Four

"For the love of God, Jason, why are you making this so hard on both of us?"

George Potts was about Sam Kennedy's age, but they could have been two different species. Or two different geographic features. Whereas Kennedy was like Mont Blanc—all high altitude, treacherous routes, and severe weather changes—George was like...a bunny slope. He kind of even looked like a rabbit with his pale skin and pale eyes and pale, thinning hair.

He had been a mediocre field agent but was actually an excellent supervisor. Jason liked him a lot. George was hardworking, fair-minded, and paid attention to details. In fact, sometimes—like now—Jason wished George would pay less attention to details.

"I'm not," Jason argued. "I'm just pointing out that Gil Hickok can get Kennedy anything he needs."

"Why the hell should a BAU chief have to go to LAPD for help when we've got our own resources right here?"

A perfectly legitimate question.

"Because my investigation into Fletcher-Durrand is at a—a critical juncture. Showing up with Kennedy on a completely different matter is going to complicate everything. It's liable to derail my own avenue of inquiry."

"Come off it." George sounded pained. He liked Jason too, but...

Jason leaned forward in his intensity. "I'm serious. I'm already having trouble getting access to Barnaby Durrand. If I show up there with Kennedy talking about serial killers and fake Monets—"

"Look, it's only a day or two. I agree it might be a little awkward at Fletcher-Durrand, but you know as well as I do you're the obvious and best person to accompany Kennedy to these galleries since he's so god-awful determined to visit them himself."

"Hickok has more experience than—"

Abruptly, George lost patience. "I don't want to hear it. I realize you don't want to work with the guy—"

Jason sat up straight. "I didn't say that."

George looked heavenward. "You don't have to. I get it. His reputation precedes him. Four minutes of him was enough for me. But it didn't go so badly the last time. Right? He even made sure you got a commendation for the Kingsfield case." George added doubtfully, apologetically, "I think he maybe even sort of likes you. In his own antisocial way."

That was almost funny, though Jason didn't feel like laughing.

"George—"

"No, Jason." George was regretful but adamant. "No more discussion. You can't seriously think I'm going to tell a BAU chief to go ask LAPD for help. Suck it up, buddy."

Jason found Kennedy in SAC Robert Wheat's office.

Wheat was fifty-three and gravely handsome in the style of golden age TV doctors. He looked kindly, wise, and sort of noble seated behind an impressive mahogany desk complete with fluted pilasters featuring acanthus leaf accents. The desktop was littered with framed photos of Wheat posing with various politicians and influential people. A large gold-framed portrait of J. Edgar Hoover looking uncharacteristically benign hung on the wall behind him.

The backchannel chatter was Wheat had set his sights on Ritchie's position as Assistant Director in Charge and planned to be in her office by next December. Jason had no strong feelings on the power struggle either way. He made it a point to steer clear of office politics. God knew, he had enough of politics and power struggles both in his non-professional life.

Kennedy sat in one of the two wingback leather chairs facing the desk. His body language was relaxed. His expression, as he listened to

Wheat, was attentive. Knowing how Kennedy privately felt about guys like Wheat, Jason felt a flicker of sardonic humor.

Kennedy glanced his way, and once again Jason had that odd impression of something lurking in the back of Kennedy's eyes, some shadowy, unreadable emotion. In this case, probably gratitude for any interruption.

"Ah, West," Wheat said with genuine pleasure. "Come in. Come in." The SAC liked Jason and made no secret of it. Or, more exactly, he liked what Jason represented in his mind. Old money and useful political connections.

"I see you made the papers again." Wheat chuckled at Jason's pained expression. He said to Kennedy, "Young West here is one of our rising stars."

"I know," Kennedy said. Both his tone and his expression were cordial. As if schmoozing was second nature by now. Jason happened to know that was not the case. Kennedy hated that part of the job. "I had the pleasure of working with Special Agent West in Massachusetts."

"That's right," Wheat said. "How could I forget?"

"When did you want to get going?" Jason asked Kennedy, equally cordial. If there was one game he knew how to play, it was that of social nicety.

"Whenever is convenient for you, Special Agent West," Kennedy said in a smooth tone that sounded mocking to Jason—but obviously not to SAC Wheat, who beamed as though he could think of nothing more delightful than his two favorite people in the world going off to fight crime together.

"No time like the present."

Kennedy nodded and rose. Wheat rose too. They shook hands. Kennedy followed Jason down the blue-carpeted hall and into the elevator.

As the elevator doors closed, Jason braced for sarcastic commentary, but Kennedy spent the ride down to the lobby checking messages on his cell, and the walk across the parking lot to Jason's car, returning phone calls.

Nothing was required of Jason. Which—go on, admit it—was a little bit of a letdown.

Kennedy was taking the high road. He'd won this battle hands down, but there was no hint of gloating. Jason remembered that from Kingsfield. Kennedy could be polite and professional, or not so polite and professional, but he was never petty.

Right now he was polite and professional, and that was a relief.

Or should have been.

"Where did you want to start?" Jason asked as they buckled up.

Kennedy looked up briefly. "I'll leave that up to you."

Okay, so a concession to Jason's "area of expertise," or did he really not care? Jason started the engine of the unmarked 2014 Dodge Charger—only on TV did the FBI get to drive around in cool cars—and glanced at Kennedy.

Kennedy's call had gone through. He said in a hard, flat voice, "Agent Russell? This is Sam Kennedy. What information do you think you have for me that can't wait until I'm back in my office?"

Okaaay. That was the other part of the job Kennedy didn't care for. People. But managing human resources was part of his job description now. A big part of it.

Jason backed out of his parking slot, trying not to listen to Kennedy slicing and dicing the unfortunate Agent Russell.

* * * * *

According to Anna Rodell at Bergamot Station, murder victim Donald Kerk had been charming but difficult to please.

Founded in Winter 2003, Bergamot Station referred to itself as a "virtual think-tank, simmering and boiling with creativity, always on the sharpest point of the cutting edge." To mix a metaphor or three. They featured five local artists a month, owned two full galleries, and employed twenty-five "full-time creatives," who were kept busy producing items for the large and lucrative gift store. It was one of the longest-standing galleries on the Downtown Art Walk and served as a hub within the art community.

"He didn't know what he wanted," Rodell told Jason and Kennedy, once Jason had explained the reason for the visit. "Which is not at all typical of our German clients."

She was in her twenties, a very thin, milky-skinned woman with severely bobbed hair that had been acid-washed silver gray. Her eyes were also gray—either naturally or thanks to contacts—and the whole effect, down to her sparkly silver fingertips, was gorgeously spectral.

"What day was that?"

Rodell said, "Wednesday."

"Did he buy anything?" Jason asked.

"No."

Jason glanced at Kennedy, expecting him to take charge of the interview, but Kennedy was studying the cloud of metal and glass mobiles hanging from the black ceiling. Stars, bees, miniature suns and satellites, winged horses, and ghosts twinkled and glittered in the long room.

Jason turned back to Rodell. "How did Kerk seem? Distracted? Worried? Uneasy?"

"It's hard to say. I'd never met him before," Rodell said. "He seemed cool to me. Upbeat. Energized. Like he was having a great time. We talked about his gallery and some of his artists. Maybe doing a house collaboration one of these days. He was interested in how we handle our openings. And everybody loves our gift shop."

"Did he drop names? Was he interested in any particular artists or works?"

"No. He just...browsed. Like I said, I don't think he knew what he wanted. Or maybe he just wanted everything. And nothing. The package but not the product? We're...pretty subversive, you know? Like, his idea of edgy and our idea of edgy would *not* be the same thing."

"No?"

"Well," Rodell said reasonably, "I mean, he was older. Like forty at least."

"Ah." Jason made an effort not to look at Kennedy. "Right."

She shrugged. "He liked what we're doing. But he wasn't going to buy anything. I think he was just enjoying the vibe. It's really sad. He didn't seem like the kind of person who would get murdered."

"How long did he stay?"

"He was here for about an hour, I'd say. I know he planned on seeing Paul Farrell at 30303."

"'Maybe he just wanted everything. And nothing,'" Kennedy murmured, once they were back in the car. His tone was ironic.

Jason's lip curled. "Yeah. But I know what she meant. Sort of."

Kennedy smiled at him. "Of course, West. That's why I wanted you along." He was teasing Jason, but it was friendly teasing.

Jason smiled obligingly, but his heart wasn't in it. He found Kennedy's efforts at friendliness as bewildering as his withdrawal from anything more.

Jason said, "I don't know if this is relevant or not, but Monet's work—certainly his iconic *Water Lilies*—is some of the most overexposed and commercialized out there. Those images turn up on chocolate boxes, bubble bath, puzzles, shopping bags, scarves, T-shirts, posters, notebook covers. I've even seen tablecloths and bath mats with them. Could that have any bearing?"

"It's too early to know what might be relevant or have bearing," Kennedy said. "Which is why your thoughts, your insights are helpful."

Jason's heart dropped. Plummeted, in fact. If Kennedy was being *kind* to him… It actually made him feel a little sick.

He said nothing, and Kennedy got back to returning phone calls on the ten-minute drive to their next stop.

Paul Farrell at 30303 Art Gallery and Lounge greeted them politely—and curiously—but had nothing useful in the way of information.

In fact, according to Farrell, Kerk had canceled—or, more accurately—rescheduled his appointment.

"For when?" Jason asked.

"For today," Farrell admitted. "For this afternoon. I couldn't believe it this morning when I found out he'd been killed over the weekend." Farrell had a soft, high voice at odds with his size and rough-hewn appearance. His wild and woolly black beard, combined with the flannel shirts and jeans he favored, made him look more like a lumberjack than the owner of a highly successful art gallery.

"How did you find out?" Kennedy asked, showing a sudden interest.

"Oh. Uh, James at Stripes phoned to ask if I'd heard the news."

"Did Kerk give any reason for canceling?" Jason asked.

"I don't think so. I have to admit, I was right in the middle of arguing with a vendor, so the conversation was brief. We'd never met, and I wasn't even familiar with his gallery until I looked it up online this morning."

In Jason's opinion this was heading nowhere fast. He looked in inquiry to Kennedy.

Farrell said suddenly, "Yes. He did say, come to think of it."

"He did say what?" Jason asked.

"He said an old friend was in town. Or he'd run into an old friend while *he* was in town. Anyway, that's why he decided to cancel. They were having lunch." Farrell beamed, clearly pleased with his newly found powers of recollection.

"And this was on Friday?"

"Yes."

"Did Kerk indicate whether the friend was male or female?" Kennedy asked.

Farrell started to answer, but then frowned. "Well, I assumed female. Now I'm not sure if he actually said *she*. But he had that note in his voice."

"What note?" Kennedy asked.

Farrell grinned. "The note of a guy who thinks he's going to get lucky."

"I don't know how much we can rely on that," Jason said as they walked back to where he'd parked on the street.

"No. The only thing we know for sure is Kerk canceled his appointment with Farrell in order to have lunch with an old friend. The lunch date wasn't in his day planner."

"Spur of the moment?"

"Very possible."

Jason glanced at Kennedy. "Are you theorizing that your unsub is flying back and forth across the country picking off members of the art world?" He couldn't help the note of skepticism that crept into his voice.

"I don't have a theory yet."

That would be the day.

"Sure. The unsub *could* be female, I guess. It doesn't take a huge amount of strength to wield an ice pick. You just need knowledge of basic anatomy—and have the ability to get close to your victim without raising his suspicions."

"True."

But? Jason didn't ask, though. It wasn't his case, and if Kennedy didn't feel like further discussion? Fine by Jason.

They got into the car, Jason started the engine, and Kennedy phoned Jonnie. He spent the thirty-minute drive from 30303 to Stripes speaking to her.

If things had still been what they were forty-eight hours earlier, Jason would have told Kennedy to say hi for him. That kind of casual camaraderie seemed unimaginable now.

Still, he had to give Kennedy credit. He did the upper-management thing very well. Hard to believe he had ever been a simple field agent. Of course, to be accurate, Kennedy hadn't been a simple field agent for many years. He'd been a legend and law unto himself even when he'd been working cases in the field. Now? He had a dozen irons in the fire and seemed to be keeping a very close watch on every single one.

Of course, another name for that was micromanaging. Kennedy would not like being told he was a micromanager, but it sounded a bit that way to Jason. And he was guessing it felt that way to experienced agents like Jonnie.

When they reached Stripes, they found the gallery unexpectedly closed.

Kennedy considered the CLOSED sign on the door and asked Jason, "How flexible are gallery hours?"

"Not particularly flexible," Jason said. "Not for a place like Stripes. They've got a decent-sized staff. If someone called in sick, they ought to be able to cover."

Kennedy nodded thoughtfully. "This is the gallery where the James who phoned Farrell with the news of Kerk's death works?"

"Correct. James T. Sterling. 'Stripes' to his friends. He's like the CNN of this community. If there's news, James knows it first. He's the most trusted name in gossip."

Kennedy's mouth twitched. "I see. Well, we certainly must have a chat with Stripes."

They were blocking the sidewalk on this already busy morning. The tide of people lugging shopping bags, peering at smartphones, slurping coffees and smoothies, dragging tiny, yappy dogs parted around them and rushed on. Jason glanced at his watch and was startled to see that it was already eleven thirty. Where the hell had the last hours gone?

There were still two more galleries on Kerk's list, including Fletcher-Durrand, which Jason was going to stall visiting as long as possible.

"It's about an hour's drive to Baus Wirther & Kimmel," he said. "You want to head out that way now?" He added unwillingly, "Or do you want to stop for lunch?"

Jason did not want to have lunch with Kennedy. The idea was enough to choke him. The chauffeur gig was bad enough.

Kennedy checked his own watch and shook his head. "No. We should head back. I've got a meeting with ADC Ritchie."

"Right." There was no hiding his relief.

Kennedy's glance was wry. He sighed. It was an unexpectedly weary sound. "It looks like I'm going to have to fly up north, so if you wouldn't mind, I'd like you to finish the interviews on your own."

Jason threw him a disbelieving look. *If he wouldn't mind?* Was Kennedy being sarcastic?

Nope. Kennedy seemed perfectly serious.

"Of course," Jason replied.

"You can send Jonnie your report. CC me."

"All right."

It wasn't until they were once more in the car and heading back toward Wilshire that Jason asked hesitantly, "Are you—will you be—flying back down after your trip north?"

Kennedy had once more returned to checking messages on his phone. He raised his head. His blue eyes met Jason's, and it was like getting kicked in the chest. He could *feel* that look in his heart.

He wasn't imagining it. There was still some link between them. Something crackled as bright and hot as an energy field. Maybe it was nothing more than sexual awareness. But there it was, and it was real.

Kennedy broke the connection. He turned his head to stare out the window. "No." He sounded...removed, distant. "I don't think it'll be necessary. You'll get me what I need."

Probably not intended to be a compliment.

Or maybe it was. Who could tell with Kennedy?

"All right," Jason said. "Er...thanks."

For a time he was occupied in playing shuffleboard with the buses and delivery trucks and taxis clogging the crowded streets, but inevitably his thoughts circled back to the passenger in the seat beside him.

Given how irate Jason had been at being conscripted into Kennedy's investigation, it was odd that what he mostly felt now was a sense of letdown, even disappointment, that Kennedy would not be returning.

But wasn't it normal that his feelings should be confused? The situation was just...so strange. All those months. And when they finally did get together...

Nothing.

Worse than nothing. It was like they had never met. Never made lov— *Oh, hell no.* Not that. Never had sex. That's what he meant.

His anger faded, leaving him depressed, disheartened. What the hell had happened to change everything? He just couldn't understand it. He was baffled.

Yeah. Baffled.

The traffic lurched to a sudden standstill. Jason's phone vibrated. He ignored it. Around them, a few impatient drivers vented their frustration with honks, but the seconds continued to tick by. Pedestrians in every size, shape, and color crowded the sidewalk beside them, darting around the cones and sawhorses and hoses of the workmen tearing up the pavement with jackhammers. The pound of the pneumatic drills was not as loud as the silence stretching between himself and Kennedy.

In disbelief, Jason heard his own voice—hesitant, slightly strained—break the silence.

"Look. Did I...do something?"

"No," Kennedy said at once. And that was a relief. A relief that Kennedy did him the courtesy of not pretending he didn't understand. In fact, it was as if he had been sitting there thinking the same thing as Jason. "It isn't you. It's nothing you've done or didn't do."

He didn't elaborate, though, so Jason—who already felt like he was out on a very flimsy limb—had to stretch still further.

"Because I don't understand." Excruciating to have to put this into words. His face felt hot, and his heart was pounding as though this was a high-risk situation. He was not used to it. Not used to…caring so much. It wasn't that he'd never been turned down before or even been dumped. It always stung, but it hadn't *hurt*. Not really. Not like this.

Kennedy didn't answer immediately, and Jason couldn't bear the silence.

"Is it the promotion? Are you thinking that I would somehow trade on our friendship? Or that other people might think I was trading on our friendship?"

"No," Kennedy said, again adamant. "I don't think that. And I don't give a shit what anyone else thinks."

So what the hell was it? Because he was not wrong, not imagining things. Kennedy was confirming it was over. But he wasn't telling him why, and that really was the part Jason needed to understand. They'd talked two weeks ago, and there had been no hint that everything was not…

Was not *what*?

Okay? Fine? Normal? None of that applied. They'd had a long-distance relationship that was more like phone tag. In other words, they'd had nothing.

And kudos to Kennedy for recognizing that fact and breaking it off.

Although this was more like passive resistance than breaking it off. But whatever. Over. Done. Finito. *Let it go, West. It only gets more embarrassing from here.*

A couple of excruciatingly long seconds passed while he tried to think of a way to change the subject, scrabble to the solid ground of… *anything*, for the love of God. *How about them Cubs?*

The traffic ahead of them crept forward, and Jason eased off the brake, letting the Dodge roll a couple of inches.

Because I care about you, Jason. More than I thought I could.

His eyes blurred.

Jesus Fucking Christ. Was he about to cr—tear up over *this*? No way. And sure as hell not when Kennedy was sitting right beside him. For God's sake.

Kennedy said suddenly, "I...like you. Nothing has changed."

Right. Except everything.

Jason made a sound in the back of his throat that was supposed to be...not what it sounded like. Which made him angry and enabled him to get out a terse, "Right."

"But it isn't...practical to try to..." Kennedy was picking words as painstakingly as somebody gathering shards of glass. "It's not enough to...build on."

Wow. Maybe he was misremembering, but getting shot three times hadn't hurt this much. And anyway, what the hell did that mean? It's not like Jason had been pushing for more. He had accepted Sam's terms. Not that Sam had really given him terms.

He wanted to say something to the effect of what he had said in Kingsfield: *Whatever. It was just supposed to be a fucking date.*

But of course it wasn't just a date. Not anymore. Somehow they had managed to move beyond that never-to-be date to something more. Something deeper. And yet less concrete than even a date.

It made no sense for him to sit here like his heart was breaking when they didn't even know each other. It was ridiculous. Pathetic.

"It's okay," he said flatly. "You're right."

He felt Kennedy look at him, but he kept staring straight ahead. He shrugged.

"I should have told you sooner," Kennedy said. "Made my position clear." Had it been anyone but Sam Kennedy, Jason would have said there was guilt—regret?—in his tone. "But I like talking to you."

"Yeah. Well." He was relieved his voice had steadied again, because inside he was a churning mess of confused emotion. Mostly pain. "I liked talking to you too."

Neither of them had anything to say after that, and the nearby crush and crash of broken cement filled the distance between them.

Chapter Five

Per usual, Barnaby Durrand was not taking Jason's calls.

After the morning he'd had, Jason was not taking any more crap from anyone, and the minute he finished lunch—or, more exactly, finished the remaining half of a stale Kind bar while typing up a list of hundreds of Native American artifacts recovered in a raid on a local Van Nuys residence to send to a professor of anthropology and museum studies over at USC—he headed straight out to the gallery in Downey.

Traffic was moderate on the I-105 East, and he made the drive in just under forty minutes, pulling into the small parking lot behind the pink and white pseudo-Empire style structure.

In continuous operation since 1903, Fletcher-Durrand was technically the oldest art gallery in Los Angeles. A second branch had opened in New York in 1938, but the California gallery and Fletcher-Durrand's early support and patronage of the Plein-Air and Modernist California School was what had established the company's brand and reputation. Currently they specialized in 19th and 20th century European and American paintings of "investment quality."

That said, the building looked more like a hair salon with a high-end security system than a reputable art gallery. Jason had been to the New York gallery once or twice, and that building was far more impressive. But despite its humble, even tawdry appearance, Jason remained convinced the Los Angeles office was where the real action was.

He got out of his car, crossed the cracked and broken asphalt lot empty of all but a large blue Dumpster and a small red Toyota, and went around to the front of the building.

"Special Agent Jason West to see Ms. Keating," he said into the intercom and held up his badge to the security camera over the gated front door.

There was no answer, but he did not have long to wait before a tall, red-haired woman of about thirty came to unlock the door.

"Agent West, I *told* you this morning Mr. Durrand was not in the office today," the woman protested as she pushed aside the security gate.

"Yes, you did, Ms. Keating," Jason said.

"Well then…but…I really *can't* help you, Agent West." All the same, she stood back and allowed him to enter the building. It was very difficult for normally law-abiding citizens to tell law enforcement officers no, especially when the LEO in question was smiling and rueful and clearly taking it for granted he was coming in.

Keating was nearly as tall as Jason and could have modeled for one of Jean Auguste Dominique Ingres' odalisques. Creamy skin, doe eyes, and voluptuous build. She favored prim white blouses and dark-colored pencil skirts that somehow only served to emphasize that repressed sexiness. Jason suspected she had watched one too many of those 1950s office romances. The ones where the mousy and devoted secretary whipped off her spectacles, was revealed to be a raving beauty, whereupon the big boss instantly fell for her and, following a few comical misunderstandings, proposed marriage.

"So where is Mr. Durrand today?" Jason asked.

"I thought I— He had to fly back East this morning."

Jason said lightly, "That's the third time he's canceled on me. I'm beginning to think he has something to hide."

Keating could not take that impugning of her god lying down. She began to protest.

"It's nothing to do with the…the investigation. It's personal business. A family matter. His mother's not well."

"I'm sorry to hear it."

And Mrs. Durrand would probably be feeling less well once her son was indicted for first and second degree grand larceny—in addition to other charges.

Two months earlier Durrand had been accused by married clients Hank and Roslyn Ontario of secretly selling off three Picassos, a Monet, and a Cézanne that he was supposed to be holding for them—and then keeping the profits for himself. Since then, another client had come forward with similar claims.

Jason believed there were more victims out there. He also believed many of those missing works had been stored and eventually sold through the Los Angeles gallery. But it had not been easy to build a case—a watertight case—against Durrand. Not all of Durrand's clients kept accurate records. Further, although it was possible in the Ontarios' case to prove Durrand had possession of the art, it was not possible to track down where it had disappeared to. A lot of business in the art world was still conducted with handshakes and notes on cocktail napkins.

It didn't help that Fletcher-Durrand had been around longer than the FBI—or that they had a sterling reputation in the art world. At least for now. The problem with the contemporary art scene was there was more money to go around than art. A lack of supply was not good for business. And when business was bad, it led people into temptation. Jason's gut told him the rot at Fletcher-Durrand went deeper than selling off collections and forgetting to pay clients, but so far he'd been unable to find proof of anything.

He'd tried hard to roll Keating, tried to impress upon her that as things stood, she was in very real danger of taking the fall for the gallery when the case eventually went to court, but either she couldn't see her jeopardy, or her faith in the Durrands was stronger than her survival instinct.

Maybe she was counting on the case never making it to court. And fair enough. Jason figured there was a good chance the Durrands would settle with the Ontarios, though so far they were hanging tough.

"What about Shepherd Durrand? Is he available?"

Shepherd was Barnaby's younger brother and the junior—so junior as to be all but nonexistent—partner at the gallery.

"Shepherd?" Keating said warily. "No. He doesn't come in on Mondays."

Or any other day as far as Jason could determine. He said, "Then I guess you're my last hope, Ms. Keating."

He could be reasonably charming when called upon, but Keating was made of stern stuff. She straightened her spine. "I'm sorry, Agent West, but my attorneys have ordered me not to answer any more questions unless they're present."

Well, hell. She had finally lawyered up. Definitely not his day. Not personally and not professionally.

"That's good advice," Jason said. "But actually I'm just checking up on whether Donald Kerk visited the gallery last week."

"No," she said without hesitation.

"You don't want to check your—"

"No," she repeated firmly.

"Hm. Okay. Well."

"If there's nothing else—" She was interrupted by a loud buzzer, and an expression that seemed to be a mix of alarm and frustration crossed her face.

Jason glanced over his shoulder at the front door, but no one stood outside the glass.

"If that's all," Keating said desperately. She actually made a little shooing motion toward the door. Jason grinned at her.

He suspected Barnaby was catching a later flight than he'd been led to believe. Or maybe Barnaby wasn't on his way out of town at all.

But the man who rounded the corner and stopped in surprise when he spotted Jason and Ms. Keating was not Barnaby Durrand.

He was shorter, stockier, younger, and better looking than Barnaby. There was a strong family resemblance, however, and Jason knew this had to be the younger brother. The rarely seen Shepherd.

"Oh!" Shepherd Durrand said. His dark eyebrows shot up, and he stopped in his tracks. He was probably in his mid-forties but looked very fit and well kept. He looked like a guy who got regular manicures and facials. Which Jason knew something about since his brother-in-law the congressman was a guy who got regular manicures and facials.

"This is the FBI," Keating said quickly, as though she feared Durrand was going to launch into some incriminating statement.

"Well, not the entire operation," Jason said. "Just one of the cogs in the wheel. Special Agent West."

Durrand chuckled and moved forward to shake hands. "I thought that Dodge parked out back looked like an unmarked police car." He had a firm grip and a pleasant, light voice. "I guess you're closing in on poor old Barnaby."

"Mr. Durrand!" protested Keating. She threw Jason a horrified look.

Durrand was sizing Jason up with a knowledgeable eye, and as their glances caught, it occurred to Jason that Shepherd might be gay. It wasn't anything he could put his finger on, but he felt an almost instant recognition.

"Not at all," Jason said easily. "In fact, I'm here on a completely different matter."

"Well, you've got *my* interest," Durrand said meaningfully, and if Jason still had any doubts as to Durrand's sexuality, that mischievous pucker of a smile put them to rest. "Why don't you come back to my office?"

Keating began, "But—"

Durrand ignored her, and Jason followed him through a rabbit warren of narrow white halls to a small office in the back of the building.

It was instantly obvious that Durrand did indeed work there and was not, as Jason had suspected, a partner in name only. A Mac computer sat on the desk. Art books and catalogs were jammed in the crowded shelves. The "incoming" file tray on the desk was empty, and the "outgoing" tray held a stack of neatly printed and signed documents.

What really caught Jason's attention was the large wood-framed oil on canvas landscape that hung behind the desk. Muted earth tones of sage and sand, a style vaguely reminiscent of Chagall or maybe Klimt, but the subject matter...

"Is that a Reuven Rubin?" he asked.

Durrand's smile indicated surprise. "Very *good*. I'm impressed. Yes. That's a Rubin. *Hills of Galilee*. Beautiful, isn't it."

"Yes. Very."

"I think I fell in love with it because it looks like Northern California. You're...an art collector?"

"I can't afford much of a collection on my salary. I'm with the Art Crime Team."

"Oh. Right." Durrand's smile fell. His brown eyes were earnest. "This situation with the Ontarios and Barnaby is *absurd*. We're all sick about it. You have to understand something. The *lawyers* are telling Barnaby not to speak with law enforcement. It's not that he's trying to hide anything. We have every intention of fighting these allegations in court. If it really does come to that. But our lawyers are telling us not to talk, and we pay them good money for that advice."

"That's the advice lawyers usually give," Jason said. "But I can tell you right now that cooperation in the early stages of an investigation can go a long way to smoothing the journey in the final stretch."

"There isn't going to be a final stretch." Durrand looked unexpectedly grim. "You can't imagine how painful this situation is. Ros and Hank were close friends. They were like *family*. That they would do this to Barnaby… It's beyond belief."

"I'd love to hear your side of it," Jason said. "If there's a simple explanation—"

"The explanation is Ros and Hank *told* us to sell those paintings and authorized us to accept payment in installments." He hurried to add, "And before you say it, *no*, there was nothing in writing. No written instructions to liquidate the collection—just as there were no written instructions to take the collection in the first place. We were friends. Then. We didn't realize a time would come when we'd need a paper trail."

Jason tried to look suitably sympathetic. "And was an initial payment made to the Ontarios?"

"Yes." An expression of discomfort fleeted across Durrand's face. "To the best of my knowledge, yes. But there's where you *do* have to talk to Barnaby. That's all his…realm."

"I'd like nothing better." Jason's smile was quizzical. "*Did* he really fly back to New York?"

"Yes. He really did. This morning. Our mother isn't well. Barnaby is her favorite, so he's usually the one who makes the trip. My sense of humor gets the better of me sometimes. Of course he's not on the lam. When he gets back to town, he'll meet with you. The lawyers will be with him, but you'll have your meeting."

"Okay. I look forward to that." Jason rose.

Durrand stood as well. "Is there anything else I can help you with, Agent...? I'm sorry. I've forgotten your name. I have a horrible memory."

"West." Jason clasped the hand Durrand offered. "Actually, there *is* something. Did you have a meeting with Donald Kerk last week?"

Durrand's hand tightened instinctively on Jason's. "*God.* I can't believe it. Yes. Or no. Not a meeting. We had dinner Friday night. He's a friend. *Was* a friend. I just got the news a few hours ago." He shook his head.

"I'm sorry for your loss," Jason said. "Then Kerk didn't come to the gallery?"

"Well, yes. He did come to the gallery. But that was on...Wednesday, I think. Tuesday? No, Wednesday."

"What was the purpose of that visit?"

Durrand's brows rose. "Er...of course, we *are* an art gallery, and Don was in the art-buying business."

"Did he purchase any works?"

"No." Although the suggestion had been his, Durrand now seemed amused at the very idea. "We're far too 20th century for Don. Mostly he came by to see the gallery and say hello. The three of us went to lunch afterward."

"The three of you?"

"Me, Barnaby, and Don. At one time we were quite close. Barnaby— Well, anyway."

Jason raised his brows in inquiry, but Durrand shook his head. Question mark beside the equation of Don and Barnaby, then.

"Would you say you knew Kerk well?"

Durrand sighed. "As I said, at one time, yes. But people change. We—I—hadn't seen him in nearly ten years. Ten years is a long time."

"Sure. How had Kerk changed?"

Durrand gave another of those sighs. "He's—*was*—a lot more successful now. I'm not saying he was arrogant, but he wasn't the shy, reticent boy I used to know."

Ten years earlier Kerk would have been in his thirties, so he hadn't been *any* kind of boy, as far as Jason could tell.

Durrand added, "Also, his partner passed away nine months ago. I think he was missing Klaus and feeling retrospective."

So...pushy and lonely? According to Anna Rodell, earlier in the day Kerk had been upbeat and happy and "enjoying the vibe." Had something happened between the visit to Bergamot Station and Fletcher-Durrand?

"Partner," Jason repeated. "Was Kerk gay?"

"Bisexual, actually." Durrand smiled meaningfully at Jason.

So. Okay. That made Paul Farrell's comment about Kerk sounding like he expected to get lucky all the more interesting.

"Do you know who Kerk had lunch with earlier that day?" Jason asked.

Durrand shook his head. "No idea."

"We know he was supposed to fly out of LAX tomorrow. Would you happen to know what his plans were for the rest of the week? Whether he was meeting with other old friends?"

"No. I really don't know. He was in good spirits on Friday. He didn't mention his plans for the rest of his stay. We talked art. You know how it is."

Yes, Jason knew how it was. And he thought it strange and unlikely that Kerk wouldn't have discussed his itinerary at all. He also thought Durrand had a way of offering and retracting information in almost the same breath.

"I see. Thank you for your help," he said. "If you should think of anything else, you can reach me here." He handed over one of his cards.

"You never know, do you?" Durrand winked at him. Jason was a winker himself, but the open invitation of that deliberate flick of eyelid surprised him.

"Uh, no. You don't."

Still smiling broadly, Durrand tucked the card in his shirt pocket and patted it as though for safekeeping.

Chapter Six

"Here comes trouble," George said with resignation as Jason strolled into his office later that afternoon.

Jason dropped into the uncomfortable plastic chair in front of George's desk and crossed one ankle over his knee. "Admit it. You're living vicariously through me, George."

George rolled his eyes. "Yes. I confess. I secretly dream of being a workaholic single guy reading art books and eating TV dinners alone every evening."

"They don't call them TV dinners anymore, FYI. Anyway, sometimes I splurge and get fast food. Hey, I want to fly to New York tonight. I think I might be able to corner Barnaby Durrand at the family estate."

George sat back, looking skeptical. "Is this your way of getting out of working with Kennedy?"

"Hell no. Anyway, Kennedy's gone."

"Oh? I didn't realize."

"Something came up. He's on his way north. He asked me to finish the interviews and send him my report."

George said in a fatherly tone, "See, that wasn't so bad, was it?"

"No."

George grinned at Jason's grudging admission. "Okay. Fill out the travel request, leave it on my desk, and I'll sign it first thing tomorrow. How long are you planning to be gone?"

"Three days including travel time ought to be more than enough."

"You don't want to take someone with you?"

Like every other field office in the country, they were suffering a personnel crunch, and ACT investigations were low priority at the best of times.

"Not necessary. Durrand will either talk to me or he won't."

"What makes you think he will?"

Jason related his interview with Shepherd Durrand.

George heard him out. "Interesting. What do you think? Is it all just a big misunderstanding?"

"No." Jason shook his head. "No way. Shepherd tells a pretty good story, but I'm not buying it. The Ontarios are very credible witnesses. I didn't share with Shepherd that we've got Ursula Martin waiting in the wings with her own complaint."

"Still not enough for the US Attorney's Office to file charges," George reminded him.

"I know. I'll get what we need."

"Okay." George glanced at the clock behind Jason. "Safe travels."

Back in his own office, Jason placed a couple of phone calls to contacts within the art community, booked a midnight flight for New York, and then phoned Karan Kapszukiewicz, chief of the Major Theft Unit of the Criminal Investigative Division. Karan oversaw the Art Crime Team agents from her Washington DC office.

Though it was after hours on the East Coast, Karan still picked up.

Jason filled her in on how the Fletcher-Durrand case was developing and his plans to travel to New York to force an interview with Barnaby Durrand.

"We're walking a fine line," Kapszukiewicz commented. "Are you sure this is where we want to focus our resources? Especially if the gallery is going to end up settling out of court?"

"I do, yeah. My gut tells me there's more here. I think we're just seeing the tip of the iceberg. Shepherd Durrand has a Reuven Rubin hanging in his office that, as far as I know, should be on display at MoMA."

"It's not illegal to purchase or display a copy of a valuable painting in your work space."

"I know. But it's unusual for an art gallery to hang a copy. And I think it's interesting Durrand didn't mention it was a copy."

"I think you're stretching," Kapszukiewicz said. There was a smile in her voice, though. Jason was one of her protégés, and they both knew she was going to extend him latitude. "But if your instinct is telling you to keep digging, then keep digging."

"Thanks, Karan," Jason said—and meant it. "I'll send my reports as soon as they're processed."

"Good deal. Have a pleasant evening." Kapszukiewicz's attention had already moved on to bigger and more important things.

Jason hung up and settled down to type up his notes on his interview with Durrand. He started an email to Jonnie—weirdly formal in tone because of Kennedy's name in the CC field—attached his notes, and sent it off.

Mission accomplished.

He glanced at the clock. It was after five by then, and the building was getting that quiet, creaky sound even skyscrapers had after they emptied for the day.

He was supposed to drive out to Diamond Bar to pick up a painting he'd purchased on eBay. The impressionist work of the rain swept Catalina coast by Granville Redmond was a birthday present to himself. The current owner would not be home until seven thirty, so Jason figured he'd work until about half past five.

Something else he and Sam had shared: a love of Granville Redmond's work. That was the kind of pointless synchronicity that could fool you into thinking there might be grounds for a relationship. So there you go. Two workaholics who traveled all the time and liked early California Impressionism. A match made in heaven.

Only not.

Jason sighed and decided to give Baus Wirther & Kimmel a call on the off chance Sabine Baus was still there. They'd been pals since their years as art history majors at UCLA.

His luck was in. Sabine verified that Kerk had been to the gallery on Thursday, had purchased three paintings, and had been in excellent spirits.

"You didn't happen to know him from before, did you?"

"From before what?" Sabine inquired.

"From before you met him on Thursday."

"Sure. I met him the last time I was in Germany. That gallery is amazing. Don was a character. He wore his hair in this Little Dutch Boy cut, and his voice was very high and airy. He had a really silly sense of humor. I liked him a lot. You'd have liked him too. It's horrible what happened to him."

"Yeah. We'll get the guy."

"Or gal, you chauvinist."

"Right. Or gal."

"Oy! I've got a question for you. Is it true Fletcher-Durrand has reached a settlement in their lawsuit?"

"Not to my knowledge."

Sabine snorted. "That was very FBI-ish, West. I heard through the grapevine they were settling."

"News to me," Jason said. "Where'd you hear that?"

"Where else. Stripes."

"Right," he said thoughtfully.

"So when are you taking me to dinner again?"

"It's your turn to take me to dinner, you chauvinist."

Sabine laughed. "True. How about next week. Maybe Thursday?"

"It's my birthday. I think I'm booked at Stately West Manor."

"Friday?"

"Friday. It's a date."

"I'll pick you up at seven. Wear something pretty."

Jason snorted and hung up. His amusement faded at the unexpected and jarring sight of Sam Kennedy standing in his office doorway.

"Knock, knock," Kennedy said.

"Thanks, I've had mine for the day," Jason returned. He was still smiling, but it was a curve of mouth and nothing more. He did not like the way his pulse jumped and fluttered just because Kennedy suddenly popped up again.

And, oddly, Kennedy's return smile was equally unamused.

"Something tells me you'll survive."

Jason's heart gave another unpleasant leap, and his temper rose with it. What the hell was *that* supposed to mean?

He opened his mouth to ask, but Kennedy cut him off with a neutral, "You're here late."

"So are you. I thought you'd be on your way north by now."

Kennedy's smile was sardonic. "Disappointed?"

Jason didn't bother to answer. He closed his laptop.

Kennedy showed no sign of being in a hurry. He folded his arms, leaning back against the door frame and studying Jason.

The steady appraisal made Jason uneasy, though he wasn't sure why. He said at random, "I sent you my notes from my interview at Fletcher-Durrand Gallery."

"I saw that," Kennedy said. "Thanks. What can you tell me about Special Agent J.J. Russell?"

Now there was a change of subject. "*Russell?*" Jason thought back with surprise to Sam's phone conversations in the car. *That* Russell? The LA Field Office's Russell? He said neutrally, "Competent. Ambitious. He's still pretty green."

"You're being diplomatic. This is between you and me. It goes no further."

Jason remembered that not overly pleasant smile. He suspected Kennedy had already formed an opinion on Russell.

"Yeah? Okay, then. I think he's a homophobic prick. And I would not trust him to guard my back. Or resist sticking his own knife in."

Kennedy looked thoughtful. "And what about Special Agent Adam Darling?"

Jason couldn't help a faint grin. "Best name I ever heard for an FBI agent."

Kennedy's mouth curved in answer, but he said gravely, "Aside from that."

"You can ask Jonnie. She was partnered with him for about a year."

"I'm asking you."

"I don't know him well. He's a little standoffish. Reserved. Obsessive about the job—like someone else I know. What happened to him last year was bullshit."

"What happened to him?" Kennedy asked.

Jason filled him in on the history of Special Agent Adam Darling—when bad things happen to good agents—and Kennedy listened without comment.

"I see," he said noncommittally at the end of Jason's recital. "Thanks."

Jason nodded. He shoved his laptop into his computer bag, grabbed his keys, and rose.

Kennedy said slowly, "So Friday's your birthday?"

Like you fucking care? Kennedy probably did care. Kennedy had said he liked him, and Jason believed him. In fact, he *knew* Kennedy liked him. Knew Kennedy was still attracted to him. Kennedy was every bit as aware of Jason as Jason was Kennedy. Besides. You didn't spend hours on the phone late at night with someone you didn't like. So why Kennedy's question made him so angry was hard to say.

"Thursday after next." He glanced at his watch. "Is that it? I've got to be somewhere."

Kennedy's brows rose. "That's it."

As Jason headed for the door, Kennedy straightened and stepped into the hallway. He waited silently as Jason closed his office door.

What the hell was he waiting for? Jason gave him a look of polite, cool inquiry.

"Have a good evening," Kennedy said.

Jason turned away. It was not easy. Not when this might be the last time they ever spoke in private. Certainly it was the last time they would ever speak as anything more than work colleagues.

He couldn't help glancing back—and surprised an unexpectedly bleak expression on Kennedy's face.

It smoothed out almost at once. It was Kennedy's turn to offer a look of cool inquiry.

"Take care of yourself, Sam." Jason's voice was just about right. Maybe a little huskier than he'd have liked, but for a time Sam Kennedy had mattered to him. A lot. Still did, in a troubling way.

There it was again. A flash of something startlingly close to pain. But Kennedy's voice was brisk. "You too, Jason."

Jason turned and walked away. He did not look back until he reached the elevator. He punched the button, glanced back. The hall was empty.

The elevator doors opened. Jason stepped inside. The elevator doors closed. Jason leaned back against the wall and watched the numbers swiftly count down to nothing.

Chapter Seven

"It's not like Mom and Dad are getting any younger. How many more birthdays will we all get to spend together?"

"Jesus, Sophie." Jason awkwardly tried to balance his phone while shifting his computer case and the oversize painting he held. He managed to shove his key in the lock of his front—well, actually side—door. The house did not technically have a front door. There was a side door accessible through a wooden gate. The only other exit was a pair of large French doors leading into the backyard and facing the canal. "Will you stop saying things like that?"

The door swung silently open on a kitchen as quaintly cozy as one of his eldest sister Charlotte's store layouts. Because it *was* one of her store layouts.

"I'm being realistic," Sophie said. "Dad's eighty-five. Mom's eighty."

"I know that." Jason stepped over the scattering of mail that had been deposited through the mail slot. He went through to the main room, put down his briefcase, and leaned the painting against the wall. "I just— I'm not in a big celebratory mood this year."

To put it mildly.

"That's silly." It wasn't that Sophie was insensitive—well, maybe it was—but mostly other people's anxieties made her feel helpless. Sophie was a born fixer. She did not like feeling helpless. "And even if it was true, that's all the *more* reason to celebrate."

Jason hung on to his patience. He knew from long experience there was no outarguing her. "I don't mind getting together for dinner, just the family, but I don't want to go out. No Melisse. No Spago. I don't want my birthday to turn into a photo op."

A photo op for Clark was what he meant, but he managed to stop himself from saying so.

Sophie laughed. "Look who's talking! You're practically a celebrity. That photo of you at Santa Monica Pier—you can't buy publicity like that."

"I don't *want* publicity," Jason said. "That's the last thing I need."

"That's how you get promoted."

"Or shot."

That gave her a moment's pause. But it was only a moment. "Which is why you need to get promoted. So you don't get shot again. Anyway, this will just be something small and private at Capo Restaurant. That's practically next door to you. Just family and a few close friends."

Jason stopped, closed his eyes, and counted to ten. Finally he managed a semi-pleasant, "When did you say you guys were heading back to Washington?"

"Next week. After your birthday party."

"Okay, well, I might have to work late that night, so take that into account for any plans you're making."

She made a *tsk-tsk* sound and promised to be in touch.

Jason clicked off. He was tired, hungry, and depressed, but no one had shot at him that day. Not even with a camera. So there was a bright side.

He went up the two stairs that led to the master bedroom, cool and green-shadowed as the garden on the other side of the French doors slid into darkness. He unfastened his hip holster and tucked gun and holster in the bedside drawer. He slipped off his Ralph Lauren navy two-button suit jacket, pulled off his tie, and glanced at himself in the trumeau mirror. He was startled at how stern he looked.

Eyes shadowy, mouth tight. For God's sake. It wasn't like...

Wasn't it?

He swore again, quietly, changed his shirt and trousers for ripped jeans and a black T-shirt with the silver MoMA logo.

A drink, a decent dinner, and a good night's sleep, and he'd be fine again. Not that he'd be getting a decent dinner or a good night's sleep. He'd need to be at the airport by eleven to catch that flight back East. That was okay. He could sleep on the plane.

Anyway, there was a lot to be happy about. Nobody but Sophie had mentioned that article in the *Valley Voice* to him. That was a big happy thing right there. Tomorrow he would, by God, talk to Barnaby Durrand or die trying. That was going to be very satisfying. And finally, he had just bought himself a fantastic birthday gift for which he had been saving up for months. So...*woohoo*! As his fourteen-year-old niece, Nora, would say. Woo-fucking-hoo. Right?

To hell with Sam Kennedy and his mixed messages, phoned in and otherwise. That had *always* been a bad idea, and Jason had *known* it was a bad idea, so this was actually more good news, if he would just make the effort to recognize it as such.

Padding into the kitchen with its oak cabinets and red tile floor, Jason poured himself a shot of Canadian Club, which he kept on hand because Sam had once revealed he preferred his whisky sours made with Canadian Club.

He knocked back the whisky, shuddered—*really, Sam? Canadian Club?*—but did feel almost instantly better. Well, warmer.

He went to examine his birthday gift, cutting away the string and brown paper, carefully removing the bubble wrap, and lifting out the seascape. The wooden frame was dinged and peeling, but the canvas itself was in wonderful shape. *Those colors.* Gorgeous. Shimmering turquoise and dazzling ultramarine. He could practically hear the sound of the waves and the cries of the gulls, smell the salty air, feel the sunlight on his face.

Jason lifted down the painting currently hanging over the fireplace—a gilt-framed study of a basket of roses and peonies on loan from Charlotte's shop—and replaced it with the Redmond, standing back to have a good look at it.

Yeah. Really beautiful and it suited the room perfectly. And it suited him. His spirits rose. At least this part of his life was coming together.

His eldest sister, Charlotte, had decorated the house, mostly pulling stock from her floor rooms at Charlotte's Le Cottage Bleu because by the time he'd bought the house, Jason's financial resources had been depleted.

Charlotte's sensibility ran to shabby chic, but she had tried to take Jason's taste into account—at least once he had complained about the lack of sturdy chairs and the abundance of floral arrangements. He'd appreciated her help, though. Even if he'd had the money, he didn't have time to furnish the place. The truth was, he traveled nearly as much as Kennedy.

He poured himself a tall glass of water, gathered the mail up from the floor, and sat down on the sofa next to the distressed library table that served as his coffee table. He began to go through his mail. Bills, junk mail—mostly art catalogs—and a large envelope that looked like a birthday card.

He tore open the envelope and sure enough. It was a hand-designed card. For a second he thought it must be from his niece. Nora was the artist of the family. But this ink and watercolor effort was a bit sophisticated for Nora. He stared at the detailed jumble of blue and green. What was it supposed to be? A mermaid and water and fish and…vines and leaves. Or was that seaweed?

Nice work, even beautiful, but something about it made him uneasy. He opened the card, and his unease increased as he studied the tiny, cramped handwriting centered on the middle of the stiff paper.

He glanced down at the signature and saw he'd guessed correctly.

Dr. Jeremy Kyser had contacted him for the second time since Kingsfield.

Jason took a slow, thoughtful swallow of water.

Not grounds for alarm. Necessarily. But it didn't make him happy either.

The first note—a Halloween card—had come to the FBI field office. He didn't like the fact that Kyser now knew where he lived. He didn't like the fact that Kyser was reaching out to him.

In fairness, Kyser had not been involved in the events of the previous summer, and he was not currently a person of interest. In fact, he was a respected psychiatrist and author of several books on aberrant psychology.

He was also a very weird guy, in Jason's opinion, and he did not want Kyser sending him greeting cards.

Dear Agent West

I was very pleased though not surprised to discover that you were born under the sign of Aquarius. I suspected this from our first meeting, as you possess the physical attributes of this air sign: good looks, beautiful eyes, angular face, and thin build.

Jason's unease mounted.

He had been afraid of this. Well, not *this*. But the Halloween card had seemed to be an indication of personal and unwelcome interest on the part of Kyser. Jason had meant to talk to Kennedy about this development, but their own communications had grown so infrequent—and Kyser had not contacted him again—that he'd eventually forgotten about it.

As you may know, Aquarians are the natural detectives of the zodiac—although they hate to have their own secrets probed. I am curious about your secrets. I sensed a natural affinity at our first meeting. My own sun sign is Leo. A fire sign. This places us in harmony. Air makes fire burn more brightly. Ours is the 7-7 sun sign pattern. Like you, I am working to build a Utopia. I will contact you soon to explain how we may work together to bring this about.

With admiration and affection,
Jeremy Kyser

Jason closed the card to once more examine the chaos on the front. He tossed the card to the table and leaned back on the sofa, staring at the Redmond painting.

He did not want to overreact.

Was this a troubling overture? Yes. Did it concern him that Kyser had taken the trouble to find out where he lived? Yes. Did the grandiose and sort of incoherent tone of the communication worry him? Yes.

But. It was only a birthday card and only the second communication in nearly a year. There was no specific nor even vaguely implied threat. On the contrary, Kyser was friendly and complimentary.

He hadn't even used Jason's first name, so it was sort of difficult to accuse him of being overly familiar.

He leaned forward and picked up the envelope. No return address. The postmark was Virginia. So Kyser was on the other side of the country, not lurking on Jason's patio, waiting to pounce. He glanced instinctively at the windows and the vine-shrouded pergola beyond—and was annoyed with himself.

He could not hope to hang on to any credibility as an FBI agent if he freaked out over something this nebulous.

It would have been nice to be able to talk it over with Kennedy, but that was out. The last thing he wanted was to look like he couldn't handle himself—or, worse, that he was coming up with lame reasons to stay in contact.

Goddamn it, Sam.

Jason's heart—hell, his whole chest—ached at the memory of that conversation in the car.

Just like that? It was *over*?

Why? What had he done?

Nothing, according to Kennedy.

It isn't you. It's nothing you've done or didn't do.

Which really didn't help.

What would help? Anger. Anger would help. But could you be legitimately angry at someone for changing their mind about wanting a relationship with you? Sure, people did rage over that—even kill each other over that. But not sane people. Not reasonable, grown-up people.

It was worrying how much this hurt. Way too much for what it was. It felt like a huge weight had landed on him last night, and it had been all he could do to keep upright and moving through the day while that weight got heavier and heavier and heavier.

But he had made it through today. And he would make it through tomorrow, and all the tomorrows that followed, and eventually the casual mention of BAU Chief Sam Kennedy would not trip his heart in his chest or cause him to lean in to listen to other people's conversations.

He swallowed the last mouthful of water and was trying to decide whether a second whisky would be a bad idea on an empty stomach, when someone knocked on his side door.

He couldn't help that surge of hope—though he knew it was ridiculous—even before he peered out the side window and spotted...

Wait.

The hell? Was that— That could *not* be—

Jason yanked the door open, and Chris Shipka, minus his hoodie and camera equipment, gazed nervously back at him.

At Jason's glare, Shipka faltered, "Uh...hi, Special Agent West."

"No comment." Jason moved to close the door.

Shipka jammed his foot in the doorway in a move time-honored by reporters and door-to-door salesmen alike.

"No, wait, man," he pleaded. "I'm not here to interview you."

Jason said stonily, "Right. You're just selling subscriptions to the *Valley Voice*. How did you find out where I live?"

Shipka's expression was a mix of apology and pride. "Hello? How much of a reporter would I be if I couldn't find out where somebody lives?"

Fair enough. Whatever else he was, Shipka did seem to be a pretty diligent reporter.

"Okay," Jason said. "You found me. Now get lost. This is private property, and you're trespassing."

He was not jumpy by nature, but he couldn't deny that Shipka's appearance, following on the heels of the card from Kyser, was unsettling.

Shipka kept his foot planted and his hand braced on the red surface of Jason's door. He was smiling, but it was a pained effort. "Wait a minute. Don't be so hostile, West. This isn't— I'm not— I've got information for you."

"What information?"

Shipka recognized Jason's hesitation and said quickly, "Information you'll need for your Fletcher-Durrand investigation."

"Then you need to come down to my office and file a complaint tomorrow—or actually, on Friday when I get back. I'm out of town for the next couple of days."

Shipka's eyes narrowed. "No way. I'm not filing a complaint. I'm not reporting a crime. I can't do that."

Jason asked, "Why's that?"

Shipka's expression twisted into a grimace. His eyes were hazel. More green than brown. His features were blunt, not unattractive. He had a dimple in his chin and a tiny scar over his lip. His hair was brown and curly. He was nice-looking. Not handsome—not the kind of looks that won TV anchor slots—but appealing.

"Because for one thing, how much credibility would I have if I was shown to be working *with* law enforcement? People are going to think I betrayed my source."

Jason was unimpressed. "*Are* you about to betray a source?"

"Of course not. But who's going to believe that? It's my job to report on your investigation. Not become part of it."

"Then what are you doing here blocking my doorway and insisting I talk to you?"

Shipka snapped, "Because these are fucking dangerous people." He seemed…genuine. About that, anyway.

Jason asked, "Who are? The Durrands?"

"Yes. Well. Yes." Shipka threw an uneasy look over his shoulder. "Look, West, can I come in or not?"

Jason hesitated. This was a breach of protocol, and he was not comfortable with it. Especially after the card from Kyser. One stalker per customer.

At the same time, he was not picking up a particularly…hinky vibe from Shipka. Working in law enforcement, you did develop a sense for when people were not on the up-and-up. Shipka seemed almost desperately sincere. And if he *did* have information? Making him wait until Jason got back from his trip to New York meant risking Shipka changing his mind about coming forward.

Jason pulled the door wide, stepping back, and Shipka came inside, looking around with unconcealed curiosity at the weathered floorboards and vintage-looking appliances.

"Wow. This is…very *Town & Country.*"

Jason led the way through to the miniature living room. "But you're not here for an interview, so don't bother taking notes."

"I'm not making notes. Anyway, it's nice," Shipka said. "I just didn't figure you for a guy who would go in for chandeliers and sideboards." They both studied the vintage coffee urn with its spill of pastel silk flowers, which sat on the peeling and battered table.

Jason admitted unwillingly, "My sister is an interior decorator."

"Right. Charlotte Baldwin. She owns Le Cottage Bleu." Shipka smiled at him.

This reminder of Shipka's nosiness into things that did not—should not—concern him refreshed Jason's hostility.

He said coldly, "Do you have information for me or not?"

The smile faded from Shipka's face. "Jeez, West. You could offer me a seat at least. We're on the same side."

Doubtful. But okay. Maybe. *Maybe* Jason was a little touchy. Maybe he had reason. Maybe he didn't. In either case… He sighed and pointed at the overstuffed white sofa. "Sit."

Shipka laughed. He seemed unoffended. "I will. I've been on my feet all day chasing down leads."

"Don't remind me."

Shipka laughed again, and…frankly, there was something unexpectedly engaging about his easygoing acceptance of Jason's lack of welcome. Something unexpectedly engaging about someone who wasn't fifty shades of grim.

Shipka sat down, looking relieved when the sofa frame didn't crack or the mounds of cushions try to swallow him whole. He wore jeans and a perfectly respectable sport shirt in a baby blue and white check. Jason said, reluctantly, "Did you want a drink?"

Shipka brightened. "Thanks." His gaze fell on Jason's tumbler. "Beer. If you've got it."

Jason poured himself another Canadian Club, got a Mass Riot IPA from the fridge and a mug from the freezer. He poured the beer into the frosty mug, carried it into the front room. As his fingers brushed Shipka's, there was a snap of electricity. Shipka gave another of those quick laughs. He looked up into Jason's eyes.

Yeah, more green than brown in those eyes.

Jason scowled, but that was because he did not want to like Shipka, let alone notice the color of his eyes. He took the matching overstuffed chair across from the sofa and said curtly, "Well?"

Shipka started to put his mug down, but then paused to look for a coaster.

Unwillingly, Jason was disarmed. After watching Shipka for a second or two, he said, "It doesn't matter. Just set it down. Apparently the table is supposed to look like a piece of junk."

Shipka grinned and set the mug on some of the scattered fake flower petals.

"So, listen, West. I'm going to put my cards on the table, but you've got to promise I get the exclusive on this when the case breaks open."

"I'm not promising anything." Honesty compelled Jason to add, "At least until I hear what you've got."

Shipka took a moment to think it over. He shrugged. "Okay. I'll meet you halfway. You're after Fletcher-Durrand for fraud and grand larceny."

Jason's interest sparked. He said steadily, "No comment."

"I know you are."

"Then I don't need to confirm or deny, do I?"

"It's bigger than you think. It's not just one or two clients. And it's not just that the Durrands are dragging their feet on paying the owners for paintings they've sold, ostensibly, on their behalf. Whole lots of paintings left in Barnaby's supposed safekeeping have disappeared. There are people out there who don't even know their entire art collections are gone."

Say what? Did Shipka actually have something here?

Jason managed to conceal his surprised interest. He raised an eyebrow and said nothing.

"I'm taking that as confirmation. You know it goes way beyond Barnaby?"

Jason continued to stare at Shipka.

Shipka said earnestly, "Okay, okay. But you need to look *beyond* Barnaby. You need to look at Shepherd."

"What would we do without the press?" Jason said. *Tell me you've got some evidence? Some kind of proof? Please don't be playing me.*

"You don't have to be sarcastic. If you hadn't got that far, there was no point me telling you the rest."

"What is the rest?"

"A missing model and art student by the name of Paris Havemeyer."

"A missing *model*?" Jason's wariness returned. "What are you talking about? What does that mean?"

"Just exactly that," Shipka said earnestly. "Twenty years ago Havemeyer disappeared and has never been seen since."

"And this relates to my case how?"

"You care about murder, right?"

Jason said, "I repeat. How does this relate to my case?"

"I don't know. But it does. Kerk's murder proves that."

"You're going to have to start at the beginning because I have no idea what the hell you're talking about."

"I only know that either Barnaby or Shepherd killed Havemeyer. I'm assuming Shepherd."

"Killed him how? When? Where? Do you have *any* proof of this?"

"Anything I have would be circumstantial. It's your job to get real evidence."

Jason's laugh was disbelieving. He shook his head, finished his drink, and set it on the table. "Right. Okay. Well, I appreciate your stopping by this evening, Mr. Ship—"

He started to rise, but Shipka said quickly, "Okay! Yes, the Havemeyer thing *is* kind of an art-world legend, but I believe those stories."

"Why?"

"Because of the source."

Jason was starting to get exasperated, but he said with reasonable— he thought—patience, "The source you refuse to reveal?"

"Look." Shipka stopped. Seemed to struggle inwardly. "You're gay, right?"

Suddenly it wasn't funny anymore. "What the hell does that have to do with anything?"

"I knew it. *I'm* gay too." Shipka was gazing at him with meaningful, even hopeful intensity.

"So what?"

"So Shepherd Durrand is gay. The kind of gay our daddies used to warn us about." By "daddies" Shipka was not referring to Shipka senior or Peter West. That much was obvious.

Jason started to speak, but Shipka hurried on, "Havemeyer was part of that whole arty scene back in New York. He was part of that circle. When Fletcher-Durrand was the biggest name in art. And Donald Kerk was there too."

Donald Kerk. Was there a connection? Maybe Jason's face revealed more than he imagined, because Shipka said hastily, "And yes, I know this is all before your time. Mine too. I know it sounds like a-a—"

"Don't say fairy tale."

"No. Look, West, I *know* what you think, and it *is* mostly rumor and speculation. Okay. I admit that. But I've got an instinct for this kind of thing. Just like you do for your kind of thing. But you don't believe me; fine. I can continue to work that angle on my own. Although I don't have your resources. I can't force anyone to talk to me."

Join the club. But Jason kept the thought to himself.

"What is *not* speculation is that Durrand is selling multiple percentages in paintings in order to finance more acquisitions."

"That's not against the law," Jason said impatiently. "That's standard practice for operations like Fletcher-Durrand. It's extremely expensive to purchase some of these 19th and 20th century masterpieces, so they get investors to put up the cash, and then—ideally—everybody makes a healthy profit when the work is sold."

"That's the theory," Shipka agreed. "But suppose Durrand is selling more shares than there is art?"

"Meaning?"

"Meaning that he's sold more than two hundred percent worth of shares in a couple of paintings currently up for sale."

"'He' being...?"

"Barnaby. I think."

"You *think*." Jason frowned, thinking. "What are the paintings? Do you know?"

Shipka smiled. "*That* I can help you with. Paul-César Helleu's *Lady with a White Umbrella.* However you say that in French. I guess it's a lot like a picture by Monet? And a 1950 painting by Toyen from his *Neither Wings nor Stones* series. Both paintings have investors holding over two hundred percent shares worth of painting."

"Can you give me the name of one of these investors?"

Shipka finished his beer and set the mug down. "Not without putting my source in jeopardy."

"Seriously?" Jason asked. Insiders joked that the art market was even less regulated than gun running and drug smuggling. The only real law was discretion.

Shipka rose. "Yes, I *am* serious. If I'm correct in my suspicions, these are very dangerous people. Maybe you haven't heard the rumors about Barnaby back in the day. Not to mention Shepherd. But I have. And before you blow me off as a conspiracy theorist or some other kind of nut, maybe you should do a little more poking around."

Jason rose too. "Have I blown you off?"

"No. Not completely. But you don't believe me about Havemeyer."

"Believe *what*? You said yourself that as far as you could tell, it— whatever *it* is supposed to be—was rumor and speculation."

"Murder is what it's supposed to be," Shipka said bluntly. "Cold-blooded murder."

Jason was silent. Shipka might have his facts wrong, but he believed what he was saying. You didn't have to be a BAU profiler to see that much. And there was no question that where there was a lot of money involved, dangerous people could always be found. The nerves in Jason's shoulder tingled in unhappy muscle memory.

"I plan on interviewing Barnaby Durrand tomorrow," he said, by way of concession.

Shipka's brows rose skeptically. "Good luck with that. He's in New York."

"I know. I'm flying out tonight."

"Well, now. A sign of initiative," Shipka murmured.

"Go to hell," Jason returned also under his breath.

Shipka laughed, unoffended, and headed for the kitchen door. Jason followed him, switching on the outside light. The night air smelled of smog and the dank smell of the canal drifting from the back of the house.

As Shipka stepped out into the artificial yellow haze, he said, "One other thing. Just a… heads-up. You know who also used to party with that arty-farty crowd? Detective Gil Hickok at LAPD."

Chapter Eight

One little thing Jason failed to take into account.

The Durrands' upstate family estate was *way* upstate. As in Jefferson County upstate. On Camden Island in the St. Lawrence River, to be precise—and the only way to get there was by boat.

Meaning a private boat rental. Not a ferry. Once upon a time there had been ferry service to the island, but that was one hell of a long time ago, and since only private residences and a few vacation cottages remained on the island, who needed ferry service anyway? Anyone who could afford to live on an island could afford their own boat.

This time of year there wasn't even, at least officially, water-taxi service. Though once Jason had offered his ID—the "Big Initials" as Gil Hickok once joked—the owner of Seaport Sloops agreed to throw in a complimentary boat ride on the even off-season gulp-inducing cottage rental rate.

Jason wasn't going to argue. It had been eight hours from LAX to ART, and he had not managed to sleep at all on the plane—on top of not sleeping the night before. It had taken practically as long to arrange for the car rental as to drive from Watertown to Cape Vincent, and he'd already lost three hours traveling west to east. By the time he arrived at the boat rental facility, he was tired, ever so slightly jetlagged, and—as it was only lunchtime—still facing a full day's work.

There was no general store—or any store—on the island. At the helpful reminder of Mrs. Seaport Sloops, he stocked up on enough groceries to see him through lunch, dinner, and a possible breakfast: a small bag of freshly ground coffee, a pint of milk, a couple of cans of soup, a package of dubious-looking mini "blueberry" muffins, and a frozen beef stroganoff dinner.

"The FBI!" Mrs. Seaport Sloops beamed, ringing up Jason's purchases. She was a medium-sized woman with frizzy brown hair and purple fingernails as long and curving as a storybook Chinese mandarin. "I guess you can't tell us what you're here for?"

"Just routine follow-up stuff."

She laughed. "But routine follow-up on *what* stuff?"

Jason was amused at her unashamed curiosity but shook his head.

She was unfazed. "Taxes, I bet. That's what it usually is with those folks."

"Which folks?"

"Island folks." She finished bagging his groceries. "Rich folks. I sure hope you don't get seasick. That water's *rough* today. Beautiful weather though."

Jason glanced out the window at the cold and drizzling day. "Is it?"

"Sure. We're having a warm spell. It was snowing last week. You want to add some Dramamine to your groceries?"

"I don't get seasick."

Which was true, but in any case, the boat ride across to the island, though wet and cold, was quick.

Mr. Seaport Sloops—or Bram, as he instructed Jason to call him—was tall, wiry and talkative. His eyes were gray. His hair too, prematurely so. He offered a quick rundown of the three-mile-long island and its inhabitants without being asked. In fact, shutting him up would have been the challenge.

"You can't hardly see the house behind the trees and fog, but those chimneys off the port side belong to the Hoveys. They've been here the longest. There have been Hoveys for as far back as anyone can remember. It's just Caroline Hovey now. Caroline Durrand, I should say. She's been living here since she and the old man separated back in 1980."

"She lives on the island alone?"

"Sure." Bram's tone was dry. "All on her own. Not counting the cook, the housekeeper, the gardener-chauffeur, and two maids."

"That's a lot of servants for one little old lady," Jason said, as if he'd never heard of such a thing as household staff.

"It sure is. Of course, used to be the sons spent a lot of time here. Especially during the summer. And *way* back in the day, the Hoveys used to hold house parties and so forth. Believe it or not, once upon a time this island was haven for the rich and famous. They'd come all the way out here to fish and play golf." Bram grinned, as if entertained by the foibles of the wealthy.

Jason studied the green, heavily forested shoreline wreathed in thready mist. "It looks deserted."

"Not far from it. There are thirteen year-round residents. You gotta love peace and quiet. It's too out of the way for most people." Bram added, "There's the ruins of an old fort on the other side of the island. The British used this place as a naval station. They'd build their ships here and then raid the coast."

"That's a lot of history for such a little island."

"It is. You can find lots of artifacts and interesting stuff if you poke around." He glanced at Jason and added hastily, "Of course, it's illegal to take anything away. I know that."

"It's illegal on federal land. This island is privately owned."

Reassured that Jason and Uncle Sam were not going to snatch his collection of arrowheads or tin cans or whatever it was he was hoarding, Bram relaxed. "We used to come out here all the time to explore when we were kids. There are a couple of graveyards near the fort."

"Graveyards?" That caught Jason's attention.

"Sure. Twenty-five military graves lie outside the north wall of the fort. The civilian graveyard is a little east of the fort. Then you've got the Indian burial grounds clear on the other side of the island." He smiled. "These days they've got more dead residents than live ones on Camden Island."

Jason nodded. "The Durrand sons don't visit anymore?"

"They come to see the old lady sometimes. They live in California now. That's where the old man was from. Some place up north. Wine and cattle country. Barnaby comes out more than Shep. Somebody told me he's out here now. I wouldn't know. They dock their boats at Trudell's Marina these days."

"What about the other son?"

"Shep? I haven't seen Shep in years. But then the estate will go to Barnaby, so I guess it makes sense he keeps an eye on it."

They rounded a rocky promontory, white rocks like a skeletal foot jutting out into restless, dark water. In the distance, Jason spotted a man— or at least a burly figure—carrying what appeared to be an ax. He was headed toward the winter-bare woods and away from the ruins of a large house.

House? Castle was probably as accurate. Four stories of what looked from a distance to be solid stone. A castle as imagined by Salvador Dalí. Right down to a giant gray and blue disk—was that really a clock face?— lying upturned in the tall grass.

"What's that place?" Jason asked Bram.

Bram glanced indifferently at the fog-shrouded shoreline. "Camden Castle. That's what people around here call it, anyway."

The man with the ax vanished into the deep surrounding woods. Jason went back to studying the structure. As architecture went, it looked like a cross between the House That Jack Built and Hogwarts. "Is that a clock tower?"

"What's left of it. If you look carefully, you can see the clock itself still lying in the garden. Lightning struck the tower a few years ago, so they dismantled it before the clock took out the whole roof. It wouldn't take much. The whole place is falling down."

Pale smoke wisped from one of the tall chimneys, rising like a question mark against the slate clouds. "Somebody still lives there."

"Sure. Eric Greenleaf. He's the last of the line. At least for now. He had a kid with a girl in town. Melanie Foster. Claims she tricked him into it. He pays support but won't recognize the kid as his own. I guess he could still marry and have a family, but I can't imagine who would want to live out here with him."

Jason nodded politely as Bram continued the good-natured gossip and slander of his neighbors.

"How many full-time residents did you say are on the island?" Jason asked when he could insert a comment.

Bram automatically corrected the tiller, heading for a distant dock looking silver in the stormy light. "If you mean households, four. The Hoveys, the Greenleafs, the Patricks, and the Jeffersons. Thirteen people. The rest of the houses are summer homes or vacation rentals."

Meaning if Jason ran into trouble, he'd be at least half an hour away from help. Not that he could picture a scenario where Barnaby turned violent.

They reached the short dock and found two other boats moored there: a pontoon and a small aluminum fishing boat.

"Who do these belong to?" Jason asked.

"The Lund belongs to Pat Patrick. The pontoon goes with the cottage to your leeside."

Jason considered what he could see of a gray roof, shingles wet with fog, half-hidden behind tall evergreens.

"Is anyone staying at the cottage?"

"Doesn't look like it. We don't own that property."

Bram tied up the boat, and they clambered onto the dock and walked up to the "lodge," Jason shouldering his carryall and clutching his meager bag of groceries.

The holiday rental was a long box of tall, narrow windows and green siding. A fieldstone chimney capped one end of the building and a large screened-in sleeping porch the other.

Bram unlocked the front door. "Home sweet home."

Jason stepped inside and set his bags down. The place smelled musty but clean, scented of a million summer vacations: a blend of fish, wet towels, fading potpourri, and disinfectant. It was chilly and a little damp, but Bram flicked a switch and the heater rumbled into life, gusting hot, stale air through the vents.

"This is great. Thanks for the ride—" Jason reached for his wallet, but Bram waved him off.

"No, no. It's all part of the service. Let me show you around."

The grand tour began with the small, dark wood kitchen.

Bram pointed to an ancient-looking machine. "Coffee maker—"

"Thank God," murmured Jason. As long as the thing turned on, he'd be happy.

Bram thumped an oak cupboard door. "Dishes. Utensils in the drawer. Dishwasher, microwave, oven, refr—"

"Thanks. This is great. I'm sure I can find everything."

Bram would not be deterred, leading the way into the next room. "I guess it must be pretty exciting working for the FBI?"

"Good days, bad days," Jason said. "Like any job."

"Have you worked any high-profile crimes? Anything I'd have read about?"

"I doubt it," Jason said.

Bram grinned. "Have you ever caught any serial killers?"

Thanks to television, most people thought the FBI spent all its time chasing kidnappers and serial killers.

"Me? No. My team mostly follows paper trails. I spend a lot of time examining old documents."

"I see." Bram smiled, clearly not believing this for a second. "Here's the family room. You can see we've got lots of games, puzzles, and books. My wife loves to read, so all her castoffs end up here. Romances mostly. Stereo, TV, DVD player—we've got a great video library. Let me think..." He brightened. "We've got *Silence of the Lambs, Manhunter, Hannibal, Suspect Zero,* and *Red Dragon.* And one other one about the FBI. I forget... Oh, *Heat.* We love that one. We love that Sandra Bullock!"

Did Bram think FBI agents only watched movies about FBI agents? Jason said gravely, "I know what I'll be doing tonight." And that, hopefully, would be sleeping. Deeply. Dreamlessly.

"It's too cold this time of year for swimming or snorkeling, but there's the outdoor grill, and you've got the kayak—"

"Sounds like the perfect vacation." Jason stayed patient. "I wish I could spend an extra day or two."

"Smuggling, I bet." Bram watched him shrewdly. "With Canada right across the water? Yeah. It'll be smuggling. Off the record?"

"Off the record?" Jason winked. "You didn't hear that from me."

"Right. Right. Well, if anything goes wrong, there's the phone. Your cell phone will work too. Mostly. It depends on your carrier, of course. When you're ready to come back, you can borrow the pontoon. If you're not comfortable driving a boat, I'll come fetch you."

"I grew up on boats. That's not a problem."

Bram seemed reluctant to leave, but at last he ran out of instructions, information, and gossip, and was forced to bid Jason so long.

Jason watched Bram's motorboat grow small, smaller, and then speck-sized in the misty distance. Good. Now maybe he could finally get to w—

His cell phone rang, the sound startling in the profound silence. He glanced at the ID and sighed. Charlotte. Sister #1. The family diplomat. He clicked to answer.

"Hi, Charlie."

"Where are you?"

"Working."

"I didn't ask what you're doing. You're *always* working. *Where* are you working?" At fifty-four, Charlotte was old enough to be his mother and had spent the last thirty-three years not letting him forget it for a moment. Granted, Sophie was old enough to be his mother too, but that technicality was not something she wanted to advertise.

"I'm in New York. As a matter of fact, I'm on Camden Island in Cape Vincent."

"Cape Vincent? Isn't that right across from Canada?"

He said patiently, "Was there something you needed?"

"I saw that photo of you in the *Valley Voice*. I hope to God you're not still planning to take part in any undercover operations."

"No plans at the moment." Those swift approaching clouds were looking more and more like rain. He began to mentally calculate how long it would take to walk to the Hovey estate. According to Bram, the island was ninety percent woodland, but in addition to tons of smaller trails and shortcuts, a walking path surrounded the entire island.

"Did you tell Sophie it was okay for her to go ahead and organize a big party for your birthday next week?"

Jason's attention abruptly refocused on Charlotte, the bearer of bad news. "No, I sure did not."

"Well, she seems to think you gave her the go-ahead, and she's putting together a dinner party at Capo Restaurant."

This was another thing you never saw on TV or the movies. The FBI agent throwing a fit about his birthday party plans.

"I told her I did *not* want a big thing made of my birthday."

"Well, I do kind of see her point. Mom and Dad aren't getting any younger—"

"Would you two stop saying that?"

"—and, after all, you did nearly get yourself killed last year, so even though it's an off number, maybe it's all right to make a little bit of a fuss."

"I don't want a fuss."

"I know. I'll try to rein her in, but since there *is* going to be a small—very small, hopefully—party, there's someone I'd really love you to meet. His name's Alexander, and he teaches art at UCLA. He and his partner split up a year ago, and he's just getting back into the dating game. I did the redesign on his dining room. He's a lovely, lovely guy, and I really think you two would hit it off."

Jason had been listening to this with mounting exasperation. "Charlie, I'm not interested in meeting anyone right now. I'm *working*. I'm in the middle of a case."

"Well, you won't be working next Thursday. It's not a date. In fact, he can come as my date."

"Come as your…"

"My date-friend. He's definitely gay. There's no pressure. I simply think you'd really hit it off. Wouldn't you like to meet someone?"

He expelled a quick, exasperated laugh. "No."

"Well, you should. All work and no play. Etcetera. Etcetera. Seriously, though. Life is too short."

"Here it comes. And *I'm* not getting any younger either."

Charlie laughed. "You? You're still a baby. There's no rush."

"Well, there kind of is." Jason staunchly ignored the "baby" comment. "I really *am* in the middle of something right now, so we'll have to talk about it when I get back later in the week."

"Later in the week when? Do you need me to go by your place and water the house plants?"

He was hoping for the swift demise of those house plants—he was not an exotic orchids kind of guy—and in any case, he didn't like the idea of anyone, even his sister, wandering through his home when he wasn't there. Working for the Bureau made everyone a little paranoid, and Jason was no exception.

"No need. I'm hoping I can get out of here tomorrow—assuming I ever get off the phone and accomplish what I came here to do."

"*Okay*, point taken." Charlotte sounded like she was humoring a small and cranky child. "I'll let you go. I just wanted to give you a heads-up."

"I appreciate that."

"No, you don't, but that's what sisters are for. Let me know as soon as you get back, will you?"

That final request, he understood. His loved ones were jumpy about his safety after he'd nearly been shot to death when an undercover operation went disastrously wrong. They had never been happy about his decision to join the Bureau, and his close call had done nothing to change their minds.

"Will do," he said neutrally, and disconnected.

It didn't take long to change into a clean pair of jeans and a fresh shirt for the interview he hoped he'd be having within the hour. He had originally anticipated this interview taking place in the Fletcher-Durrand New York gallery, but the navy blazer he'd brought wasn't warm enough for a hike through the wintery woods. He opted for his FBI jacket, and hoped he wouldn't tip Durrand off from a mile away.

In fact, that was another thing that annoyed him about how the Bureau was portrayed in film and TV. Wardrobe. Apparently, Hollywood had never heard of polo shirts and chinos. Let alone jeans when they made sense—which today they did. Hollywood FBI agents wore suits and ties regardless of weather. And even if the men were right, the women always dressed like classy hookers or college students.

He checked his weapon, rechecked his weapon, and set off through the woods.

Thanks to the helpful and garrulous Bram, he knew where he was headed, and the brisk cedar-scented cold air revived his energy and determination. Unfortunately, the long silent walk also gave him too much time to think about things that had nothing to do with the job.

At least, he didn't believe they had anything to do with the job. But adding to his general disquiet was the growing certainty that Kennedy had deliberately staged things the way he had to minimize how much fallout he had to deal with from Jason. He had profiled Jason from the first, and he continued to profile him. He knew that by framing their breakup—if you could call it that—in a professional context, Jason's behavior was automatically constrained.

Whether it came down to the difference in their ages or job titles or just their very different personalities, Kennedy knew that Jason would cue off him. That it would be all but impossible for Jason to do other than follow his lead on this.

Not that Jason had wanted a big scene, but a little emotional honesty would have been nice. Would have helped him understand. He deeply resented feeling that he had been manipulated. Not in the relationship itself—although, maybe—but in how Kennedy had decided to terminate things.

He had waited to do it in person, so point. But he had also held off doing it—and when he had got around to doing it, he'd done it in such a way that he might as well have cut Jason loose over the phone. It had been that impersonal. Certainly it had felt that impersonal to Jason.

And because Sam—Kennedy—had delayed, Jason also could not help feeling that he'd strung him along.

Okay, in fairness, a little long-distance flirtation and a few late-night conversations that verged on confessional weren't much of a string. No real lines had been crossed. But.

But all the same he was pissed off.

And yes, hurt.

"Grow the hell up," Jason muttered. He brushed by a juniper bush, startling several small, winged somethings, which circled overhead, twittering, and disappeared into the network of bare branch oak and birch trees.

Bats.

Perfect. Just what the day had been missing.

Anyway, it wasn't childish to care about someone, to be open emotionally to...possibility. Jason wasn't in the wrong for that. For starting to feel something for Sam. Back in June, Sam had indicated a willingness to pursue...something. Once he'd changed his mind, the right thing to do would have been to let Jason know ASAP. So that Jason didn't continue to— Well, it was painful and stupid to even think about.

But I like talking to you.

Yeah, that was the truth. Sam *did* like talking to him. There weren't a lot of people in Sam's universe he could talk to as openly and easily as he'd talked to Jason when they were both unguarded and off the clock. Sam didn't have a lot of friends. It was possible he didn't have any friends beyond Jason. Jason couldn't remember any mention of friends in all those phone calls. In fact, although the word "solitary" seemed to suggest an emotional vulnerability Sam didn't possess, he was in a lot of ways a solitary guy. Or at least in any other person, Sam's isolation would have seemed lonely.

But one thing Jason had figured out over the past eight months: *alone* was the way Sam liked it. Alone was his default.

The wild oaks and birches gave way to ornamental trees, including a ten-foot wall of winter-bare lilacs. Beyond the straw-colored stretch of muddy lawn, Jason spotted the house.

After the sight of the Greenleafs' crumbling clock tower and the news of Indian burial grounds, he was ready for anything, but the house was a perfectly ordinary three-story mansion. Reinforced concrete and brick veneer with lots of detail lifted from 13th Century Gothic architecture, including a slate mansard roof and rows of French windows.

He crossed the long expanse of mushy yellow-gray grass, wondering if his approach was being observed by someone standing at those elegant windows. Even so, not a lot of room to run on an island.

He reached the double front doors—nine-foot-tall and painted black and gold—and rang the bell.

He could almost feel the shock reverberating through the house as the chimes died away.

Nothing happened for a long minute.

Two long minutes.

He was about to ring the bell again when the towering door suddenly swung open.

The tall forty-something brunette standing before him was undoubtedly the housekeeper. That demure brown shirt dress communicated her job title as effectively as a name plate on an office desk. She wore her dark hair in the sleek flip still favored by so many wives of conservative politicians—not including his own sister.

Same make but different model as the devoted Ms. Keating, if Jason was any judge.

"May I help you?" she asked after a surprised moment. Her voice was pleasant, her brown eyes curious. She gave the impression of looking Jason up and down without ever moving her gaze.

Jason introduced himself, offering his ID.

"FBI?" she repeated mechanically, staring at his badge.

"Correct. I'd like to have a word with Barnaby Durrand, Mrs....?"

She was frowning. "Merriam. I'm Mrs. Durrand's housekeeper. You came all the way out here looking for Mr. Durrand?"

"That's right. I—"

"Without calling first?"

"I understand Mr. Durrand is visiting his mother."

"Well, yes, but..." She hesitated, still frowning, still clearly taken aback. "Yes," she repeated. "But he's not here at the moment."

"Really?" Jason didn't bother to hide his disbelief. "According to the manager of his Los Angeles gallery, *here* is exactly where he is."

"He sailed over to Cape Vincent this morning."

She was too genuinely bewildered to be lying, but there was more than a tinge of exasperation in Jason's instinctive, "You've *got* to be kidding."

"No. I'm certainly not kidding you. I believe he had a business meeting."

"I see." Jason recovered his self-control. "And when is Mr. Durrand expected back?" He held his breath, waiting. If she told him Durrand wasn't coming back, he was going to end his misery and jump in the St. Lawrence River.

Her expression grew wary. "Tomorrow afternoon."

"What time tomorrow afternoon?"

"I don't know. He didn't say."

Jason opened his mouth, and she added hastily, "He'll be back in time for dinner, naturally."

Naturally.

"I see." If he didn't know better, he'd say Barnaby had received advance warning he was coming. The only person with that knowledge outside the Bureau was Chris Shipka, and Jason had trouble believing Shipka would tip Barnaby off, given his attempt to further implicate the Durrands in fraud, larceny, and what had sounded a lot like a possible murder. But you never could tell.

"Was Mr. Durrand expecting you?" Mrs. Merriam inquired, recovering her own equilibrium. She had to know the answer to that one, but her expression was one of polite inquiry.

"He should be." Jason was aware he'd lost the element of surprise; there wasn't a chance in hell she wouldn't notify Barnaby that the FBI had shown up at his front door.

He considered his limited options. "Okay, Mrs. Merriam. I assume you've got some way of getting in touch with Mr. Durrand. Please let him know that I'll be back tomorrow afternoon. If he's not available, perhaps I could speak to Mrs. Durrand."

Mrs. Merriam looked startled. "*Mrs.* Durrand? Mrs. Durrand doesn't—isn't—" Her gaze went automatically to the badge once more clipped to his belt. Yeah. The Big Initials.

"She'll see me," Jason said ominously. "Either Barnaby or Mrs. Durrand. I plan on talking to somebody in this house tomorrow. I'll leave it to Mr. Durrand as to who that's going to be."

Her jaw dropped. And so would George Potts' if he ever heard about this exchange, but Jason had well and truly had it with the runaround. He was not really going to insist on interviewing a sick old woman—had no legal jurisdiction to do so even if he was ruthless enough to try—but Barnaby couldn't know that, and, if Jason's instinct was correct, wouldn't risk such a meeting in any case.

He delivered a formal and professional smile to the wide-eyed Mrs. Merriam and departed.

Chapter Nine

Mostly it was academic curiosity that sent Jason in the direction of Camden Castle.

For one thing, he now had a day to cool his heels before he could interview Barnaby Durrand. For another, the former art historian in him wanted to see that grandiose structure up close.

Alluring as was the idea of spending a day watching Sandra Bullock movies… Yeeeah, no.

He spied the pointy tilt of the witch's hat towers above the bare white tree branches as he hiked toward the Greenleaf property. No question that there was something eerie about these woods. Maybe it had to do with all those different burial grounds scattered across the island. Maybe it was something else. A lot of this forest predated the fort and the graveyards. These trees were very old—the shining trunks, knotted limbs, and bony twigs reminded him of an army of skeletons—and the silence had a listening quality to it.

In fact, "silence" was relative. The steady thud of his boots on damp soil, the furtive rustle of underbrush as unseen life watched and waited for him to pass, the occasional tentative birdsong served to remind him that he was just another traveler on a very long road.

The sun was making a half-hearted attempt to warm things up. Patches of yellow light filtered through naked branches and pooled beneath the twisted roots. His shadow appeared and then vanished on the path as he crossed beneath towering trees filtering the sun with crisscrossed twigs and branches. It was not yet spring, but the butterflies didn't seem to know it, furling and unfurling mystery-colored wings before vanishing into the gray, filmy shadows.

The cool silence was ruptured by the sound of distant gunfire.

Rifle shots.

One.

Two.

Jason halted in his tracks, counting.

Boom. Three.

His heart paused for the length of a couple of beats while he tried to place the direction they were coming from. It was not hunting season, but this was a rural space and people in wilderness areas used firearms more casually than people in suburbia. These shots were coming from the south side of the island—well away from him—and Jason was irritated with himself for his irrational reaction.

Reaction? *Fear.*

Call it what it was.

The unexpected sound of gunshots still scared him. It was stupid and infuriating. He had been on the weapons range plenty of times since Miami, he had been involved in a shooting incident in Massachusetts, and—on top of everything else—he had not been injured by rifle fire, and yet his immediate response to the sound of a rifle was fear.

How the hell long was this going to go on? For the rest of his career? He'd hoped after Massachusetts he was past it—and he *was* much, much better—but even so.

Even so, the unexpected sound of gunfire sent his pulse rocketing, caused him to break out in a cold sweat.

Anyway, it was a momentary reaction. He was fine again. Irritated with himself, but steady.

He jumped as his cell phone rang, the sound weirdly loud in the enclosed and secret silence of the trees. Okay. *Mostly* steady. He thought he'd put the damn thing on vibrate.

He reached for his phone and snapped out, "Yes? West here."

"Yo, G-man," came a cheerful male voice.

"Lucius." Jason relaxed. Lucius Lux was one of his top informants. A genuinely gifted young artist who had, unfortunately, turned his gift to forgery. Jason had pulled a lot of strings to keep Lux out of jail—and more strings to get him into a top-notch art program at Otis College of Art and Design. Lux was always threatening to quit Otis, but he'd lasted a year so far, and so far was so good in Jason's opinion.

"What up? Busy chasing bad guys and harassing little old ladies?"

Jason thought of his threat to interrogate Caroline Durrand, and winced. "Something like that. How's it going?"

"Haven't flunked out yet. What can I do you for?"

"I'm looking for information."

Lux's sigh was noisy and exaggerated. "Tell me something I don't know."

Jason smiled to himself. He was fond of the kid. While it was true that most forgers were failed artists, unable to break into the brutally competitive market on their own creative merits, that wasn't the case with Lux. He'd been sidetracked by the lure of quick and easy money, but his ego was healthy enough that more and more he wanted his own career.

"What have you heard about forged works making their way into Fletcher-Durrand?"

"Fletcher-Durrand?" Lux sounded slightly less breezy. "Me? Nothing."

Until that moment, Jason had been willing to believe he was making a felony out of a bit of harmless fakery. But that infinitesimal change in Lux's tone alerted him that he just might be onto something.

"Nothing at all?"

"No, man. Was that all you wanted?"

Jason felt a flicker of concern. Lux was naturally both curious and chatty. Yet he showed zero interest in the possibility of forgeries at one of the best-known galleries in the state. Hopefully that was not a hint as to his own involvement.

He said neutrally, "If I was looking for someone to copy a Reuven Rubin, who would I talk to?"

"Nobody, man. What you'd want is someone to do you a nice long-lost Monet. That's what sells. That's where the money is. Monet. Mon*ay*."

"Monet. Really?" That at least sounded like the normal Lux, and Monet was a frequent and favorite target for forgery, so Jason didn't want to leap to the conclusion that two and two made eight. But the sudden mention of Monet in this context made him uneasy.

"Funny you say that. I saw a really lousy forgery of Monet the other night."

"Yeah? Well, there are a lot of them around." Lux stopped there, again noticeably unlike his usual self.

"If I'm in the market for a Reuven Rubin, who do I talk to?" Jason tried again, and this time Lux's tone was edged.

"I thought the feds were after F-D for selling off what don't belong to them."

"We are. But I noticed a copy of a Reuven Rubin last time I visited the gallery."

"Maybe it wasn't a copy."

"The original is hanging in MoMA. I got an email verification this morning."

Lux made a noncommittal noise.

Jason gave up on diplomacy. "I need to know who's supplying forged works to Fletcher-Durrand."

"Not me."

"I know not you. But someone."

Lux said seriously, "You want to stay away from them, G-man."

"I'm not in the stay-away business," Jason pointed out. "I'm in the bring-people-to-justice business."

"I'm just saying…there are rumors."

"Fill me in. What kind of rumors?"

"More like whispers."

"Okay. What kind of whispers?"

"That bad things happen to people who get on the wrong side of the Durrands."

Jason was silent for a moment. This might be something. Or it might not. He said casually, "Like? Give me an example. Give me a name."

"I don't *have* names. I don't *have* an example. If I *had* an example, it wouldn't be a rumor!"

"Okay. Don't get excited. I have to ask, right?"

"No. You don't. You don't have to ask me. I can't be your only snitch."

"You're not a snitch. You're a friend."

Lux said sulkily, sounding younger than his twenty years, "Yeah, well."

"You're a friend able to move in circles I can't. That's why I'm asking you."

"Oh, I owe you, believe me, I get that," Lux's tone was unexpectedly bitter.

That *was* the truth, but it pained Jason to hear it. He liked Lux; he genuinely wanted to help him—hoped he *was* helping him—but he had cultivated their friendship with this end in mind: Lux's continued usefulness.

All the same, Lux was too young to be that cynical.

"Forget it," Jason said. "You're right. I have other informants. How do you like your classes this semester?"

Silence.

Lux burst out, "Rabab Doody. That's who you need to talk to."

Before Jason could respond, Lux disconnected.

Jason sighed, pocketed his phone, and strode on toward the Greenleaf estate.

His angle of approach brought him up behind the house on a hillside overlooking the deep bay of a small, sheltered harbor. From this distance, the mansion looked more like an insane asylum for witches. An abandoned asylum. There were large holes in sections of the roof, and a number of the windows were shuttered or boarded up.

Not entirely abandoned, though. There was smoke drifting from one of the chimneys, and laundry hung from a clothesline in a small courtyard.

It was one thing for the Durrands to continue to inhabit ye old family estate. Their ancestral holdings were still in excellent repair, from what Jason could see. Who the hell would choose to live in a relic like this one? It would take millions to restore the house to its former glory, and clearly there was no spare change in the Greenleaf family coffers. If restoration was out of the question, the next best bet would be to sell the property to some organization that could preserve and protect the building, while profiting from the real estate. A resort chain maybe. Although that might be easier said than done. Camden Island was not exactly on the beaten path. But then that was also what might make it a very enticing property to an investor with vision.

Jason hiked down an steep trail to the burned ruins of a yacht house and then checked out the crumbling remains of a nearby skiff house. It was probably a five-minute walk to the mansion itself, but back in the day, a carriage would have been sent down to the harbor to transport guests and goods.

As he neared the house, he was struck again by the sheer size of the building. That was typical of these Gilded Age palaces. It was built for weekend house parties and lavish summer retreats. It would comfortably house a large extended family as well as a fleet of servants.

He couldn't quite pin down the architectural style, but Walt Disney would probably have given it a thumbs-up. The mansion seemed to be the end result of a collision of ideas and creative impulses, almost sculptural in effect with its advancing and receding turrets, dormers, and massive chimneys crowning high, steep roofs. Whatever the guiding principle of design might have been, the result was a big and complicated structure, richly, even ornately decorated. The exterior walls of the upper stories were paneled in a variety of silvery diamond and scalloped wood shingles, framed in a semi-Tudor half-timber pattern of wood beams. The lower story and a half were constructed of masonry and clad in a fortune's worth of beautifully carved gray marble.

The final effect was neither graceful nor stately, and yet it was weirdly appealing. Jason walked to the end of the stone path and glanced down.

A double tier of retaining walls lifted the villa's gardens—draped in a tangle of dead vines—high above the water.

Even from the garden level, that was one hell of a drop. Stunning view, though.

He ascended a broad flight of steps to a terrace pockmarked with missing stones and littered with broken slats and shingles. He gazed upward.

When whole, the clock tower had probably served as both a landmark and a beacon for miles and miles. The great tower still dominated the scene, rising from a massive stone base toward the clouds. There was something almost shocking about the giant black hole at the summit where the clock face had formerly rested, but it had probably been a wise idea to take the thing down when they had. The wooden framework showed a number of alarming gaps in its trunk. Birds, large and small, flew in and out of the openings.

He walked around the smaller corner tower, to find himself at the true front of the house, and started toward the massive arched entrance—stopping dead when someone shouted, "Hey! What are you doing?"

Jason glanced around. A man was approaching from the other side of the terrace. He wore a red and black plaid hunting jacket, dirty jeans, and a formidable scowl.

"Mr. Greenleaf?" Jason asked.

"I asked what you're doing here."

Greenleaf—if this was indeed Greenleaf—was a big man. It wasn't all muscle, but there was enough muscle to pose a threat—assuming he knew how to handle himself. His hair was yellow-blond; long, but balding on top. A look only legendary rock stars could pull off. His eyes were close set and brown, a shade so dark they looked black.

"I was admiring your clock tower," Jason replied. His curiosity was aroused by the other man's instant hostility. Not that people weren't hostile for all kinds of reasons, but an antisocial attitude just naturally caught Jason's interest.

"Didn't you see the sign? Private property. No trespassing."

"I did. Yeah." Jason offered his ID. "Federal agent Jason West. You're Eric Greenleaf?"

"FBI?" Greenleaf scrutinized the badge. It was not the cursory look most people gave official ID. His black gaze raised to study Jason. "Jason West." He sounded like he was committing it to memory.

"That's right. Do you live here alone, sir?"

Greenleaf nodded. A man of few words, or experience with the legal system?

"I was hoping to ask you a couple of questions about your neighbors. The Durrands."

Greenleaf's look of distrust deepened. "What about them?"

"Well, to start with, how well do you know them?"

He shook his head. Shrugged.

"You've lived on the island your entire life?"

"Off and on."

"Did you know the Durrand brothers when you were growing up?"

"Sure."

Greenleaf was about the age of the Durrands. The Durrands had spent summers on the island—and Greenleaf was their closest neighbor. It seemed likely the boys would have gravitated toward each other.

"Would you say you were friendly with the Durrand brothers?"

Greenleaf's smile was humorless. "I knew them."

"What were they like?"

"Spoiled rich kids."

Jason glanced instinctively at the crumbling structure behind Greenleaf. "Not like you?"

"Depends who you ask."

"I'm asking you."

The black look that flittered behind Greenleaf's pale gaze prickled the hair at the back of Jason's neck. Yeah, there was something about this guy...

That didn't mean Greenleaf had anything to do with the Durrands and Jason's case. Not everybody loved law enforcement or the federal government. It would still be a good idea to stay sharp while in Mr. Greenleaf's presence.

"I work for a living," Greenleaf said. "I'm an underwriter for Cape Vincent Savings Bank."

"I see. Then you're able to work from home?"

"Why are you so interested?"

Jason wasn't particularly interested—this had been purely a fishing expedition—but Greenleaf's hostile and defensive attitude continued to raise flags.

"When was the last time you spoke to Barnaby Durrand?" he asked.

"Barnaby? Years. I haven't seen or spoken to him in probably twenty years."

"Do you keep in touch with Shepherd Durrand?"

Greenleaf snarled, "I told you we're not friends! Now unless you have a warrant, get off my property."

Whoa. Jason considered Greenleaf's flushed and angry face. Here was a guy who believed he had something to hide. That didn't mean what he had to hide was any concern of Jason's. People could behave strangely and unpredictably for reasons of their own, reasons that would not make sense to anyone else.

He said, "Sorry to have disturbed you, sir."

Greenleaf stared at him without answering. His demeanor set off alarm bells for Jason. Again, it didn't mean he had any connection to Jason's investigation.

And it didn't mean he *didn't* have any connection...

Chapter Ten

There really was—or at least had been—a Paris Havemeyer.

The nineteen-year-old German exchange student had been working as a model and taking classes at the Art Institute of New York when he'd disappeared twenty years earlier.

Jason blew on his steaming mug of Campbell's tomato soup and studied Havemeyer's black and white photo. Several square-jawed images of the kid popped up in a Google search, though they all seemed to originate from one photo shoot. Havemeyer wore the same bulky wool sweater and retro Jheri Curl do in all five photos. His hair looked white blond in the pics, and his eyes were that colorless glitter that usually indicated blue.

Bad hair decisions aside, there was no question he had been a very handsome—even beautiful—young man.

And after several hours of searching, that was the extent of what Jason knew about Paris Havemeyer. He had existed, and he had disappeared without a trace—if internet forums were to be believed.

ASK SHEPHERD DURRAND!!! an anonymous poster advised in one such forum.

Whose Shepherd Durrand? came an ungrammatical and equally anonymous reply.

Anonymous #1 responded with a link to the Durrand gallery in New York and the comment THIS MAN IS A MURDERER!!!

Art should be free. This gallery sucks! riposted commenter "donuts."

That was the extent of the exchange. As leads went, it wasn't much.

Presumably Chris Shipka had more—a lot more than this. What *was* his connection to the case, given that he'd have been about ten at the time of Havemeyer's disappearance? Further, this seemed to be an East Coast incident, and Shipka's crime beat was the West Coast. California's Southland, to be precise.

The more Jason looked into Havemeyer's supposed disappearance, the more curious he grew about Chris Shipka.

He swallowed a mouthful of soup and considered.

A few finger taps brought up a heart-stopping list of bylines on stories featuring yours truly, intrepid FBI agent Jason West. Shipka was the crime reporter for the *Valley Voice*, so he wrote about other cases and ongoing investigations—he was energetic in his pursuit and prolific in his output—and it was abundantly, embarrassingly clear to Jason that a lot, certainly some of the most favorable press he received over the past couple of years, had been coming from one source: Chris Shipka.

It's the president of your fan club, Hickok had joked, and that was maybe a little too close to the truth for comfort.

A lot of Shipka's investigations seemed to revolve around the art world, so fair enough, but he wasn't writing about Hickok's clearance rate, and in his own unassuming way, Hickok was a legend.

Maybe FBI agents made for better headlines. Or maybe it had to do with Jason's orientation. Maybe it had to do with something else. He'd felt a connection...no, that was the wrong word. He'd sensed Shipka's... awareness. Yes. That was it. He'd picked up signs of interest from Shipka. So maybe it was that simple. Shipka personally found him appealing, maybe even attractive.

Or maybe it *was* something else.

Or maybe Jason was getting paranoid in his old age. Spending too much time with a guy like Sam Kennedy would make anyone start to see the dark side of every human interaction.

Other than a preoccupation with Jason's investigations, there seemed nothing remotely sinister about Shipka. His life appeared to be an open book. Or at least an open internet article.

He had graduated from San Diego State University's School of Journalism and Media Studies and landed his first job at the *San Diego Reader*. From there he had worked his way to the *Voice of San Diego* and then the *San Diego Union-Tribune*. After the *Union-Tribune*, he had moved north and taken the job at the *Valley Voice*. Since the *Valley Voice* was a smaller and less prestigious paper, maybe there was something there. Or maybe Shipka had liked being a big fish in a little pond. There was no difficulty getting bylines at the *Valley Voice*.

Glancing over Shipka's online articles, Jason was disconcerted to realize that on several occasions Shipka had contacted him directly for comments or to confirm facts. Yet on Sunday night, Jason would have sworn he had no prior contact with Shipka. Partly that was because it was routine to now and again confirm or deny facts for various news media outlets. Evidently his occasional interactions with Shipka had triggered no alarms.

As for the stories themselves, Jason had kind of a...not exactly antipathy, but a determined disinterest in any attention from the press. Maybe it had to do with growing up never quite sure if he was being singled out for his own achievements or those of his family.

And in return you'll be the guy who gets to pose in front of the cameras...

Kennedy had unknowingly struck a nerve eight months ago.

Jason was ambitious and had been aware of receiving favorable press, but it was a point of pride not to read that stuff. It was enough to know he was getting the right kind of attention for his work. Had he bothered to read Shipka's stories, he'd have likely recognized him at the museum wing dedication—he'd have likely been aware of Shipka long before that.

But other than being a little obsessive about his job—gee, who did that remind him of?—Shipka seemed normal enough, at least on cursory examination. Jason intended to dig deeper, of course. Whether he'd intended to or not, Shipka had made himself part of the investigation by coming forward. Inevitably his motives and possible connection to the Durrand case had to be evaluated.

Jason swallowed the last mouthful of soup and checked his messages and email. He'd received an automated response from Jonnie regarding the interview notes he'd sent on the Kerk investigation. No word from Kennedy, of course. Nor was he expecting one.

After answering the most urgent of his email, he phoned the Information Technology Branch and asked Bernadette to run a basic wants and warrants on Shipka. Then he phoned The New York State Missing

Persons Clearinghouse to see if any official investigation had been initiated into Havemeyer's disappearance.

Though originally created to provide assistance to law enforcement handling cases involving missing children under the age of eighteen, in 1999 the Clearinghouse had expanded their purview to include college students of any age. Unfortunately, Havemeyer had disappeared in '98, and Jason drew a blank. That did not necessarily mean no report had been filed, just that Havemeyer's case had never been kicked upstairs.

Jason went back to the beginning and phoned NYPD's Missing Persons Squad, which had its own cold case unit. It took some time, but at last he got the information he was seeking. A missing person report had been filed four days after Havemeyer disappeared. The case was still open, but that was a technicality. Nobody had given a thought to Paris Havemeyer in a very long time.

Understandable, given that hundreds of thousands of people across the country were reported missing every year. About 87 percent of those cases resolved within 30 days. The remaining 13 percent—more than 84,000 people in 2016—became long-term missing persons cases. Unsolved—hell, unidentified—homicides in most cases. And if that wasn't depressing enough, the DOJ estimated that there were more than 40,000 sets of unclaimed human remains in medical examiner or coroner offices—with several hundred new cases reported annually.

The facts of this case were few. Paris Havemeyer had last been seen entering his apartment house on West 26th Street at 1:30 a.m. on June 22. He was with two friends—the friends who would later report him missing—and the three men had just returned from a private party at the Fletcher-Durrand gallery. Havemeyer had informed his companions he wanted to keep partying. He had given no indication of where he intended to find this next party. His friends had continued on to their own apartment several blocks away.

Jason told himself not to make too much of this tenuous, highly circumstantial connection to the Durrands, but it offered insight into Shipka's insistence that Barnaby and Shepherd were dangerous to know.

It had taken a couple of days for Havemeyer's friends to determine that he really was unaccounted for. Because he was a young sexually active gay male—and an art student to boot—the police had not broken down any doors looking for him. In fact, listening between the lines, it sounded to Jason like no real investigation had taken place. The prevailing theory was that he had returned to Germany.

Times had changed, and that was a good thing. Twenty years ago, the circumstances surrounding Havemeyer's case were such that it was unlikely any other police department in the country would have handled anything differently.

"Could you email me a copy of that MP report?" Jason asked Lt. Hanna, head of the Missing Persons Squad.

"You bet," she said. "Knock yourself out. The sad truth is we have more of these cases than we could solve if the entire NYPD devoted itself to nothing but missing persons."

She was a woman of her word. The missing person report on Havemeyer landed in Jason's inbox ten minutes later. He glanced it over, not expecting to find anything ground-breaking, but one of the names of Havemeyer's companions on the night in question jumped out at him.

Donald Kerk.

The buyer for the Nacht Galerie in Berlin who had turned up dead beneath Santa Monica pier on Sunday appeared to be the same person who, twenty years earlier, had been one of the last people to see Paris Havemeyer alive.

Now *that* was some coincidence.

Jason glanced at the name of Havemeyer's second companion. The name Rodney Berguan rang no bells, but it would be interesting to have a word with this witness, if he could be located after so much time had passed. Jason made a note of Berguan's then-address.

Despite access to NCIC and all the other resources available to him, it would take some time before he had any answers. Even when you worked for the FBI, everything took longer than it did on TV, and a twenty-year-old missing person case was not anyone's priority. It was somebody's tragedy, though, and he felt initiating the first steps of a genuine investigation into Havemeyer's disappearance was the right thing to have done.

He was going to have to push Shipka on the link between Havemeyer and Durrand, as well as the name of his mysterious source. Was the party at the gallery the sole basis for Shipka's claims, or did he have something more concrete? Jason assumed Shipka had managed to access the missing person report on Havemeyer, which would explain why he'd been so sure Paris Havemeyer's disappearance would prove relevant to Jason's investigation into Fletcher-Durrand.

Regardless of what Shipka knew or didn't know, Jason needed more to go on than a couple of pieces of highly circumstantial evidence and an unsubstantiated claim from a source who was, so far, an unknown quantity.

The pressing question was should he bring this nebulous connection between Kennedy's hunt for a serial killer targeting members of the art world and his own investigation into the potentially shady dealings of the Durrand brothers, to Kennedy's attention? Given that what he'd uncovered seemed to spin the case in Kennedy's direction.

Or did he wait to see how these various and disparate leads developed? Leads? More like rumors and speculation.

Rumors, speculation…and a feeling in his bones that there was something to the whispers. Call it gut instinct—that was what Sam had called it when they'd talked about hunches and intuition and that sixth sense the best law enforcement officers developed over the years.

"Always go with your gut," Sam had advised. "Better red than dead."

Well, Jason's gut was telling him that there was something here, something not right, something that needed to be, at the least, followed up on.

Before he could change his mind, he phoned Kennedy's cell, hearing out the familiar message with a weird feeling in the pit of his stomach.

"Hi." Once again he was confronted with the difficulty of what to call his former…friend. "It's me."

In a way this was worse, given that the phone had been their direct line of communication. Once upon a time he had been comfortable in the knowledge that if he called, sooner or later Kennedy was going to call back. And that however lousy Jason's day, he would be smiling by the end of that conversation.

Jesus. Get over it, West.

He said briskly, "I'm in upstate New York—on Camden Island near Cape Vincent—to interview Barnaby Durrand, the primary suspect in my fraud case. Anyway, I've been following up a couple of leads, and

I think it's possible our two investigations may intersect. I spoke to that reporter from the *Valley Voice* before I left LA, and Shipka believes one or both of the Durrands may be involved in the cold case disappearance of a German art student about twenty years ago. I've come across information that might support that theory. It's a tenuous connection, but I still think it's worth pursuing."

God. He was starting to ramble.

"Obviously, that's your call."

Worse, maybe it sounded like he was hoping for continued interaction? He wasn't. He didn't want anything. Except to do his job to the best of his ability.

Jason concluded formally, idiotically, "Thank you," and disconnected.

That was at three thirty.

By three thirty-one he was questioning why he had not phoned Jonnie with his information, given that Kennedy had told him she was taking point on the case.

Was he hoping for further interaction with Kennedy? If so, that was just embarrassing.

At three forty-five his cell rang. Kennedy's number flashed up, and Jason's heart seemed to light up with it.

"West," Jason answered stiffly, formally, as if he didn't know who was on the other end of the call—but assumed the worst.

Kennedy said crisply, "Sorry for the delay. I was in a meeting."

This uncharacteristically courteous response had the reverse effect of further unsettling Jason. Since when did Kennedy concern himself with inconveniencing or irritating others—including Jason?

He said automatically, forgetting for a moment they were no longer on such casually intimate terms, "Right. How's it going up there?"

"The situation is not what I was led to believe." Judging by Kennedy's implacable tone, someone would pay for that. "What have you got?"

"A tenuous connection. And I do mean tenuous. In fact, I'm not sure I should have brought it to your attention. Not yet anyway."

Kennedy said—his tone unnervingly tolerant, "Noted. Let's hear what you've got, West."

"Mostly a rumor the Durrands may be behind the disappearance of a German art student twenty years ago. The kid disappeared after a private party at the Fletcher-Durrand gallery."

Kennedy was a silent for a moment. "You got this lead from the reporter who's making a career out of covering your cases?"

"Chris Shipka at the *Valley Voice* tipped me off, yes. But I've seen the missing person report."

"I see."

"I know what you're thinking, and again, I realize the link is—"

Kennedy said crisply, "We've got a dead German art dealer who met with—and had a long-standing connection with—two American art dealers who may be implicated in the earlier disappearance of another German, also involved in the art scene. Is that correct?"

Nice to know his emails were not going unread. As usual Jason was impressed with Kennedy's swift and concise assessment of the pertinent facts.

"Correct. And there's more. Kerk was also at that party. In fact, he was one of the last two people to see the kid alive. He filed the MPR."

"I see. You're taking it for granted this missing art student is dead?"

"Well, yes," said Jason. "I do think he's dead."

"Meanwhile, you believe that the Durrands are guilty of fraud and grand larceny, and you're working to build a case against them that will hold up in court."

It wasn't a question, but Jason answered, "Also correct."

Another pause while Kennedy considered. He said finally, neutrally, "You might be onto something."

It was a relief to know he wasn't blowing a couple of weird parallels out of proportion. Jason admitted, "It could just be a coincidence."

"Sure. It could. Life is full of coincidence. Or we might be looking at the faint outline of an actual pattern. It's too soon to know."

"How did you want to proceed?" Nothing Jason had discovered that day helped his own case. He did not want to lose control of his investigation, but inevitably BAU's claims would take precedence.

To his surprise, Kennedy said, "Continue to pursue your line of investigation, and keep me posted on your progress. I'm reassigning Agent Gould for the time being."

"Right. Okay," Jason said, doubtfully. Just what he did not want and did not need—staying in regular contact with Kennedy.

In response to whatever he heard in Jason's tone, Kennedy said, "The situation up here is more complicated than I anticipated. And since I can't be everywhere at once—"

"Since when?" It popped out, a leftover reflex from their previous interactions.

Kennedy laughed, which was unexpected. As was the way Jason's heart lifted. He had liked knowing he could make Kennedy laugh. Liked the fact that Kennedy let down his guard with him. He still liked it—and that was just sad.

"I've got to go," he said.

"Right. I'll talk to you later."

Not if I can help it, Jason thought, and disconnected. These days, email was about as close as he wanted to get to BAU Chief Sam Kennedy.

It was past five o'clock, and he was researching everything he could find on the provenance of Paul-César Helleu's *Lady with a White Umbrella*—he had to start somewhere in tracking down these alleged multiple shareholders in the painting—when Jason caught the faint buzz of an approaching motorboat.

He rose from the table in the dining area and went to the window facing the mist-shrouded dock. In the purple-gray twilight he could just make out the swift approaching outline of a white cruiser.

Barnaby Durrand arriving home early? But no. Barnaby would land at his own private dock. As would any of the island's residents. So…a stray vacationer renting an off-season cottage?

He swallowed a mouthful of coffee, watching as the boat drew up at the dock. There were two men aboard. Jason set his coffee cup down, frowning, and peered more closely through the gently misting glass.

He didn't recognize the man at the helm, but the passenger was Chris Shipka.

Chapter Eleven

"Hey!" Shipka called in greeting as he spotted Jason striding down the hillside toward the deck. His smile slipped at the noticeable lack of welcome on Jason's face.

Shipka turned to wave to the boat's captain. The captain raised a hand in answer and called something, lost beneath the rumble of the boat's motor. Shipka picked up his bags.

The captain goosed the engine, doing a back and fill maneuver to rotate the cruiser from the dock. The water churned green and foamy, slopping over the boards, turning the faded posts dark.

"This is a surprise." Jason reached the end of the dock at the same time as Shipka.

Shipka called back, "I know. Look. Before you get too worked up, this was my story first. I have every right to be here."

"And I have every right to have your ass thrown in jail if you interfere in my investigation."

Shipka gave him another of those pained looks. "I'm not going to interfere. I'm trying to help you."

Jason opened his mouth—and Shipka rushed on. "I'm suggesting we work together."

As the roar of the cruiser's engine faded into the twilight, Jason was able to answer in normal tones. "No, you're not."

"I am. Really. I think it's a great idea."

"It's not a great idea. It's fu—" Jason tempered his original thought. "Impossible. For one thing, we work for two different and occasionally *adversarial* organizations. For another we're not the-the goddamned Hardy Boys."

Shipka frowned, seeming genuinely taken aback. "Since when am I an adversary? You've only gotten good press from me. And okay, yes, we work for two different organizations, but ultimately, we're just different branches of truth seekers. Right? We both want the same thing. We can make that happen if we pool our resources."

This was ridiculous. Maybe funny on some level, but mostly exasperating. Jason could not have—sure as hell did not intend to have—Shipka looking over his shoulder while he worked this case, even if he did appreciate the tip he'd been given.

He said, striving for patience, "First of all, who says we want the same thing? Secondly, I work for the FBI. I have all the resources I need. Thirdly, what happened to worrying about your credibility if word got out you were working with law enforcement?"

Shipka's jaw took on a pugnacious slant. "I'll take that chance."

"I won't."

Shipka stared into Jason's eyes. "That's disappointing." His tone was flat. He shrugged. "But suit yourself." He nodded to the small white cottage a few yards down, partially concealed behind hedges and trees. "That's where I'm staying if you change your mind."

"Shipka, I'm dead serious about arresting you if you interfere with my investigation."

Shipka met his stare without blinking. "And I'm dead serious about this being my story first. You don't want to team up, fine. Your loss. But I've been working this case for nearly two years. I'm not backing off now."

Great. The thing was, Shipka *had* been helpful. His tip regarding Paris Havemeyer's disappearance might even prove to be crucial in breaking the case. It was too soon to know.

Also unknown was the extent of Shipka's personal involvement. There were too many question marks when it came to Chris Shipka.

Jason nodded curtly. Shipka turned, shoulders squared, and marched off down the rocky beach. Jason watched him for a moment—hard to retreat with dignity when you were slip-sliding over rocks and mushy grass—then returned to the lodge. He phoned Bernadette at ITB once more.

"Anything on Shipka yet?"

She responded testily, "Heck no. You know how many requests I have ahead of yours? You didn't say it was a priority."

"Didn't I? Can I upgrade my request with a pretty please on it?"

She groaned. "Give me a break, West." But he could hear a speedy *click-clickety-click* in the background. She muttered, "All right. Hang on."

He hung on, watching through the window as lights went on in the cottage across the way.

After a couple of minutes Bernadette said in a different tone of voice, "*Oh.* This is interesting."

Jason felt a flash of alarm. "What?" he demanded.

"No results."

Jason leaned back against the wall, happy no one was around to see his expression. "Funny."

"I thought so." Bernadette was still laughing when she hung up.

Jason was trying to decide between the second can of Campbell's soup and the frozen beef stroganoff when he spotted Shipka leaving his cottage to begin the trek across the grassy divide to the lodge.

In the gloom, Shipka was no more than a swiftly moving bulky shadow, and Jason felt a little too much like Chandler Bing spying on Ugly Naked Guy, watching his progress through the kitchen window.

After all, Jason was the one running computer checks and doing internet searches on a guy who had so far only been helpful to his investigation—although, in all likelihood, Shipka was already done with the internet and computer searches.

He went to answer the *knock-knock-knock* at his front door, pistol jammed in the back of his waistband.

He flipped on the porch light and opened the door. Shipka held up a bottle of wine. His eyes were shining. He had shaved, but the damp was causing his hair to frizz in a wild halo about his face. "Peace offering, neighbor." He smiled, his cheeks pink with the cold.

It was the dimple that undermined Jason's resolve. Shipka looked hopeful and boyish and uncomplicated.

Wouldn't uncomplicated be a nice change?

Plus it was hard to stay mad at someone who had written so many nice things about you.

Jason sighed. He felt like a jerk. He probably was a jerk. It didn't change the fact that this was an odd situation. "Look," he began.

Shipka said earnestly, "No. It's okay. I get it. You think this is just about me getting an exclusive. You don't trust me not to run my story before you've closed the case."

Partly, yes. Shipka struck him as ambitious and aggressive in his pursuit of the truth—and they were liable to trip over each other. But partly... he'd have to be blind not to notice Shipka was interested in him. Too interested. So, *uncomplicated* was already wishful thinking.

On the other hand, Shipka had already proved a useful resource.

Jason stepped back, opening the door. "Okay. Truce."

"Were you able to talk to Barnaby?" Shipka said as Jason waved him ahead to the kitchen.

"No."

"No surprise there."

"He had to return to the mainland. He's supposed to be back tomorrow afternoon."

Shipka glanced around the kitchen with automatic interest—probably thinking how he would describe the room in whatever article was simmering in the back of his brain. "Not if he hears from Mrs. Merriam first. Do you have a corkscrew?"

"A—I don't know." Jason opened one of the counter drawers, considering the fact that Shipka knew the name of the Durrands' housekeeper.

"I forgot my cottage doesn't have one."

"Your cottage? You've been out here before?"

"Yep. Six months ago I tried to interview Barnaby. And got about as far as you did."

"I'm not giving up yet."

"No. That's why you're so good at what you do." Shipka was smiling, seemingly sincere, and again Jason felt that flicker of discomfort. Not that he didn't like compliments, but—this was probably unfair—that much admiration was off-putting. Or maybe it only seemed like undue admiration in comparison to Kennedy, who offered praise like he was spilling his life's blood. The thing was, when Kennedy did break down and give a compliment, you damn well knew you deserved it.

Jason rifled through the utensils drawer and then the silverware drawer. No corkscrew. "Plan B." He reached in his jeans, pulled out his pocketknife, and flicked open the flimsy corkscrew tool.

Shipka laughed. "Former boy scout?"

"Not me. I thought the Boy Scouts were very uncool."

"They were. Back then."

Their glances caught, and Jason knew Shipka was also thinking of the Scouts' recent decision to accept transgender boys into the ranks.

It was a nice moment. Jason looked away first. "There are glasses in one of these cupboards." He pried out the rubber cork while Shipka hunted for glasses.

No wineglasses being found, they settled for plastic juice glasses. Jason poured the Merlot.

"*Skol.*" Shipka pushed his glass against Jason's, and the plastic bent inward. Shipka laughed. He seemed to laugh easily, and that was kind of nice too.

"*Skol.*" Jason sampled the wine. It seemed like a decent vintage. He was no expert, although everybody else in his family considered themselves to be. He preferred beer or, if he was looking to get drunk, Kamikazes.

Shipka swished his wine around like mouthwash and swallowed with a satisfied sigh. "Ye gods. That was a hella long trip. Even before my connection flight was canceled."

"Kind of a sudden decision, wasn't it? You didn't say anything about flying back here last night." Was it only last night that Shipka had stopped by his place? It seemed like a week ago. Jason's own trip—or the not sleeping for two nights—was catching up with him.

"It was spur of the moment, yeah." Shipka's warm hazel gaze met Jason's. "I realized it was a chance to talk to you on neutral ground."

"Neutral ground? Now there's a concept." Was that what they called it nowadays? Jason swallowed another mouthful of wine. He knew if he raised his lashes, he'd find Shipka still watching him with smiling approval.

Well? What about it?

Since when was someone finding him attractive a problem for Jason?

Since Sam Kennedy.

But Sam Kennedy was no longer a factor. And the sooner he accepted that and moved on, the better.

Shipka was nice-looking. They had a lot in common. He was also, unofficially, a complainant in Jason's case. But then Jason wasn't planning on starting a relationship.

Actually, he wasn't planning on anything. He set his plastic cup on the granite countertop and leaned back against the sink.

Shipka said, "Did you always want to be an FBI agent?"

"Nope. I thought the FBI was as uncool as the Boy Scouts. I wanted to be Indiana Jones. And paint."

"I wanted to be Clark Kent," Shipka volunteered.

"And instead you turned out to be Superman."

Shipka laughed—and flushed. The flush was…endearing.

"I've got to ask," Jason said. He was surprised at how reluctant he was to break the relaxed mood between them. "What's your connection to Paris Havemeyer?"

Shipka was immediately serious. "There's no personal connection, if that's what you think." He held Jason's gaze. "My old journalism professor, the guy I consider to be my mentor, was Phil Belichick."

"And Phil Belichick is…?"

"Have you ever heard of Jimmy Breslin?"

"Sure. Famous New York columnist. He chronicled the Son of Sam murders."

Shipka made a face. "He wrote about a lot more than serial killers, but yeah. Okay. David Berkowitz sent him letters and because he published parts of them, Breslin was accused by the FBI of promoting and publicizing the slayings. My point is, Phil was San Diego's Jimmy Breslin."

"I don't think I like where this is headed."

Shipka refilled his glass and topped up Jason's. "No, you've got it wrong. Phil was one of the best crime reporters on the West Coast, maybe in the country. He was even nominated for a Pulitzer prize."

Jason took another swallow of wine. "What does a San Diego crime writer have to do with a German exchange student who went missing in New York twenty years ago?"

"Twenty years ago, Phil was hired by the *Times-Herald Observer* to be their Jimmy Breslin. He moved to New York and set about building a network of sources and informants like he had in San Diego. That's how he first heard about this missing kid, a German art student who had disappeared after spending the weekend with an infamous pair of brothers well known to the New York art scene."

"Go on." Already the story was verging from the police report, but okay. That happened.

Shipka leaned toward Jason in his earnestness. "Phil believed what he was hearing from his informants. There were a lot of rumors about the Durrands. A number of people corroborated that Shepherd had been pursuing Havemeyer all over the club scene."

"The Havemeyer kid was gay?"

"Yes. That's part of what caught Phil's attention. What drew his sympathy."

Naturally. And part of what had caught Shipka's attention and sympathy—it was part of what was now tickling Jason's interest.

"Belichick was also gay?" Jason was just verifying, getting everything clear in his mind.

"Yes. He'd run into Shepherd a few times, which is why he figured there might be truth to the rumors. But here's where it gets interesting. When he asked for the go-ahead to pursue the story, he was told no. When he decided to follow it on his own time, he got canned."

"He was fired from his paper for pursuing the story on his own dime?"

"Yep. He sure was. Phil always believed it was because of the family connection. The Durrands were related through marriage to the owners of the *Times-Herald Observer*."

Jason said skeptically, "Belichick could have taken the story elsewhere."

"Nobody wanted to touch it."

"Maybe because there was nothing there." But there was no denying this account raised some intriguing possibilities. The scenario Shipka described was plausible. Up to a point.

"Rich people stick together," Shipka said.

Jason retorted, "Any group sticks together when the perception is it's us against them." He studied Shipka. "I'll give you that it's an interesting story, but what it comes down to is, although your former professor believed the Durrands had something to do with the kid's disappearance, he had no proof. Which means *you* don't have any evidence either."

"Right. I mean, there's circumstantial evidence."

"Not really. Not if all you have is that this kid partied with Shepherd a few times."

"But I think Kerk's murder *is* evidence."

Now they were getting down to it.

Jason shook his head. "Because Kerk was German and Havemeyer was German? You'll need more of a connection than that. Havemeyer disappeared twenty years ago."

"Because Kerk was one of the last people to see Havemeyer alive. He reported him missing. That can't be a coincidence."

"It could be. Absolutely it could be."

Shipka's face was flushed, his eyes bright. Partly that was the wine—they had killed the bottle in record time—and partly that was passion for his cause. Jason recognized a crusading spirit when he saw one. Frankly, that passion was one of the most attractive things about Shipka.

"But they were both part of that scene," Shipka said. "Kerk was part of that scene. Now, after all these years, he comes back into the Durrands' orbit, and he's murdered."

Jason said, "We're getting ahead of ourselves. We don't know that Havemeyer didn't return to Germany where he's been living happily for twenty years." Shipka started to object, and Jason added, "But okay, let that go for now. Let's say Havemeyer *is* dead. Why wait twenty years to get rid of Kerk? You're assuming Kerk wasn't in contact with the Durrands, but according to Shepherd, they've never been out of contact. In fact, they all met up ten years ago. So why didn't they knock him off then?"

Shipka thought it over, frowning. "Obviously something changed."

That held either way. Jason was silent, thinking. It wasn't simply the facts of the case. It was that the facts had caught the attention of two crusading reporters. He respected that instinct. So while he might question, he couldn't outright dismiss their interest in the case.

He said, "You speculated in your article for the *Valley Voice* that Kerk's death was part of a larger pattern."

"Sam Kennedy is a BAU Chief, so yeah, obviously, I'm not the only one who thinks Kerk's death is part of a pattern." At Jason's expression, Shipka added, "Google Image Search."

It was a given Shipka would figure out who Kennedy was before long. He wouldn't be much of a reporter if he couldn't manage that. He didn't seem to have made the connection to the the Earnst and Lapham slayings yet.

Shipka said, "If these two deaths are connected, then for sure there are more."

Probably. Kennedy seemed to think so, and how often was he wrong about this kind of thing? Rarely, if ever. Kerk's death was unquestionably connected to the Earnst and Lapham killings. The method of execution and the creepy, fake Monets proved that. The fact that the first two killings had taken place on the East Coast meant nothing. The Durrands traveled across the country on a regular basis. The world was their playground. Logistics was not an issue in this case.

Kerk's connection to Havemeyer was the tricky part. It was difficult to believe three people had been knocked off because of a twenty-year-old cold case. But if Kerk's death *was* somehow connected to Havemeyer's disappearance—if it was not simply a gruesome coincidence—then it would seem to follow that Earnst and Lapham's deaths were also connected.

Talk about circumstantial. Still. Once the circumstantial evidence piled high enough, it became too compelling to ignore.

"*Now* I've got your attention," Shipka said softly.

Jason glanced up in surprise. Well, semi-surprise. He'd been aware that Shipka had gradually closed the counter distance between them and was starting to crowd Jason's space. Okay, it was more lurking on the perimeter than an actual intrusion, but...he was there, gazing into Jason's eyes with that mix of hope and recognition.

What about it? Chris Shipka was not really his type—did he have a type? Tonight his type was anyone who was not Sam Kennedy. There was something sort of rumpled and comfortable about Shipka. His eyes were warm and intelligent. Even his hair seemed to crackle with energy. He smelled like soap and a woodsy aftershave. Pleasant. His jacket carried the scent of the damp night.

Jason smiled. Shipka's eyes lit, although there was a trace of doubt in his expression.

"That you have," Jason said. And when Shipka continued to eye him with that mix of wary longing, he reached for Shipka's belt and drew him in.

Chapter Twelve

"**Y**ou're *wonderful*," Shipka whispered, breaking off his sucking and licking to find Jason's mouth.

Jason smiled bleakly and returned the kiss, tasting himself on Shipka's lips. Well, that was fitting. If "wonderful" meant lying there and accepting the attention Shipka was lavishing on him, yes, he was Mr. Wonderful personified.

They had moved to the bedroom, neutral territory for both of them, and the darkness made it easier. Easier to be selfish.

In fairness, he had tried not to be selfish, tried to give as well as receive. But Shipka was a man on a mission, and that mission was to woo and win Jason with his sexual prowess.

Shipka's mouth brushed his Adam's apple, nuzzled Jason's ear till he shivered, traveled pleasurably, deliberately down the length of Jason's body until it closed once again on the head of Jason's cock. He sucked strongly, wetly, hotly, and Jason groaned his appreciation.

Better than doing it himself, that was for damned sure. The tight, tight knot of tension in the pit of his belly eased. They were both getting what they wanted, right?

Or maybe not. What Shipka wanted probably didn't exist. And what Jason wanted… Well, it wasn't that Jason wanted this so much as he didn't want to keep hurting over what he couldn't have. He needed to stop wanting Kennedy. Needed to stop missing him. How the hell could you miss what you had never really even *had*?

This was about exorcising a ghost.

Besides, it was nice to be wanted again.

Very nice…

Shipka's mouth moved hotly down the length of Jason's cock, nosed and nuzzled his balls. Jason lifted his hips, closed his eyes, though it was too dark to see anything really. The occasional gleam of eyes or teeth or pale skin. The room smelled of musty sheets and musky sweat. Familiar and unfamiliar.

Hot sweat prickled all over his body, his heart thundered in his ears. Flashpoint. His eyes opened to stare into the void as orgasm drew up, poised to strike.

"Going to come," he warned, and Shipka mumbled acknowledgment and withdrew to courteous if not safe distance.

They definitely did not know each other well enough to exchange body fluids. The fact that they were not using protection didn't change that. That was about not being prepared rather than intimacy.

Orgasm was simple biology, a release that was almost convulsive, a huge, wet stream over his belly. Afterward he felt weirdly emotional, trembling and hollow, but better. Right?

Sex had to be pretty damned awful not to feel good at all. This felt great compared to lying awake all night. Even after orgasm, Shipka continued to be appreciative and attentive. There was nothing to not like here.

Except that Chris Shipka wasn't Sam Kennedy.

He did not sleep well.

He was out of the habit of sharing a bed with a stranger. Not that there had been any understanding with Sam about seeing or not seeing other people. No promises. No commitment. But somehow Jason had stopped finding time for other possibilities.

Last night's sex had been good—especially good after eight months of nothing but his own right hand for company—but somewhere along the line he had lost the ability to fall into deep sleep beside someone he didn't know and didn't trust.

He was awake before Shipka, showering while the coffee heated, and drinking his first cup while staring out the dining room window, watching a red fox hunting along the hedge that separated this property from its neighbor.

There were no messages on his phone. He was three hours ahead of the West Coast and had not expected to hear from Kennedy in any case, so in that he was not disappointed.

When he heard sounds of stirring from the bedroom, Jason popped the mini blueberry muffins in the microwave.

Shipka finally appeared, rumpled and unkempt in jeans and unbuttoned flannel shirt. He was barefoot, and his curly, brown hair stood on end. He was smiling and cheerful, exuding a surprisingly sexy contentment.

"Morning. How'd you sleep?"

"Okay," Jason said with unnecessary briskness. "How do you like your coffee?"

"Cream. Two sugars."

"I'm not sure why I asked. I don't have anything but milk and coffee."

Shipka laughed. "That's okay. Milk is fine."

Jason poured the coffee, splashed in a little milk, and handed the steaming mug to Shipka.

Shipka took it, smiling. "Last night was great," he said.

Jason's face warmed, but that was guilt, not embarrassment. "Yeah. It was," he admitted. And why wouldn't it be, since he'd basically lain there and let Shipka do all the work. And a very nice performance it had been. Shipka deserved a better audience. Honesty compelled him to try to clarify his position. "I don't usually—"

"Good," Shipka said.

No, not good. Not good if Shipka thought last night had been about anything more than being in the right place at the right time.

"What are your plans for the day?" Jason asked.

"Don't worry. I'm not going to try to talk to Barnaby before you. I'm going to have another crack at the neighbors. The Patricks were away the last time I visited."

Jason's brows drew together. "The Patricks?"

"I've been able to verify they were on the island that weekend."

"Okay, but why are you interviewing any of the neighbors?" The penny dropped. "You think Havemeyer came *here*?"

Shipka looked surprised. "Of course. I thought you understood that. It didn't happen in New York. It didn't happen at the gallery. The police searched the gallery. That's the one thing they did do."

"I don't see any 'of course' about it. The last time anyone saw Havemeyer, he was standing on his front doorstep in New York City. How do you get him from there to here?"

"I think he either went back to the party at the gallery or Shepherd came looking for him."

"Neither scenario explains how he ended up over three hundred miles away on an island in the St. Lawrence river. That's almost a six-hour drive. Are you suggesting—"

"It was a Friday night. What do people do on Friday nights?"

"Work," Jason replied. "Sleep."

Shipka grinned. "We have to change that, West. But no, most people, and for sure people like the Durrands, go *out of town* for the weekend. And back then 'out of town' for the Durrands meant this island. They spent a lot of time here. It was the perfect place to party, and they had a lot of parties. Lots of drugs and sex and skinny-dipping."

Jason managed not to choke on his coffee at that casual "we." He said more crisply than ever, "Do you actually have some evidence Havemeyer came to the island, or is this just more speculation?"

"It's a logical deduction. Do I have proof Shepherd brought Havemeyer here? Not yet. But I do have evidence of a precedent."

"Go on." Jason remembered he'd zapped the blueberry muffins to warm them. He opened the microwave and set the steaming plate on the counter.

Shipka brightened. "And breakfast too." He picked up one of the mini muffins, peeled the paper, and popped it into his apparently asbestos-lined mouth. Through a spray of blue crumbs, he said, "Eleven months before Havemeyer disappeared, Shepherd was charged with kidnapping and raping a young man who he allegedly lured to the New York gallery with the promise of sex and drugs." He washed the muffin down with a gulp of coffee. "Now that's a matter of record. Not legal record, because the charges were dismissed and the whole thing was hushed up, but you can find it if you know where to look—and I know you do."

"The charges were dismissed?" They had to have been more than dismissed because none of this had come up in Jason's delving into the Durrands' background. This was more like erasure. Jason shook his head. "Then you've got nothing."

"We've got precedent. The first victim was hushed up. Bought off. The next guy wasn't so lucky."

"There is no precedent without proof."

"The hell!"

Jason tried again. "Do you have *any* hard evidence that this alleged victim was paid to go away?"

"No. If I had hard evidence, I'd have written the story, not come to you for help. Why are you in such a hurry to sweep all my work on this case under the rug?"

I'd have written the story, not come to you.

That was the simple, unadorned truth and the reason why journalists and law enforcement agents made uneasy bedfellows. Literally.

"I'm not dismissing your work, let alone trying to sweep it under the rug—and, by the way, that's a pretty damned offensive thing to say." Jason kept his voice even, although he was, no lie, pretty damned offended. "It does seem to me that you've already got your mind made up about what happened to the Havemeyer kid, and that means you're liable to conflate the facts that support your theory and ignore those that don't."

Shipka glowered at him. "You don't know me at all."

"No, that's right. I don't. I met you two days ago. I think we're on the same side—you seemed to think we're on the same side—but I'm being honest when I say I'm not one hundred percent convinced you're on the right track. Isn't it far more likely the Havemeyer kid went out for a drink at one of the bars and clubs near where he lived, and either hooked up with the wrong guy or got mugged on his way home?"

"Then where's the body?"

"Buried in someone's basement. He could have ended up in a Dumpster and then in a landfill. People disappear in the city as easily as the country. I know it and you know it."

"And what about Donald Kerk winding up dead in Santa Monica? Is that supposed to be a coincidence?"

"It could be a coincidence. You have to at least consider the possibility."

"I'll leave you to consider that possibility," Shipka said shortly. "The Durrands' first victim—although who's to say he was the first?—went by the name of Marco Poveda. He was an artist who met Shepherd at the gallery where they did a lot of coke and had, by all accounts, some very freaky sex. Shepherd talked him into going back to the island for the weekend. Poveda agreed. But when the weekend was over, Shepherd wouldn't let him leave. Poveda claimed Shepherd kept him locked up in a crypt on the family estate for another three days. He finally escaped back to the mainland where he filed charges with the Cape Vincent Police. Who promptly notified the Durrands' family lawyer." Shipka shrugged.

None of this had anything to do with his own case, but despite the hard line he was taking with Shipka regarding real and solid evidence, Jason remained interested in this particular line of investigation. He didn't want to pin too much on it, but he did think Shipka was onto something.

"Did the case ever come to trial?"

"No. All charges were dropped."

Jason grimaced.

"The Durrands paid him off," Shipka said.

"Again. Do you have any proof of that?"

"Poveda told friends that's what happened."

"That's hearsay. Is Poveda still around? Can he be questioned?"

"No. He died two years ago."

Jason sighed.

"Look, that's the breaks." Shipka shrugged, picked up another muffin. "Sometimes witnesses die. I can forward you my interview notes with him and the copy of the police report he originally filed. I found his story compelling. Your mileage may differ." He downed the muffin in one bite.

"Sure. Send it. How did Poveda get off the island?"

"Grabbed a ride on one of the water taxis. It was July. Summer vacation for a lot of people. Most of the cottages were rented. There was a lot of coming and going."

Jason asked, "Which water taxi service?"

Shipka's lip curled. "Seaport Sloops. I tried to talk to them, but nobody remembered anything. Which is not surprising given the stranglehold the Durrands have on this community."

"Here's the thing." Jason cradled his coffee cup in his hands. "And I realize how much work you've put into this, and I'm not saying that your theory isn't plausible. Even if you're right about Shepherd Durrand murdering the Havemeyer kid...why wait twenty years to kill a possible witness to that crime? That's your theory, right? Your theory is that Kerk was killed because he knows something about the Havemeyer kid's disappearance?"

"It's the only thing that makes sense." Shipka snagged another muffin.

"Yeah, but it *doesn't* make sense. The Havemeyer case may not be closed, but it's stone cold. I'm having trouble coming up with reasons why it would suddenly be crucial to shut up a remaining witness."

"Then all I can say is you lack imagination."

Ouch. This was a less likable side of Shipka. Sure, no one liked having their pet theories challenged, but it should be possible to debate an idea without getting personal. Then again, maybe Jason sounded more dismissive than he meant to.

He said neutrally, "That could be. How about this. Send me what you have. I promise to look at it with an open mind."

Shipka's face twisted. "Okay. Fair enough. I realize this isn't really your area of expertise. But you were involved in that murder case in Massachusetts, and you seem to be part of this taskforce."

"There is no taskforce. The BAU is working directly with Santa Monica PD on the Kerk homicide. I was brought in for about five minutes' worth of consulting." He was briefly tempted to share with Shipka the real problem with his theory: the fact that Kerk's death was part of a definite pattern that did not seem likely to dovetail with the Havemeyer case. But Kerk's homicide was part of Sam's case, and no way in hell would Sam be okay with sharing any such information with the press.

It must have been obvious he was holding something back, because Shipka's eyes narrowed. "It's a two-way street, West."

"I'm not part of any taskforce," Jason said.

Shipka said with sudden shrewdness, "There is no taskforce, or you're not part of any taskforce? Which?"

Well, hell.

Jason was forced to admit, "I'm not part of any taskforce."

"Ah-ha." Shipka grinned. "I thought so."

Jason refused the bait. He said, "There's something I wanted to ask you about a comment you made regarding Gil Hickok. You said—implied, anyway—he might not be entirely impartial in any investigation into the business dealings of Fletcher-Durrand."

The sour expression sat awkwardly on Shipka's normally good-natured features. "Are you telling me you never noticed how good old Hick always manages to get himself invited to all these premier art shows and exhibitions? He likes hobnobbing with the rich and famous a little too much."

"Is that your opinion, or do you have some basis for saying so?"

"I'm not saying he doesn't do his job—he's happy enough to go after street artists or small fry like your protégé Lux—but he's not looking for a reason to get kicked off the Getty's guest list."

The Getty being one institution with past problems purchasing works of dubious provenance?

"My protégé?"

"That's what Lux is, isn't he? A little flexing of the noblesse oblige?"

Jason let that pass. "It wouldn't be useful getting kicked off anybody's guest list." He considered Shipka's flushed face and heated tone. "Did you bring your theories on the Havemeyer case to Hickok?"

"Yep. I sure did. Right after Phil died. Hickok wasn't interested. Said there was nothing there, and even if there was, it was out of his jurisdiction."

"It *is* out of his jurisdiction."

"Whatever. He basically warned me off."

"When you say 'warned you off'…"

"Just that. He told me not to waste my time, said it wouldn't be smart." Reading Jason's expression correctly, Shipka said, "Sure, he did it like he was offering friendly advice, but I know a threat when I hear one."

"Hm." Jason was unconvinced. There were non-sinister reasons for Hick to warn off Shipka, including the fact that Shipka could be a little overzealous in his pursuit of a story—case in point, sneaking into the Hotel Casa del Mar.

And as far as the events at the Hotel Casa del Mar... Hick hadn't given any sign that he knew Shipka. Maybe he didn't remember him, in which case there couldn't have been much behind the warning off. Maybe he remembered him but dismissed him as that same pesky reporter, in which case—again—there couldn't have been much behind the so-called warning off.

Hick would regard Shipka as a not always necessary nuisance, which is how most law enforcement—including Jason—regarded the news media.

Shipka said, "Yeah, the thin blue line. I know."

"I'm not a cop," Jason said. "I'm not going to turn a blind eye to police wrongdoing, but so far all I see is you think Hick enjoys the perks of his job a little too much and several years ago he told you he couldn't investigate a missing person case in New York. That's not grounds for involving IA."

He didn't like the disappointment in Shipka's eyes, but he was being honest. The fact that they'd slept together didn't mean he'd suddenly lost his objectivity—any more than Shipka had lost his. Or maybe that was the problem. Maybe Shipka had held an idealized image of Jason, and now he was confronted with the reality of plain old puts-his-jeans-on-one-leg-at-a-time Jason.

"What I'm saying is don't trust him."

Jason said, "I don't trust anyone."

Chapter Thirteen

Mrs. Merriam was ready for Jason.

"Mr. Durrand is out walking," she announced defiantly. "He likes to take a walk after lunch."

Jason smiled. This was actually the good news. Barnaby was back. He'd been right to follow his instincts and head over to the estate early. "Great," he said. "Which direction did he go?"

She did not like his smile. "I have no idea," she said stiffly.

What was it about the Barnabys of the world that made the Merriams and Keatings so ready and willing to jump in front of a firing squad for them?

"Where does he usually like to walk?"

"I have no i—"

Jason said gently, "Maybe Mrs. Durrand might have an idea where her son likes to walk."

It wasn't subtle.

Mrs. Merriam flushed. "I think he was headed toward the old fort. He sometimes goes in that direction."

"I'll have a look. Thank y—"

The door banged shut.

The woods smelled wet, dank and earthy, like a newly dug grave.

Full moons, thunder and lightning, dark and stormy nights were the staples of both thriller and horror films, but in Jason's opinion there was nothing more mysterious or eerie than fog winding its silent, sinuous way through the woods, smothering sight and sound in a soft white shroud.

He found himself walking more quietly, carefully down the uneven trail. He was not trying to sneak up on Barnaby. The idea of Barnaby running from him was kind of funny. Barnaby was far too dignified to flee or skulk behind bushes. He might walk away briskly, but that would be about it. Still, Jason couldn't shake the feeling of, well, foreboding.

Every snap of a branch stopped him in his tracks, eyes scanning the tree-punctured gloom. It was so quiet that every *drip, drip, drip* of moisture off pine needles seemed magnified. He could hear a dog barking clear on the other side of the island.

It would be way too easy to lose direction in this murky soup of trees and mist. Better to take his time.

About ten minutes or half a mile from the Hovey mansion, Jason heard a man speaking. He couldn't make out the words. He drew closer and almost fell over a short iron fence.

He looked beyond the fence and could just make out moss-covered headstones and a tilted cross. A graveyard.

He stepped over the low fence and took a look at some of the gravestones. Marble stones carved with the image of an urn and/or weeping willows were typical of the early-to-mid-1800s. Sure enough.

HIRAH KELLY
WAS DROWNED
OFF NORTH BAY
Nov. 8, 1834
AGED 34 YEARS

The next stone read:

IN MEMORY OF
MARY GAGE
DAUGHTER OF
ELI & CAROLINE HINCKLEY
DIED JULY 2, 1860
AGED 1 YEAR 10 MONTHS
AND 12 DAYS

This would be the civilian burial ground.

What had Bram said? The civilian graveyard was slightly to the east of the old fort?

"Ambrose, put that down!"

Jason looked up, trying to see through the lazily shifting mist. The voice came from a short distance away. Despite the words, the tone was calm, even exasperated. This was confirmed by the short, excited bark of a dog.

The voice said, "You're too old to chase sticks, and I'm too old to throw them."

Jason followed the sound of the voice through the length of the grave-yard and up a steep embankment. A man in a green hunting jacket and a tweed cap stood near the ruins of a tall stone fireplace.

He turned in surprise at the sound of Jason's approach. The dog, a springer spaniel, changed barks and ran toward Jason.

"No, Ambrose. Come," the man called. "Come here!"

Ambrose's ears twitched acknowledgment. He did not come, but his tail began to wag. He advanced on Jason with friendly snuffling curiosity.

"Mr. Durrand?" Jason closed the gap between himself and Barnaby.

Barnaby's face immediately closed down. "Special Agent West, I presume?"

"That's right, sir." Jason offered his ID. Barnaby did not deign to glance at it.

He looked like an older and more refined version of Shepherd. His hair had been allowed to go silver. His features were sharper, more patrician. He was the physical type companies such as Barbour and Morgan Stanley chose to star in their advertisements. Shepherd was the type who showed up in commercials for Club Med.

"My lawyers have ordered me not to speak with you."

Jason smiled. "Mr. Durrand, your lawyers work for *you*. They don't give you orders, they give you advice, and they're giving you the advice lawyers usually give clients in your situation. But you should be aware that your cooperation now could make all the difference later on. Could determine whether there *is* a later on. No decision to prosecute has been made yet. There's still room for discussion, for negotiation, for deals."

Barnaby stared down his long, elegant nose. His eyes were the shade of hazel that could appear almost yellow, but doubt lingered in those wolfish depths.

"According to your brother, this is all one big misunderstanding," Jason added.

Barnaby frowned. "When did you speak to Shepherd?"

"Monday morning at the Downey gallery. I also spoke to Ms. Keating."

Barnaby pursed his lips—or maybe that was a tight little smile. "Ms. Keating has retained her own legal counsel."

Jason smiled again. "Yes, she has."

Barnaby's gaze sharpened. He scanned Jason's face for further hints as to his meaning, but didn't break down and ask what Keating had said.

"Shepherd is correct. This is not going to end up in court. Though I'm not sure it's a misunderstanding so much as financial desperation on the part of former friends."

"The Ontarios would have to be fairly desperate to file federal charges."

"They would have to be fairly desperate to liquidate their art collection," Barnaby retorted, "but that's what they instructed us to do. And that is what we did."

"These instructions were put into writing?"

"No. Hank phoned me up in May of last year and said he and Ros had decided to sell their collection."

"Did he give a reason?"

"He was vague. He spoke of financial pressures, which I think we can all understand. I told him we would do the best we could. I specifically asked if they were willing to take payment in installments, and Hank agreed."

"So...nothing in writing."

"Nothing. Unless you count the check we wrote as the first installment on the Monet. The Ontarios were friends as well as clients. We were used to communicating by phone."

The sudden mention of Monet gave Jason a moment's pause. Unexpectedly, he was in excellent position to pursue Kennedy's—the BAU's—investigation.

"Can you provide a copy of that check, sir?"

"Of course I can."

"Were other payments made to the Ontarios?"

"Only the first installment is due at this time."

"On the Monet? But according to the Ontarios, the gallery also sold three Picassos and a Cézanne that were being held for them."

"And your point is?"

"Are you saying you don't recall the sale of these highly valuable works?"

"Highly valuable?" Barnaby said scathingly, "What do you imagine we are? Art.com? All we sell are *highly valuable works*. Do you know how many paintings we've sold in the past six months?"

"No, sir, I don't."

"Enough that I don't know off the top of my head where we are with every single payment on every single transaction."

This was good. Barnaby was on defense, beginning to bluster, starting to dissemble.

Jason said pleasantly, "I realize that, sir. I merely thought that since the Ontarios had filed charges, you might be a little more familiar with the status of their particular collection."

Barnaby glared. "Then you're doomed to disappointment, Agent West. We've sold many, many valuable and significant works. Works far more important than anything belonging to the Ontarios."

Riiiight. So many Picassos, so little time!

"Just one more question, sir. I believe you had lunch with Donald Kerk last Wednesday. Did he give any indication that he was in fear for his life?"

Barnaby looked confused. "Don? In fear for his life? Of course not." His expression changed. "Why?"

Shit. This was not feigning ignorance. Barnaby really didn't know Kerk was dead. Unbelievably, Shepherd had not informed his brother that their old friend had been slaughtered on Santa Monica beach.

Which left it to Jason to break the bad news.

Happily, there wasn't a lot of talking to bereaved loved ones on the ACT. True, the loss of a priceless painting was no laughing matter, but it still wasn't like losing a child or a beloved spouse. Especially now days when so many people bought art strictly for investment purposes—sometimes not even bothering to take their acquisitions out of storage.

Jason said in that wooden tone they all got when they had to deliver the worst possible news—basically bracing against someone else's pain, "I'm very sorry to inform you, sir, that Donald Kerk was murdered Sunday night."

He knew it was crucial to observe and memorize every detail of Barnaby's reaction. It wouldn't be difficult, because Barnaby was stricken and silent. No automatic denial, no emotional outburst. He stood perfectly still, staring into the distance as though watching a train wreck from...not far enough away. He seemed mesmerized.

"How?" he asked finally.

"I can't share the details, only that his death is being investigated as a homicide."

Life came back into Barnaby's face. "You can't share the details? Why for God's sake? Was he robbed? Was he shot? Was he— Do they have anyone in custody? Is there a suspect?"

"No one is in custody. The investigation is ongoing."

Barnaby's brows drew together. "Why is the FBI involved?"

Kennedy had given no directive on how he wanted this handled. Everyone they had interviewed together had already heard about Kerk's death. No one had questioned the FBI's involvement, but it was a good question. And the fact that Barnaby thought to ask it was probably indicative. But indicative of what?

Jason said reluctantly, "There are indications Kerk's death may be part of a larger pattern."

Barnaby stared at Jason as though he couldn't quite hear him. "Does Shepherd know?" he asked.

Again, not the question Jason anticipated. He replied, "Yes. Your brother was already aware of Mr. Kerk's homicide when I spoke to him."

Barnaby muttered something, whistled for the dog which had wandered off, and said to Jason, "I've told you everything. If you have more questions, you'll have to direct them to our attorney. I'm quite confident the matter with Ros and Hank will be resolved without further legal action, but if the federal government wants to waste additional taxpayer time and money on harassing me and my family, well, we'll see where that leads."

He stalked off, whistling again for the dog, which burst out of the undergrowth like it thought a bear was after it.

Jason watched man and dog until they reached the top of the trail and vanished into the fog.

Barnaby had not known Kerk was dead. That, Jason would stake his career on. But from the point he had learned of Kerk's death, his reactions became hard to read. He had been shocked, upset. That was to be expected. But he had also seemed to experience a light-bulb moment. That gazing into space as though transfixed? That had been an instant of horrible recognition.

But what or whom had he recognized? That was the question.

Does Shepherd know?

Clearly he did not think his brother had killed Kerk.

And beyond that? He was difficult to scan, but Jason thought Barnaby had seemed more angry than afraid.

He had been a little afraid, though, and that was interesting.

Jason walked down the hillside and glanced around the lonely graveyard.

Where better to hide a body?

Might as well have a look. He started up the nearest crooked row of graves, studying the weather-beaten markers.

A number of sunburst-style headstones. Those would be from the 1800s. Those coy half-suns peeking over the horizon could be interpreted two ways: the setting sun of an ended life or the rising sun of the eternal hereafter.

IN MEMORY OF
EMELINE COOK
DAU'R OF
JESSE & THANKFUL COOK
SHE DIED MARCH 14
1811
AGED 11 MOS

A lot of babies and small children.

A lot of Hoveys and Greenleafs too.

Everybody seemed present and accounted for. No graves missing markers. No new-looking headstones. In fact, the most recent headstone was 1953. A large hollow-metal monument of a beautiful white bronze decorated with anchors and chains.

IN MEMORY OF
CAPTAIN JACOB HOVEY
HE DIED
NOV. 27TH 1950
IN THE 82ND YEAR
OF HIS AGE

HULDAH K. GREENLEAF
HIS WIFE
DEC. 14, 1916–SEPT. 2, 1953
HOPE WE HAVE AS AN ANCHOR TO THE SOUL.

That was interesting. Not the part about Captain Hovey being a cradle robber. The part where the Hoveys and Greenleafs turned out to be kissing cousins.

Families did feud. Just ask the Hatfields and the McCoys—or anybody in Scotland.

The fact that Eric Greenleaf hadn't mentioned being distantly related to the Hovey/Durrands didn't necessarily mean anything. Maybe it was something he preferred to forget.

In any case, Jacob's and Huldah's seemed to be the first and final union between the two families.

If Havemeyer had died on the island, it didn't look like his body had been hidden in this graveyard. Granted, there were two other burial grounds to check: the twenty-five military graves on the north side of the fort, and the Native American burial site on the other side of the island.

Jason took another look around the graveyard. The fog shifted, gauzy white whorls tumbling languidly over gravestones, spilling into urns, winding through bushes. A small building stood revealed.

A mausoleum?

Jason's interest spiked. Was this possibly the so-called "crypt" in which Marco Poveda claimed to have been imprisoned?

He hiked over the muddy grass and weeds for a better look.

Yes, a mausoleum. A beautiful example of Gothic architecture with its pointed arches, ornate stonework, stained glass windows. A tall and ornate bronze grate served as the door.

In fact... Jason moved in closer. The door was slightly ajar, resting lightly against its keeper.

He gently tugged on the heavy door, and it swung open with silent and suspicious ease.

Those hinges were pretty well maintained for a building out in the middle of nowhere.

Jason stepped inside.

The single room was about the size of a large garden shed—if garden sheds had vaulted ceilings and flying buttresses. A single marble tomb rested beneath a pair of stained glass lancet windows below a trefoil oculus.

Jason moved closer, peering down at the inscription carved into the tomb.

On a sunny day visibility would be better. As it was, he could just make out the words.

Blessed sleep to which we all return.

The bronze door behind him swung shut with a heavy and decisive *clang.*

Chapter Fourteen

"*H*ey!" Jason sprang for the door. "I'm in here. Someone's in here!"

No one answered. He listened hard but heard no sound but his own agitated breathing.

"*Hey!*" He tugged fruitlessly on the grate.

Nothing. No footsteps, either retreating or approaching. No sign that anyone was out there beyond his range of sight. He scanned the copse of nearby evergreens. No movement. No color behind the blue-green branches. Not so much as a fucking squirrel.

But the door hadn't closed on its own. There was no breeze, let alone the gale force wind it would take to move those ornate swirls of bronze. Therefore...what the hell?

He gripped the metal carving, again pushed hard against the grating. Nope. It was locked tight and built to last.

"Goddamn it." Jason tried yelling again. "Hey! Can anybody hear me? I need some help."

Good luck with that.

If anyone was out there, they were not coming to his rescue.

If anyone was out there, they had likely slammed the door on him.

Jason stopped yelling.

He pulled out his cell phone and checked for a signal.

Nada.

The walls of most crypts around the age of this one were ten-inch thick. The roofs were typically twelve-inch thick. That was another bit of arcane knowledge, courtesy of a degree in art history. He had once taken a course on funeral art and different death rituals. Some things just stuck in your memory. Like what coffin liquor was, for example.

Anyway, the thickness of the walls and roof were irrelevant. The door was basically a giant grate and the windows... Jason stepped near to get a closer look at the windows—and then a still closer look. He whistled, temporarily forgetting about his plight.

Unless he was very much mistaken, those stained-glass windows were original Tiffany. The workmanship was unmistakable. The stylized, exquisitely detailed flowers and swans, the rich, luminous blues and greens and golds. If these were indeed Tiffany glass, it would put the value of the windows somewhere in the hundreds of thousands of dollars range. For windows that size? A quarter of a million at least.

At the turn of the last century, wealthy families frequently commissioned valuable art and glass to furnish family mausoleums. Those items—Tiffany glass in particular—were now in high demand with overseas collectors willing to pay just about anything. But because so much of Tiffany's work was in churches and mausoleums, it never went on sale. Over the past few decades, enterprising thieves had turned to robbing upscale cemeteries where security was guaranteed to be minimal.

In fact, in 1999, one of the world's foremost experts on Tiffany glass had been convicted in federal court of knowingly buying and selling Tiffany windows stolen by a career grave robber.

To stumble over a find like this in the middle of nowhere? It was incredible. In fact, it was a miracle that no one had yet targeted these.

Jason studied the jewel-bright panels of white snowdrops, ivory roses, and purple and yellow pansies against crystal blue water and blazing azure sky. Tiffany had perfected a technique of layering glass that created a kind of 3-D effect. More real than real. These particular flowers reminded him a little of Monet's paintings of his spring garden at Giverny. He felt as though he could almost step through the window onto the sunlit grass.

Monet. He shivered. Yeah. Maybe better not to think of Monet right now.

He tore his gaze from the windows. Even on this drizzly gray day, they seemed to glow warmly with the promise of life and hope and eternal sunshine.

No locked doors in that world.

Jason swore quietly.

Now what?

He walked back to the door, took his phone out, and thrust his arm through the grating to see if he could get a signal.

He didn't have Shipka's number, but if Shipka had sent his notes as promised, Jason could check his mail and possibly retrieve Shipka's contact info.

But no.

The two miniscule signal bars that popped up faded out again immediately.

He'd have better luck yelling for Shipka.

Yelling for anyone.

He could try firing a couple of shots in the air, but they would almost certainly be put down to someone hunting—as he'd done the day before when he'd heard rifle shots.

Or he could try shooting the lock off the door. That's what he'd do if this was a movie. In real life, he wasn't eager to risk getting hit by a ricochet, and the chances of damaging the keeper plate and locking mechanism were higher than managing to somehow disable the latch.

As a last resort he could break the window and climb out, but that really would have to be a last resort. He'd as soon cut a hand off as destroy an irreplaceable work of art.

The remaining options were even sketchier. Rely on Shipka to come looking for him eventually? Wait for whoever had locked him in to come looking for him eventually? And if no one had locked him in? Wait for Barnaby to take the dog for another walk? Wait for someone, anyone to stroll by?

What the hell was the point of locking him in? Was it supposed to be a prank? A threat?

He really couldn't picture Barnaby tiptoeing back to lock him in the family chapel, and who else would have a motive?

Was this even the Hovey/Durrand family chapel?

He went back to the tomb and looked for a name. But there was only the carved inscription on the lid.

Blessed sleep to which we all return.

Yeah, hopefully. And ideally in our own bed.

He took a couple of frustrated turns around his cell, noting a couple of very large, though apparently abandoned, spider webs over the door.

"I don't believe this."

One thing he could do, since he was stuck here anyway. He could make sure that whoever was in that tomb—or sarcophagus, to be more precise—was who it was supposed to be, and not a missing German art student.

Louis Comfort Tiffany had died in 1933, which gave Jason a rough idea of the age of the sarcophagus and its contents. He was looking for a body or, more likely, a coffin dating circa 1878 thru the early 1930s. He knelt down, put his shoulder to the heavy marble lid, and shoved. Lifting it was out of the question, but he could, in theory, lever it—

The lid scraped a few inches sideways with a grating, stony scrape.

A peculiar, almost sweet odor wafted out. Not the stench of recent decay, thank God, but Jason's stomach did an unhappy flop all the same.

The opening was wide enough to look inside. He turned on the flashlight utility of his phone and shone the light into the stone interior.

He could make out the glimmer of black lacquer and dull gold fittings. A coffin. An old coffin.

So far so good.

The coffin appeared to be firmly sealed.

Even better.

Of course, if someone was really determined to conceal a murder, it would be possible to open the coffin and dump Havemeyer's body in with Great-Great Grandma Ermine or whoever this was. But determining that would require a court order, and no way in hell was that going to happen.

Besides, why bother desecrating the family tomb when there were so many other, more permanent ways on this island to dispose of a body?

No. It had been worth checking, but no.

Jason dragged the heavy lid back into place and settled on the floor leaning back against the sarcophagus and staring out the grating at the fog-obscured world beyond.

Back to his original question. Now what?

Okay. If someone had locked him in, it had been with some purpose in mind. Correct? Why not wait and find out exactly what the plan was?

Jason pulled out his pistol, rest it on his knee, and prepared to wait.

All you need is a fresh perspective.

That was a little Art Crime Team joke.

It was also the truth.

As frustrated and angry as Jason was—in addition to being curious about whatever the end game was—it was surprisingly useful having time to do nothing but think.

First there was Kennedy's—or rather, the BAU's—case. A series of gruesome homicides by an unsub able to travel across the country. An ice pick had been the murder weapon in all three cases. The victims were all members of the art world, though possibly—probably?—another connection existed. Depictions of the murders, painted in the style of Monet, had been left at each crime scene—indicating premeditation. But more than that. The paintings, bad though they were, indicated a genuine interest in, and likely strong ties to, the art world. That shouldn't be discounted.

Kennedy had not yet identified a main suspect—or at least had not shared that information with Jason—but the offender was organized, disciplined, and evolving. Motive unknown. There did not appear to be a sexual element to the crimes.

Shipka's investigation potentially connected to Kennedy's in that Kennedy's latest victim, Donald Kerk, was one of Shipka's witnesses. Shipka was looking into the twenty-year-old cold case disappearance of a German art student. Paris Havemeyer had last been seen alive by Donald Kerk and Rodney Berguan.

Had Shipka managed to interview Kerk or Berguan? He hadn't said, and now that Jason thought about it, it was an odd oversight.

Shipka's working theory was that Havemeyer had been killed by Shepherd Durrand at the Durrands' remote family estate. There was very likely a sexual element to this crime—if there was, in fact, a crime. That was the first problem with Shipka's case. There were any number of things that might happen to a young, sexually active gay man looking for a good time in 1990s New York City.

As a suspect, Shepherd Durrand did not, in Jason's opinion, fit the profile of an organized, disciplined, and steadily evolving serial killer. But Jason would also be the first to admit serial killers were not his area of expertise. Shepherd seemed organized enough in his professional life. And he had previously been accused of kidnapping, torture, and rape, but those charges had been dropped. Still.

Shepherd's movements at the time of Kennedy's three serial killings needed to be tracked to see if he had an alibi for any or all of the slayings. If so, he could be quickly eliminated as a suspect, and the connection between Shipka's investigation and Kennedy's could be dismissed as pure, if tragic, coincidence.

Which still left a connection between Jason's case and Shipka's investigation.

Jason was investigating charges of fraud and first and second degree grand larceny against the Fletcher-Durrand gallery co-owned and operated by Barnaby and Shepherd Durrand. The motive here was plain and simple. Financial gain. Millions of dollars were at stake.

The complainants had specifically named Barnaby in their filing, but in Jason's opinion, Shepherd was as good or even better a candidate for the defrauding of Fletcher-Durrand clients. Although Barnaby had certainly reacted with guilty knowledge when questioned.

Jason also suspected Shepherd of commissioning and selling forged paintings, though so far that was only a suspicion. He had absolutely no proof besides a single faked painting, the odd, edgy behavior of a trusted informant, and his own gut instinct.

Donald Kerk again provided a connection, this time between Jason's case and the BAU's, in that he had seen the Durrand brothers—or at least Shepherd—twice in the days before his death.

In conclusion?

All three cases revolved around the art world.

The Durrands, through their connection to Donald Kerk, seemed at least peripherally attached to all three cases.

What else?

Sitting here locked in a fucking mausoleum was not getting him any further ahead in his investigation.

His jacket and jeans, though plenty warm when he was hiking through the woods, was not heavy enough for sitting in a stone cell in winter.

He was starving. He would kill for one of those shriveled, dried-out petroleum-based blueberry muffins now.

Sam Kennedy—

No. Do not go there.

By five o'clock Jason was ready to commit a murder of his own.

He had now been imprisoned for over four hours, and he was just about ready to try shooting the lock off the gate. Just about. He still vividly recalled what it felt like to be shot, and that was a real disincentive. A ricochet in a small enclosed stone space was a high possibility, and even if he was ready to gamble on his own safety, he couldn't risk that Tiffany window.

Repeated efforts to use his phone had failed.

The good news was the fog had dissipated. The bad news was it had started to rain.

It was dark, it was cold and damp, he was tired, hungry, and starting to get a little freaked out.

He needed to pee. Which shouldn't technically be a problem, but the presence of the sarcophagus had an inhibiting effect.

What the hell was the plan here?

Was there a plan?

Had he been locked in by accident? Not likely, but not impossible either.

The whole situation was fucking *ridiculous.*

He stopped pacing at a faint jingling sound and drew his weapon.

Keys?

No. Dog tags. Ambrose was back, sniffing loudly, frantically at the bronze gate and then proceeding to bark at Jason.

"Good dog," Jason muttered. "*Hey,*" he yelled. "Who's out there?"

Footsteps approached.

Barnaby's voice muttered, "What on earth?"

A high-powered flashlight beam spotlighted him, momentarily blinding him.

If Barnaby noticed Jason was holding a pistol, he didn't comment on it. "Agent West, what do you think you're doing in there?"

The irate tone was almost funny, given the circumstances. Almost.

Jason holstered his weapon, saying crisply, "Waiting for whoever locked me in to let me out."

It seemed Barnaby was ready for this because he charged instantly to the defense. "*Locked you in!* What nonsense is this? No one locked you in. Who was around to lock you in?" His keys jingled as he unlocked the ornate heavy gate and dragged it open.

"You triggered the mechanism yourself—while trespassing on private property. You're just lucky Ambrose wanted a second walk. You could have been stuck in there until tomorrow."

Don't think I don't know it. Jason didn't say it aloud. He was convinced Barnaby had come looking for him, had *known* he was locked in that crypt, and had shown up simply and solely to release him. Who the hell walked their dog in a graveyard at night?

But that was just a gut feeling. He had no proof. What was the point of doing such a thing anyway? To punish him for forcing an interview? To irritate him? Because if the idea had been to scare or intimidate, Barnaby had missed by a mile and merely succeeded in aggravating the shit out of him.

Besides, he was pretty sure Barnaby hadn't—couldn't have—locked him in, and sneaking through the woods didn't really seem like Mrs. Merriam's style.

Which left two questions: who had locked him in, and why?

"That was lucky all right. For all of us," Jason said.

Barnaby's stiff figure seemed to grow more rigid. "I don't think I like your tone, Agent West."

"I'm not crazy about yours. No way did I accidentally lock myself in there, but if that's what you want to believe..." Jason shrugged.

This was not the time or place to make a federal case out of something. He was on his own out here, standing in the glare of Barnaby's flashlight, surrounded by the deep and silent woods, Jason was acutely aware of just how alone he was. Someone on this island had no problem tackling an FBI agent—had been willing to risk whatever the consequences to put Jason out of action for a while. What were the odds that person might be willing to put Jason out of action permanently? Not something he wanted to find out.

If Shipka was right, other people had disappeared for good on this island. Maybe the only reason Jason was still standing here talking to Barnaby was Barnaby.

Shipka. For the first time Jason considered the possibility that Shipka had followed him and then locked him in the crypt.

Why would he? What could he hope to gain?

But why would anyone lock Jason in? Looking at it from that angle, Shipka was as likely a suspect as anyone.

Barnaby was speaking in a nervous, huffy voice—as though he feared they were being overheard? "This kind of intrusion is absolutely intolerable. My lawyers will be contacting your supervisor in Los Angeles."

"That's certainly your prerogative." Jason added a belated, "Sir."

Barnaby had turned away, but the flashlight beam pinned Jason once more. "Furthermore, I'd suggest you don't continue to wander around this island in the dark, young man. This can be a very dangerous place."

Without further comment, he strode off through the gravestones. The dog, Ambrose, abandoned whatever he was grubbing for in the stand of nearby bushes to streak after him.

Watching the pale blur of the dog, the hair on the back of Jason's neck rose. Ambrose had been snuffling around the bushes earlier that afternoon. Had someone hidden out there spying on Jason? Someone familiar to Ambrose and Barnaby?

Was that person watching him now?

Chapter Fifteen

"**H**ey. Just touching base," Kennedy's recorded voice said. "Wondering how your interview with Durrand went."

Standing in the kitchen at the lodge, Jason listened to the messages which had stacked up in his voicemail over the course of the afternoon, and contemplated the dark windows of the cottage next door.

Kennedy made a sound that might have been an abbreviated laugh. "I'm taking it for granted you managed to corral him." There was a pause as though he didn't know how to end the message, and then he disconnected.

Jason glanced down at his phone. That was just...weird.

That was all too much like it had been back when they were whatever they were. Kennedy couldn't think they were going to continue on as pals? Right? Mr. Hot and Cold couldn't be that oblivious. That, well, insensitive.

Yeah, he could.

He was.

From Kennedy's point of view, there was no logical reason they couldn't be friends. At the very least, they could be friendly. Kennedy, by his own admission, liked talking to Jason, and surprisingly, until the past week, they did always somehow seem to have a lot to talk about. Jason had enjoyed their discussions and occasional debates. He had liked Sam in addition to being attracted to him. He had not imagined that he really understood him, and he sure as hell didn't understand him now.

It was just not possible for Jason to switch his feelings on and off like that. Not this fast. Maybe at some point down the line, but not now. Now he was still hurt and disappointed and a little angry. And maybe it wasn't logical—maybe it was even emotionally immature—but that's how it was.

He could—and would—work with Kennedy, but he did not want to be friends. *Scroll left, Jason.*

He turned his attention back to the cottage behind the hedge. Not a single window was lit. Not one. Was Shipka napping? Was he still out interviewing the Patricks? Had he left the island?

It was odd.

He listened to the next voicemail message.

George simply confirming he'd received Jason's message from the previous evening that he needed to stay over in New York another day.

Two messages from his sisters—double-teaming him. The message after those was from James T. Sterling, known to his friends as "Stripes," returning Jason's earlier call.

"Hi, Jay." Stripes and Jason had gone to high school together. Although they'd ended up sharing every available art class at Beverly Hills High School—back then they'd both dreamed of earning their living as artists—they were never close. Stripes regularly made a point of letting Jason know he had "sold out" by working for the Federal Bureau of Investigation. "Got your message. Not sure what you're really after. You can call me back."

Click.

"Ass," Jason muttered.

He didn't think Stripes was going to be able to offer any real information or insight into Kerk's death, but there was something uncanny about the way he always seemed to know all the juicy gossip before anyone else in town. One thing about Stripes, he was a good listener.

Jason listened to the rest of his messages, all having to do with other cases he was working.

He thought Shipka might have left word, but there was no message.

He glanced out the kitchen window again, but there was still no sign of life at the other cottage.

Had Shipka left the island without leaving word for him? It seemed strange. But the morning had been, well, a little strained after their conversation about Hickok. Jason knew his defense of Hick—even though it had really been more questioning than actual defense—had disappointed Shipka. Probably a number of things had disappointed Shipka. Which

Jason felt sort of bad about, but it was probably better in the long run that Shipka understand Jason was not good boyfriend material.

Not right now, anyway. Not while he was still smarting over getting dumped by Sam Kennedy.

Even if Shipka didn't feel like spending the evening with Jason, it was weird he hadn't turned any lights on. Why would he choose to stumble around in the dark?

Was it possible he hadn't made it back from interviewing the Patricks?

That was a worrying thought. Shipka didn't strike Jason as the outdoorsy type. If he'd gotten lost or taken a tumble, he could be lying out there in the drizzly cold night right now.

Shit. Awkward or not, Jason needed to make sure Shipka was okay.

He shrugged back into his jacket and left his cottage, squelching across the expanse of frosty grass and mud until he found the opening in the hedge. Frigid rain stung his cheeks. The sound of the lake lapping against the pylons, the ghostly knocking of the boats against the dock seemed to fill the night. He crossed the little rocky beach and climbed the wooden steps to Shipka's cottage.

Up close, the dark windows and resounding silence seemed even more unsettling. Jason rested his hand lightly on the butt of his Glock.

Something was not right.

He knocked firmly on the front door.

A long moment passed.

Jason knocked again, more loudly.

"Shipka?" he called. "Chris?"

Silence.

Jason tried the door handle. The latch clicked and the door swung open with a tiny squeak. Jason pulled his weapon. His heart was kettle-drumming in his chest.

"Shipka?" he called. "Are you there? It's West."

The hush was terrifyingly absolute.

Why? Maybe Shipka had simply gone out and left the door unlocked. Why assume the worst?

But Jason did. His scalp crawled with unease.

Shit. Shit. Shit.

He brought his weapon up in high ready and took a couple of deep, steadying breaths. In recent years, the Bureau's handgun training had focused heavily on tight quarters and close-range shooting scenarios. At least sixty-five percent of law enforcement officers were killed by assailants from less than ten feet away. Even so, it was a very long time since he'd had to make a dynamic entry—and never on his own. On your own was always a bad idea.

But with backup at least half an hour away?

"FBI," he yelled. "Show yourself." Using his free hand to push open the door, Jason stepped across the threshold, scanning as much of the interior as he could see—which was not much. The room was unlit, full of black angles and deep shadows. He could make out the bulky outline of furniture. No entry hall. The front door led straight into the living room.

Even standing outside, Jason could feel a rush of heat. The cottage was unnaturally warm. Like the temperature had been cranked to high.

He flattened himself to the door entry point, hugged his way around the jamb to "slice the pie" with his pistol, and entered the room. Now that he was in motion, it was easier. His training kicked in, and he was moving automatically, punching that first, deep corner, flipping around and clearing the opposing corner.

He swept the room with his weapon. No one was waiting for him, no one was hiding behind the rattan chairs and sofa, the trunk-style coffee table and side tables. Nothing seemed out of place. There was no sign of a disturbance.

He leaned back against the wall, breathing quietly, listening. Maybe he'd got this wrong. Was he overreacting after his own bizarre experience? Maybe Shipka had simply left the island.

It was raining harder. He could hear the guzzling sound of water rushing through the roof gutters, and the soggy chime of a ship's bell. No other sounds. Not so much as the creak of a floorboard.

The smell of rain and damp earth drifted into the too-hot room. They couldn't quite mask the other thing he smelled.

His stomach lurched.

That weird metallic smell? That was blood. A lot of blood. No mistaking it for anything else.

As his eyes adjusted to the lack of light, Jason was able to scan the layout of the room. To his right was a hall leading to the rest of the cottage. From an open doorway on the right side of the hall, he could pick out a dim glow. That was likely the kitchen. On the left side of the hall were three more doors—two bedrooms and a bathroom, he was guessing—and at the end of the hall was another closed doorway. Probably the master bedroom.

Jason stuck close to the wall, moving slowly, cautiously toward the mouth of the hall.

When he reached the doorjamb, he threw a quick look around the opening, cornered his way around the door frame, and, gun at low ready, headed for the kitchen.

Same tactical maneuver. Hug the corner, slice the pie, enter the room, and make for the deep corner.

The deep corner turned out to be beside a large window. Jason listened to the rain picking at the glass, his gaze—and weapon—staying trained on the room.

Silence and shadows, nothing more.

The only points of light came from the clock on the microwave, the coffeemaker button indicating the machine was still heating...and the light from the refrigerator which stood wide open.

Jason's heart stopped.

By the glow of the refrigerator light he could see the breakfast counter. On top of the counter sat a mousepad, mouse, coffee cup, and computer cable. What he did not see was a laptop.

He expelled a long breath and moved back toward the doorway, feeling for the wall light switch.

The light came on, cheery and bright, illuminating a scene of horror. Blood spray arced across the cupboards to the left of the refrigerator, spattered the interior of the refrigerator, and completed its arc on the cabinets to the right of the refrigerator. Jason looked upwards.

Beads of blood and other matter were dotted halfway across the ceiling.

He closed his eyes for a moment, then blinked a couple of times. Black spots danced before his eyes. There was a peculiar singing in his ears. He was not trained for this. No one was trained for this. Discovering the body of someone you knew?

But he had not found a body.

He looked down at the floor and saw the lake of blood shining at the base of the refrigerator. "*Jesus Christ,*" he whispered.

He *should* have found a body, because no one could survive that kind of blood loss.

He wiped his forehead, which was wet with sweat. It was like an oven in there. Despite the cold knot of horror in his gut, his shirt stuck to his underarms and back with perspiration.

A thick swath of smeared blood led from the pool of congealing blood toward the opposite doorway. The body of the victim had been dragged, probably bleeding out, from the kitchen and down the hallway toward the back of the cottage.

Jason followed the blood trail, weapon at ready.

Beyond the fan of light from the kitchen, the hallway was dark. A small boat-shaped night light illuminated the black streaks down the length of the hall.

Despite the gory path marker, Jason carefully and methodically checked and cleared the first bedroom and bathroom off the hall. All the while his brain was racing. Why try to hide the body? Given the amount of forensic evidence, what was the point of this?

The offender was long gone—taking Shipka's laptop with him. That would have been his next-to-last move. The last move had been to turn the thermostat to Fahrenheit Hell.

Unless this was not what it seemed?

Now there was wishful thinking.

What did he imagine? That Shipka was faking his death to lend credence to his theory that the Havemeyer kid had been killed on this island?

Jason cleared the second bedroom.

Only the master bedroom to go.

His heart was thumping loudly in his ears. His hands were ice cold as he gripped his Glock.

The door to the master bedroom was half shut. Jason used his left hand to push the door wide, and hit the smell of death like a wall. It stopped him in his tracks. His stomach rose in protest. He swallowed down the sickness and turned on the wall light.

The gleam through frosted globes in an overhead ceiling fan light was cozy and soft, revealing nothing sinister.

The bed was empty. The navy-blue bedspread was slightly crooked, but otherwise undisturbed. Shipka's clothes and belongings were strewn around, but it didn't look like a search so much as Shipka making himself at home. Jason was vaguely aware of lighthouse-shaped lamps on the nightstands flanking the bed, a white rattan chair beside a sliding glass door which led out onto a rain-wet deck.

Nor was there a body on the floor. Jason looked to the closed bathroom door, then noticed the sled tracks of blood across the jute carpet that led all the way to the closed louvered closet doors. He stared at those unmoving white doors.

He could stop right here. Back out and phone Cape Vincent Police Department, or the sheriff's department, or the state police, or whoever was responsible for this godforsaken neck of the woods. He could say he hadn't wanted to contaminate the crime scene. That he had already known it was too late by then. The smell. The blood loss. The total and complete silence. Too late.

But. He still felt that tiny niggle of doubt. Hope? Suppose it wasn't Shipka? Suppose Shipka was more closely involved—*with what?*—suppose this was not what it seemed?

Anyway, it seemed like the least you could do for someone you'd been with was not turn away from them in their...extremity. Shipka had died alone and horribly. He had died as no one should ever die. And as much as Jason didn't want to see, didn't want to know, he felt like it was his duty not to abandon Shipka now.

He crossed the final stretch of carpet, careful not to step in the blood trail, and opened the doors.

The bloody, meaty mass slumped against the side of the closet was all that was left of Chris Shipka. Jason recognized the gore-soaked jeans and shirt and tennis shoes as Shipka's. That was all he recognized. All he tried to recognize. The rest...he didn't want to see, would try to forget.

The rest would haunt his dreams. The rest was the stuff of nightmares.

"Why…" Jason wasn't even sure what he was asking.

Why would someone think this was necessary?

Why didn't you tell me everything you knew?

He gently closed the closet door, sat down on the side of the mattress, and pulled out his phone.

Chapter Sixteen

"I don't have to be in the FBI to know you're not telling me everything you know about this homicide," Detective O'Neill was saying.

Jason said wearily, "I've told you what I know."

Well, sort of. They had been at this since Jason had been taken into custody by the Jefferson County Sheriff's Department the previous evening. It was now eight in the morning. He had not been questioned the whole time. Following the initial interview, he'd been left in a holding cell several hours for "processing."

He was familiar with the tactic. He had not been charged, and he did not believe he would be charged, though technically there was probably enough evidence to build some kind of case against him. And more would turn up if they ran forensics on his bedroom at the lodge. Whatever O'Neill thought, his sergeant was not jumping to any conclusions; a lot of the hostile attitude stemmed from indignation that the FBI had been investigating in their own backyard without so much as a by-your-leave.

"Bullshit," O'Neill said. "What did you do with Shipka's laptop?"

He was probably a little younger than Jason. Dark-haired, handsome, sure of himself. No doubt a rising star in the Detective Unit. Jason recognized the breed, being the same kind of bird dog.

Unlike Jason, O'Neill had had a couple of hours' sleep, a decent breakfast, and plenty of coffee. He was bristling with antagonism and energy and looking forward to cutting the "Big Initials"—and Jason— down to size.

"The laptop had been removed by the time I arrived on scene," Jason repeated for the fourth—or was it the fifth?—time. "Shipka and I were following different avenues of investigation. I was on the island to interview Barnaby Durrand about allegations of fraud and larceny. Shipka was looking into an old missing person case."

"*You're lying!*"

"I'm not lying."

This was old-school interrogation. A lot of yelling and pounding of tabletops, coupled with the implicit threat of incarceration. Jason could put an end to it by insisting they either charge him or let him go, but that could backfire. O'Neill was irate enough to charge him, even if he still believed Jason's ultimate sin was obstruction of justice. They were not seriously looking at him as a suspect in Shipka's homicide. Not yet, anyway. That could change at any moment, but he couldn't let himself be rattled into yelling for a lawyer. If he lawyered up, they would take another, closer, look. *That*, he did not want. Could not afford. Much better to stick to their script, that this was an interagency pissing match, a game of the thrones, with adversarial LEO agencies squaring off against each other.

But the clock was ticking.

Jason had used his phone call to notify George, and George had instructed him to hang tight. That had been over six hours ago, and Jason's anxiety had ratcheted up several notches. He knew the Bureau would be working behind the scenes to secure his release, but they would also take pains to be completely transparent and cooperative in their interactions with the Sheriff's Office. That was how these situations—not that there were so many of these situations—were handled. The proper channels would be followed. There could be no appearance of throwing the weight of the federal government around.

Intellectually, Jason understood all that. But he was still exhausted and emotionally wrung out. He told himself he was not worried, but he knew innocent people did sometimes get charged, convicted, and imprisoned. He was hoping this was not one of those times.

"I didn't take Shipka's laptop," Jason said again. "I have nothing to gain by interfering with your investigation. We'd already discussed where we thought our cases intersected. If you're asking me, I think there's every indication Shipka's killer took his laptop."

"*Exactly,*" O'Neill said. Maybe he was just being an asshole. Maybe he could sense Jason was hiding something. If so, he continued to bark up the wrong tree.

Meeting his smug look, Jason's lip curled. "Give me a break," he said, forgetting his resolution not to do anything to further annoy and antagonize.

The interrogation room door opened. Jason sat back in his chair, swallowing the rest of what he'd been about to say. O'Neill swung around in his chair and glared.

A deputy sheriff who looked like a stunt double for The Rock said, "His boss is here."

"Goddamn it, Harris. Do you mind not announcing—never mind." O'Neill threw Jason a *this isn't over* look, shoved back his chair, and left the room. The heavy door swung shut.

Jason scrubbed his face with his hands and sat up straight, waiting for the next development. He was relieved someone had shown up. It wouldn't be George. It would be someone from the Albany field office. Either way, news of reinforcements was a relief.

On the wall across from him a placard read:

We operate with the desire to enhance the quality of life and maintain a pleasant experience for our residents and visitors. Our officers understand the importance of community involvement through community policing and work diligently to foster good working relationships with its residents. The agency works for a successful conclusion of every incident, balancing the outcome based on the need of the community.

Jason rolled his eyes.

O'Neill was back in a couple of minutes, his expression noticeably bleaker. "You're free to go for now, Agent West. We'll be in touch."

Jason rose without a word and walked past O'Neill who stared stonily straight ahead as though this escape was the final proof of Jason's malfeasance.

The industrial-sized deputy led Jason down a couple of narrow hallways lined with bulletin boards and wanted posters to an office where his coat, wallet, cell phone, and holstered weapon were returned to him. A side door opened, and he was facing Sam Kennedy.

Kennedy was dressed as though he'd come straight from a search-and-rescue op. Jeans, a white cable knit sweater, and his blue and gold FBI jacket. But casual dress or no, he looked like the guy in charge. Of everything. Everywhere.

"Agent West."

"Sir."

Jason's heart was thudding with astonished, even joyful relief. He had no idea why Kennedy was the one to show up, but he was passionately grateful he had.

Kennedy nodded curtly to the deputy sheriff who scrambled to get the glass front door open and see them out. Whatever had transpired in the minutes previous to Jason's release had not been pleasant, and clearly the Jefferson County Sheriff's Department could not wait to see the back of Jason—or, more likely, the back of his "boss."

Sparkling sunshine and fresh air came as a surprise. The breeze carried the scent of the ocean, though it was actually the St. Lawrence river, a glittering band of blue beyond the faded buildings of the ferry depot. The seagulls circling the boats in the harbor didn't seem to know the difference.

Jason drew in a deep lungful of clean, crisp morning—he felt like he'd been holding his breath since he'd been taken into custody.

"All right?" Kennedy asked quietly. Behind the shades, his face was inscrutable. A sphinx in Foster Grants.

"I've been better."

He was surprised when Kennedy dropped a firm hand on his shoulder and gave him a quick squeeze. "The car's this way."

Now that Jason had a chance to really look, he could see Kennedy looked bone-weary. Maybe it was the light, but his skin had a sallow undertone. Lines of fatigue were carved into his face. What the hell was happening in Oregon to make him look like that? And why had George sent Kennedy of all people?

No, that made no sense. George wouldn't—couldn't—ask a BAU chief to step in. Jason had to be even more tired than he knew because he just couldn't seem to work it out.

Neither said anything else until they were inside the black rental sedan neatly parked between two blue and white SUVs lining the white street.

"Why didn't you call me?" Kennedy asked. He made no move to start the car. He took his sunglasses off as though to better scrutinize Jason.

"Call *you*? For one thing, I don't work for you. For another—" He'd been about to say *what could you do*? But that was a silly question. Jason said instead, honestly, "It never occurred to me."

Kennedy threw him a quick, disbelieving look, but it was the truth. It had never crossed Jason's mind to call for Kennedy. Frankly, he'd have gone to jail for a thousand years before asking Kennedy's help. Not that he wasn't sincerely grateful that Kennedy had stepped in. "Did George ask you to come? How did you find out what was happening?"

Kennedy said dryly, "I phoned you last night. A deputy sheriff from the Jefferson County Sheriff's Cape Vincent Station was monitoring your cell phone calls, so I heard the whole story."

Jason gaped. He latched on to the one piece of information he could understand. "*Monitoring* my calls? They can't do that."

"Small town PDs have their own way of policing."

"I wasn't under arrest. And even if I had been, they have zero legal right." It was outrageous, but given everything else that happened, Jason was having trouble drumming up the energy for suitable protest.

"What the hell went down on that island?"

Jason gave the bare bones, and Kennedy's frown grew blacker and blacker.

"Jesus Christ." Kennedy was silent for a moment after Jason finished his recital. "You should have called for backup, West. You had no idea what you were walking into. You could have b—" He broke off.

Jason gave him a quick, disbelieving look. "Really? You think I should have called the sheriffs to see whether Shipka had left the island? Because for all I knew, that was the case."

Kennedy gave him a dark look, but they both knew Jason was right. He had no reason to expect the worst, and once he understood what the worst was, he was already on scene and committed.

Typically, Kennedy wasted no additional time on debate—let alone sympathy. It probably didn't occur to him Jason might have found the events of the previous night extraordinarily stressful. "Why didn't they question you at the scene?"

"They did."

"Then why were you taken into custody?"

"The suspicion that I was out here conducting an investigation without letting local PD know what was happening on their home front?"

"A turf war?"

"I'm not sure. Another possibility is someone phoned Barnaby Durrand, and he told them to keep me on ice."

Kennedy's brows rose in not-so-polite skepticism. "You think Durrand is behind this?"

"I told you Shipka believed the Durrands were behind the disappearance of Paris Havemeyer. I'm not sure how Shipka spent the day, but I know he planned on interviewing at least one resident. Maybe Durrand got wind of his investigation."

It sounded unlikely even to Jason's ears, and Kennedy looked equally unconvinced. "The real threat to Durrand would be the FBI's investigation, so why take out Shipka and not you?"

Jason shook his head. "I'll tell you one thing. I think whoever locked me in that crypt went after Shipka."

Kennedy grunted noncommittally.

The problem was, Jason couldn't really picture Barnaby going after someone with a machete or whatever weapon had been used on Shipka either. Besides, he'd been horrified at the news of Kerk's death. Horrified and...flabbergasted. Yeah, he'd been genuinely shocked to learn of Kerk's murder. It was hard to believe he'd have turned around and vented homicidal rage on Shipka.

"No," Kennedy said, coming to his own conclusion. "They took you into custody because you're the most likely suspect."

"*What?* How do you figure that? What the hell is my motive?"

Kennedy's glance was impatient. "You know cases aren't built on motive. Motive is icing on the cake. The *cake* is opportunity and means. You were staying next door to Shipka in a rental cottage full, I'm guessing, of knives and other suitable weapons. There's your opportunity and means."

Jason had already worked all this out for himself, and yet he still felt outraged at the idea that anyone could seriously suspect him of homicide.

"Why wouldn't I just shoot him?"

"With your own service weapon?" Kennedy shook his head. "Add in the fact that you're the only person who knew Shipka, and it's pretty obvious why you were taken into custody." As though that finalized it, he turned the key in the ignition, and the sedan returned to life with an impatient roar.

They drove, unspeaking, down a couple of shady blocks. Kennedy was preoccupied with his own thoughts, and Jason was simply numb. But when they pulled into the parking lot of a small hotel facing the water, he said, "I've got to get out to that island."

Meeting Kennedy's gaze, he said, "All my stuff is out there. My laptop. Which contains my case notes on Fletcher-Durrand."

"If you're worried about Durrand's interference, the area will be crawling with sheriff deputies. If you're worried about the sheriff's office, even these yahoos know that laptop is the property of the federal government."

"After last night, that doesn't reassure me."

Kennedy continued to eye him in that steady, unimpressed way. Jason drew a sharp breath. "Okay. Yes. There's a...potential problem."

Kennedy's eyes looked gray, almost colorless. "What kind of potential problem?"

"Depending on how bad JC's Sheriff's Department wants me for this, there's physical evidence at the lodge where I was staying. Evidence that might be open to interpretation."

Kennedy considered him for a moment. "All evidence is open to interpretation. Go on."

"Sheets in the master bedroom. Shipka and I had sex the night before last."

Kennedy didn't move a muscle.

Or did Jason imagine that almost eerie stillness? Because Kennedy's voice sounded normal enough when, after a moment, he said, "I thought you didn't know Shipka."

"I didn't. I didn't remember him, anyway. But we've been in communication since Monday evening." He resented feeling like he had to explain or defend his choice to have sex with Shipka. And he really resented that nebulous feeling of guilt. Kennedy had dumped *him*. He had nothing to explain or feel guilty about.

And maybe Kennedy agreed, because he was immediately back on point. "Right. A sexual relationship certainly presents more possibilities for a fatal feud. Not to mention the fact there's always a chance gay relationships might be viewed through the homophobic perspective of the rural socio-political mind-set."

Not that Jason wanted to make Kennedy jealous, but *that* response seemed to verge on clinical. *Dōmo arigatō, Mr. Roboto.*

"Yes. There's always that."

"Running out there to destroy physical evidence doesn't exactly bolster your claim of innocence."

"I'm not destroying physical evidence. I didn't have anything to do with Shipka's death. It's reasonable that I would go back and retrieve my stuff. And it's also reasonable that while I'm there I'd clean up, because that's what I *would* do in normal circumstances."

Kennedy stared out the windshield at the ships moving slowly up the St. Lawrence. "You want my opinion? I think the smartest thing for you to do would be to get on a plane to LA ASAP."

Jason stared. "Wait a minute. You don't— I'm not— I don't have anything to hide."

"I realize that. But your—"

"*Do* you realize that?" Jason broke in. "Because I didn't do it, Sam. You *can't* think I did. That I-I *killed* him." He couldn't hide his reaction, embarrassing and painful as it was. Hopefully Kennedy would put it down to exhaustion and not hurt that Kennedy could think such a thing of him.

He *was* exhausted. But also it was the strain and shock of the night before, and yes, the grief. He hadn't loved Chris Shipka, wasn't even on a first-name basis with him, but they had connected, they had shared something. There was a reason sex was called "being intimate." Jason was stricken by what had happened to Shipka. Nobody should die like that. Certainly not a guy like Shipka whose only crime had turned out to be caring too much. Caring about cases everyone else had forgotten, caring about people who just didn't feel the same. Jason wasn't crying, but it was close. The struggle to keep his breathing quiet and his face blank was probably as revealing as the expression of emotion would have been. His throat had locked so fiercely that further words were impossible.

He thought Kennedy leaned toward him, but that must have been the sudden blur in his eyes, because when Jason hastily wiped his face on his shoulder, Kennedy was still sitting behind the wheel. Unmoving and probably unmoved. His gaze was as bright and sharp as surgical steel.

"No, Jason. I don't think you killed him. But your effectiveness here is at an end. And I have to get back to Oregon. I've got an injured agent and an investigation to wind up. I can't run interference for you if the sheriff does decide to haul you in again."

That was flaying an already open wound. Jason snapped out, "I don't need you to run interference!"

Kennedy laughed. It was not a pleasant sound. "You don't think so? The sheriff's department doesn't have a lot of suspects for the Shipka slaying. In fact, I'm guessing they have exactly one. You. You're the only person in the entire county who knew Shipka, you had sex with him the night before he died, and you're the guy who discovered the body. Your alibi is that you were locked up all day in a crypt on a nearby graveyard but, conveniently, were released in time to discover Shipka had been slaughtered. Right there, that's enough circumstantial evidence for plenty of DAs."

"It's the truth."

"It's too ridiculous to be anything other than the truth," Sam said. "Which doesn't change the fact that you wouldn't be the first guilty person to cook up some laughable excuse of an alibi."

"But it *is* an alibi, and Barnaby Durrand can confirm it."

"He can confirm he let you out of the crypt. How would he know how long you were locked up inside? Unless he's going to admit to locking you in. A halfway competent prosecutor could argue that you killed Shipka and then locked yourself in the crypt in an attempt to concoct some cockamamy defense."

"Then how would he have known to come back and let me out?"

"Maybe he didn't know. Maybe it went down exactly as he said. He was out for a walk, and the dog tracked you to the crypt."

Jason shook his head. He was too tired. The effort to marshal an argument that would stand up against Kennedy's line of attack was like trying to push a car out of quicksand. Not happening. He said, mostly out of stubbornness, "I've got to go back. It will look more suspicious if I don't go back."

Kennedy sighed. It was a very weary sound. "We should have access to the island either late today or early tomorrow. That's the best we can hope for. Pushing for immediate access is going to raise questions. We'll wait for clearance. Then, after we…retrieve your belongings, we both need to catch planes."

Jason nodded.

"You need to be aware they may have already got a search warrant for your lodge. In fact, all they really need is permission from the owner to look around."

"I know."

Kennedy studied him for a long moment.

"Look, Jason," he said in a different voice. "You need sleep. You're dead on your feet. And I've got a conference call in eighteen minutes." He glanced at his wristwatch. "Seventeen minutes. I've booked us rooms here."

Jason nodded again. He didn't trust his voice.

Kennedy started to speak, stopped. He said instead, "One thing at a time, okay?"

"Yep," Jason said.

They got out of the car and walked across the parking lot to the two-story hotel. The Buccaneer's Cove was a pink and white clapboard building, which had probably begun life in a spiffy, eye-catching pirate red. Surrounded by tall trees and shady lawns. A pirate flag and an American flag hung side by side. Green Adirondack chairs and large pots of dead or dormant flowers were strategically placed around the building.

Inside it was…dated. Not as far back as the days of buccaneers. More like the days of shag carpeting and crocheted couch covers. The décor leaned starboard. Vintage life preservers, porthole art, and seascapes by, presumably, local artists.

The check-in process was quick and painless, which probably indicated the hotel did not do a lot of trade off-season.

Their rooms were next door to each other on the ground floor. Jason unlocked his room and glanced over at Sam, who was doing the same, a few feet away.

"I didn't thank you," Jason said. "For springing me. Thanks. I mean that."

Sam's mouth twisted. "Call it an early birthday present."

Right. In some forgotten corner of the universe life was going on as normal. His sisters were plotting a birthday party he didn't want, his parents were comfortably unaware their only son was a suspect in a murder case, and George Potts was probably typing up his formal discharge papers right now.

"Does George—my SAC—know what's going on?"

"This wasn't a rogue operation. I spoke to Potts before I left Medford."

Jason nodded.

Once again, he could see Kennedy wanted to say something. Frankly, sympathy from Kennedy was even worse than when he was being a dick.

Jason nodded again politely, stepped inside the room, and let the door swing shut.

"*Jesus*," he whispered.

But like Kennedy said, one thing at a time. He was out of the slammer. That was something—and he'd back Kennedy over Detective O'Neill any day of the week. Suppose Kennedy was right and Jason was genuinely under suspicion, the case was entirely circumstantial. Even if he couldn't get out to the island in time to dispose of physical evidence that he and Shipka had, if only once, done more than collaborate on a case, it was all circumstantial.

He went into the bathroom and splashed cold water on his face, then filled one of the glasses and drank a couple of glasses of hose-flavored water.

According to the clock by the bed it was now nine o'clock. Six o'clock in the morning Los Angeles time. He tried George at home and was informed by his wife that George was on the other line, but she'd let him know Jason had phoned.

Conference calls before the official work-day began? Never a good sign.

Well, there wasn't a hell of a lot he could do about it from here.

He phoned George's extension at the office and left a message explaining that he was out of jail, planning to get over to the island that afternoon to retrieve his laptop and belongings, and hoped to catch a plane home that evening.

He began to scroll through his email and texts, waiting for George to phone back, but his cell remained stubbornly silently.

As promised, Shipka had sent his notes on his investigation into Paris Havemeyer's disappearance. The email read: *Even The Man does not live by blueberry muffins alone. Dinner at my place. Five o'clock.*

Jason stared at it for a long time.

There had been no chance that he'd conveniently transfer his affections from Sam to Chris Shipka, but he wished they'd had that dinner. He wished he had been there to stop the attack on Shipka.

He was almost convinced he had been locked up in order to ensure two things: that he would be unable to interfere in the attack on Shipka and that he would have no alibi for Shipka's murder. Almost. The problem with that theory was it entailed both foreknowledge and a plan—premeditation—on someone's part.

Foreknowledge that included knowing who both Jason and Shipka were and that they were working together. That wasn't impossible. Barnaby's entire household probably knew who Jason was and why he was on the island. And Shipka had been to Cape Vincent a couple of times previously, asking questions.

The real hitch was the plan to get rid of Shipka. Nobody could know that Jason and Shipka would go their separate ways that day or that Jason would walk into that crypt like a complete dumbass.

The only way that scenario worked was if Kennedy's unsub had tracked either Jason or Shipka to the island—and in either case that meant the unsub was someone closely following the investigation. All three investigations, in fact. Jason's investigation into Fletcher-Durrand, the BAU's investigation into the Monet murders, and Shipka's private crusade to find out what had happened to Paris Havemeyer.

That was pretty hard to believe. For one thing, the MO was completely different. No fake Monet with a death scene. No clean, cold, merciless ice pick to the back of the brain. Whoever had gone after Shipka had done so in a frenzy of rage.

That said, it was even harder to believe Shipka had fallen victim to some random homicidal maniac.

Jason glanced at the bedside clock. George had still not called back.

It didn't necessarily mean anything. George might still be talking to the SAC, or the ADC, or even Karan Kapszukiewicz in DC. Come to think of it, Jason should give Karan a call as well and update her on everything that had happened.

But later.

Kennedy was correct about this too. Right now, what Jason needed more than anything was sleep.

He fell back on the pillows, closed his eyes, and was instantly out.

Chapter Seventeen

Blood pooled from beneath the bottom of the door.

Dark and glossy as crimson. You could almost mistake it for oil paint, if not for the smell.

He knew what lay behind that door and knew he *had* to open it. But sick dread paralyzed him. He couldn't make himself reach for the handle. Couldn't walk away either. Then from inside the closet, Shipka began to pound on the door, louder and louder—

With a gasp, Jason sat up, heart in his mouth, hair in his eyes. It took him a bewildered moment to realize someone *was* pounding. Banging on the hotel room door. He jumped off the bed and stumbled to the door.

Kennedy stood in the hallway, scowling ferociously. The ferocity faded as he took in Jason's sleep-dazed appearance.

"You okay?"

"Yeah. Of course."

Kennedy was still frowning, studying him closely. "I've been out here knocking for almost a full minute."

"I was just…out. I'm fine. Have you heard anything?"

It didn't look like Kennedy had slept. In fact, Kennedy didn't appear to have even taken his jacket off since they'd arrived. Had he been on the phone the whole time?

"We've got the all-clear to head out to the island."

That dispelled the lingering cobwebs. "Great. Let me get my shoes on."

Kennedy held the door as Jason grabbed his boots, fastened his holster, and reached for his jacket. "We can hire a boat at Seaport Sloops. I wanted to talk to the owner anyway."

"Okay. Let's get this done."

At the stern note in Kennedy's voice, Jason looked up quickly. "You don't have to be involved in this. It's my mess. I can clean it up on my own." As a matter of fact, he'd prefer to do it on his own.

"I'm coming," Kennedy said. "I want to see this island for myself."

"There's something strange about it," Jason admitted. "It's got an atmosphere I can't explain. Somewhere between peaceful and sinister."

Kennedy gave a brief laugh.

"I know. But that's the truth. I felt uneasy all the time I was there."

"With good reason."

"Yes. Shipka was convinced the Havemeyer kid was killed on the island."

"Based on?"

"Not a lot. Largely the alleged rape and kidnapping of another young man the year before. But as a point of interest, there are three separate graveyards, including Native American burial grounds. Plenty of places to conceal a body."

"You don't need a graveyard to get rid of a body," Kennedy said.

And recalling those dark woods and rocky coastlines, Jason had to agree.

On the drive to Seaport Sloops, Kennedy requested Jason bring him up to speed on everything Shipka had shared. Jason related the story about Marco Poveda and the dropped rape charges as well as the other various rumors surrounding Shepherd Durrand.

At the end of it, Kennedy said, "It would be interesting to know where Shepherd Durrand was yesterday, but your guy is the older brother. Barnaby. Correct?"

"I'm not ruling Shepherd's participation out. But yes, Barnaby is the complainee in the charges filed against the gallery. He hasn't denied selling the paintings either. That said, there are no rumors about Barnaby.

Which is to say, not like there are about Shepherd. Even before Shipka contacted me, I'd heard the whispers about drugs, rough sex and S&M clubs. He has a reputation for spending money like water. He's a playboy. In fact, I'd say he takes pride in that reputation. What nobody ever whispered was that he has a head for business. But I saw his office. I spoke to him. I think he's a lot sharper than people give him credit for. I think he's full-fledged partner in that gallery. The question is not does Shepherd know everything Barnaby is up to. I'd say the question is does Barnaby know everything Shepherd is up to."

"What do you think? Does he?"

"I don't know yet. But I plan to," Jason said.

"While we're on the topic of Barnaby, your pal Detective O'Neill informed me that Durrand left the island at the crack of dawn this morning."

"Before he could be questioned about my alibi?" Jason demanded.

"Yes."

"Goddamn it. That's not a coincidence."

"Probably not."

"Are they going to pursue this? They're not just going to let this go, are they? Where is he headed? Do they know?"

"Slow down," Kennedy told him. "Durrand is back in Los Angeles. I've already received confirmation on that. And no, according to Detective O'Neill, they're not going to just let this go."

"The Durrands own that town and everyone in it."

"Whoa," Kennedy said. "That's a little dramatic, don't you think? I spoke directly to O'Neill. I don't think he's a fan of the Durrands."

"He's not a fan of mine either."

"No, but I believe he'll do his job. I believe he'll show due diligence."

Jason glowered out the window.

Kennedy glanced at him. There was the faintest note of humor in his voice as he said, "Anyway, you've still got a couple of things working in your favor. First, nobody at the Jefferson County Sheriff's Office is going to leap to the conclusion you're gay, so the idea that you had a relationship with Shipka is not likely to occur."

"It wasn't a relationship. We had sex. One time," Jason said. Why did he feel the need to make that point? Oh, right. Because it was the truth.

Kennedy's gaze did not leave the road ahead. "Secondly, you're a special agent with the FBI, and most people outside the bureau can't picture an FBI agent having sex with anyone."

Jason snorted. Now there was the truth. He'd certainly never pictured Sam having sex—until Sam had propositioned him.

*   *   *   *   *

"We were wondering if you were going to show up today. It's all anyone in the village can talk about." Mrs. Seaport Sloop—whose first name turned out to be Daisy—greeted them. She finished ringing up the rental shop's only other customer, a stooped, elderly man in a pea coat and navy toque.

Bram came out of the back office, saying cheerfully, "To think you were right there. The FBI was right next door when it happened. That's crazy."

Yep. Not exactly a career booster.

"The sheriff's department was asking for permission to search the lodge," Daisy said. Her gaze, meeting Jason's, was speculative.

"Standard practice," Jason said. "I found the victim, so." He shrugged and glanced at Kennedy, who was watching him with a curious expression. "This is my, er, boss. Unit Chief Sam Kennedy."

"Don't worry," Bram said. "We told them to get a search warrant. I don't like Jefferson County poking their nose in. I guess you want to go back to the island?" He looked from Jason to Kennedy—and then back to Kennedy. Kennedy tended to have that effect on people.

Jason said, "Just to pick up my gear."

"There you go, Mr. Bundy," Daisy said brightly. "You have a nice day!"

Mr. Bundy gathered his bag of chocolate milk, mini donuts, and cigarettes, and departed reluctantly, with several curious glances over his shoulder.

Bram muttered, "That old busybody. Now it's going to be all over town. Is it true the sheriffs arrested you?"

"No," Jason said. "They questioned me. Of course."

"Well, yeah. You were right *there*." He shook his head in disbelief.

"You're lucky it wasn't *you*," Daisy said. "If there's a maniac on that island…" She looked at Bram.

He gave her a warning glance.

Now that was an odd little exchange, but it gave Jason the opening he'd been looking for. "I understand Mr. Shipka questioned you about an incident on the island that happened about twenty years ago? Someone from Seaport Sloops picked up a young man who claimed he'd been held prisoner on the island?"

"Oh my God," Daisy exclaimed. "Was that the same guy? That reporter?"

"I don't know why he wanted to bring that whole situation up." Bram seemed to be in no doubt as to who Shipka was. "It's *decades* ago. What good was going to come out of it? The guy's dead."

"How'd you know Poveda was dead?" Jason asked.

Bram looked blank for an instant. "Oh. The reporter told us. When he was trying to get us to talk. Said the guy was dead now, so he needed someone to corroborate his statement."

Right. Of course. Obviously.

Kennedy said, "Maybe what happened last night is why it matters."

The Seaport Sloops looked as startled as if one of the bilge pumps had spoken up. "No," Bram said. "That was a different kind of thing. That was Shep."

"*Bram*," his wife said in alarm.

"*Allegedly* Shep," Bram corrected, proving that he *had* been paying attention while watching all those FBI movies.

"Are you the one who transported Mr. Poveda from the island?" Jason asked. Twenty years ago Bram would have been in his late teens, early twenties. Not much more than a kid himself.

Bram hesitated. "No."

"I know it's awkward," Jason said. "The Durrands are important people around here. But what if these two crimes are connected? That's something law enforcement needs to know. It's too late to pursue the first case. You're not going to get dragged into a courtroom."

"They're not connected," Bram said.

"You can't know that. At this juncture—"

Kennedy interrupted, "You're the one who picked up Poveda. Correct?" He was talking to Daisy.

Daisy's brown eyes opened wide in alarm. She looked at Bram, her expression guilty.

Bram rolled his eyes. "Hell," he said. "Go ahead, Miss Chatterbox. I don't see what the point is now, but go ahead and tell them."

"There isn't a lot to tell," Daisy admitted. "I took a group of tourists over to see the old fort. They were going to have lunch and explore the island. That's typical of our summer business. A boy about my age came bursting out of the bushes. He was stark naked, holding a branch in front of his crotch like he thought it was a fig leaf." She gave a nervous giggle. "He claimed he'd been locked up in the Durrand family's crypt for days and that he'd been, um, molested."

"Molested?" Jason repeated.

"Raped. He claimed he was being held prisoner. A sexual slave. By Shepherd."

"There were other witnesses to this claim?" Kennedy asked.

"No. It was just me by then. He'd waited until everyone was gone, and then he ran down to the dock as I was about to set sail. He said he believed they were going to kill him—"

"They?" Jason questioned.

"Shepherd and whoever. Barnaby, I guess. He begged me to take him with me—the kid, that is—and I did." The look she threw Bram was slightly defiant. "*I* believed him."

"If he was locked inside the crypt, how did he explain getting free?" Jason asked.

"He said someone opened the door. He couldn't see who. He thought it was a trap at first, and he was afraid to come out. Like in the *Dangerous Game*."

"Huh?" Bram said.

"Like the story. Or maybe he watched the movie. We read it in high school."

Bram shook his head.

"Yes. We read it in Mrs. De Haan's English class."

Bram shook his head again.

"Yes. We did. You loved that story!"

Kennedy sighed.

Jason prompted, "Poveda thought the open door might be a trap?"

Daisy nodded eagerly. "Right. But finally he realized it might be his only chance to get away, and he ran into the woods."

"He didn't say who opened the door?"

"He didn't see. He figured it was one of the servants at the house. Someone who couldn't go along with murder. But he didn't know. I can tell you one thing, he was scared to death. He wasn't faking that."

Bram made a face.

"Why was he so sure he was going to be murdered?" Jason asked.

"He said Shepherd told him they would have to kill him. That he couldn't trust him not to tell what happened."

Sam said, "They again."

Daisy looked apologetic. "It was a *long* time ago. I think he said *they*, but I don't remember word for word. I had the impression he thought there was someone else besides Shepherd, but he never said another name. I'd have remembered that."

"Yes," Bram said. "She'd have remembered."

"What happened after you reached Cape Vincent?"

"Nothing. I mean, I'd given him some old clothes that were on the boat to wear. He didn't have any money or anything. No ID. He was still slightly stoned; he said Shep was feeding him drugs. Anyway, he thanked me, and then he went to talk to the police."

Where, according to Shipka, the Durrands had been immediately notified that the houseguest from hell had escaped.

Poveda's mistake was understandable. He had no way of knowing that the Cape Vincent Police Department was a part-time agency. Or that their so-called mission statement read in part: *Balancing the outcome based on the need of the community.*

Right. In other words, don't call us, we'll call you.

Major crime was handled by Jefferson County Sheriff's Department, and it was unfortunate that no one at CVPD had seen fit to escalate Poveda's complaint to that agency. But it was also easy to see how the wild accusations of a slightly stoned outsider against one of the community's leading families might be dismissed.

It wasn't right. It wasn't okay. But it was the way things were too often handled—and, unfortunately, that still held true.

After the rain and fog of the day before, the boat trip to the island was unexpectedly sunny and beautiful.

Jason and Kennedy got the complete rundown from Bram on the Who's Who at the Jefferson County Sheriff's Department. "Rundown" being the correct word for it.

Kennedy said little, leaving it to Jason to keep feeding Bram the "oh yeahs" and "is that sos."

As they drew close to the dock near the lodge, they could see several black and gold Jefferson County patrol boats moored along the shoreline. The cottage was a hive of activity, with uniformed officers swarming the crime scene.

Bram's eyes lit up with enjoyment, and he offered to wait to motor them back.

"Not necessary," Jason said. "I can bring us back on one of the boats."

"It's easier this way." Bram grinned his wide, mischievous grin. "Besides, I want to see what the cops are up to."

Ah, yes. The Cape Vincent rumor mill needed a steady supply of grist to stay operational.

Jason glanced at Kennedy, who was watching Bram with a thoughtful expression. Feeling Jason's gaze, Kennedy raised his brows in inquiry.

Jason casually asked Bram, "What would you like me to do with the dirty towels and sheets?"

Bram shrugged, still eyeing the cottage next door. "Just throw them in the machine."

Jason didn't have to look at Kennedy to know his expression would be disapproving.

They landed, disembarked, and Bram took himself off to get a closer view of what the sheriff deputies were up to.

Jason preceded Kennedy up the walk to the lodge. It seemed to Jason that there was something censorious in the bite of Kennedy's heels on stone.

Jason looked over his shoulder.

"Again, it's not evidence. I'm not involved. I don't have anything to hide."

"Everybody's got something to hide."

"Even you?"

Kennedy gave him an oddly resolute look from beneath the blond line of his brows. "Of course."

His answer took Jason aback. Or rather, not the answer, but the honesty of the answer.

"It's about the first forty-eight. If the sheriff department focuses on me, they're losing valuable time in the first hours of the investigation."

Kennedy said, "I'm not arguing with you."

"But you disapprove."

To his surprise—maybe to both their surprise—Kennedy gave a funny laugh. "Yes. I disapprove. But maybe what I really..."

Kennedy didn't finish the thought, but Jason's heart leaped at that rueful half-admission.

They reached the lodge. Jason unlocked the door, and they went inside.

Jason headed straight for the bedroom and quickly stripped the bed.

"It didn't take you long to get friendly with Shipka," Kennedy said from the doorway.

Jason shot back, "It didn't take me long to get friendly with you."

Kennedy nodded as though conceding a point, but Jason already regretted the comment. His relationship with Kennedy had been completely different from his relationship with Shipka. Although maybe not from Kennedy's standpoint.

"I was tired and depressed. Half a bottle of wine helped." He shrugged. "Or didn't help."

"You don't have to explain your choices to me."

"No. I don't." Jason bundled up the sheets with the towels from the bathroom and carried them through to the small laundry area. He stuffed them in the machine, added soap, and turned the machine on.

When he went into the kitchen, he found Kennedy searching the utensil drawers.

His heart stopped. "What are you doing?"

Kennedy didn't bother to glance up. "Making sure the murder weapon wasn't planted in here while you were gone."

Jason's lips parted, but it took him a few seconds to come up with anything to say. "The doors and windows were locked."

"Yep." Kennedy shut the drawer and moved to the next one. "But this is a rental property, and over the years, hundreds of people have had the opportunity to make duplicate keys."

After a stunned moment, Jason began to search the cabinets on the other side of the kitchen. "Then you do believe I was locked up in that mausoleum so I wouldn't have an alibi for Shipka's murder?"

The first cabinet contained empty tins, nothing more.

"Maybe. Maybe to keep you from interfering. Maybe locking you up was an impulse, and the decision to kill Shipka grew out of that opportunity."

Decision sounded too rational for the mayhem that had been inflicted on Shipka.

"Whoever killed Shipka would have been covered in blood. There would be forensic evidence all over this place," Jason pointed out.

"You want to take that chance?"

"No."

They continued to search in silence.

When they'd finished with the kitchen, Kennedy said, "Detective O'Neill is smart enough to realize the thermostat at the cottage was cranked up to help confuse time of death. That works both for and against you. He believes an FBI agent is more likely to think of that than the average person."

"What do you believe?"

"I believe people love watching those CSI shows." Kennedy added, "I'm going to take the living room. You take the bedroom and bath."

"Right."

They searched the lodge top to bottom, from the sleeping porch to the fireplace chimney. No weapon was hidden on the premises.

"That's a relief," Jason said at the end of their hunt.

"Yes." Kennedy looked thoughtful.

"No?"

Kennedy said, "Now the question becomes why *wasn't* the weapon hidden here?"

"Because there wasn't time? Because he couldn't get in? Because he had to leave the island?"

Kennedy nodded, but it was more acknowledgment that Jason was speaking than agreement. He said abruptly, "I'm going to see how they're doing processing the crime scene."

"Okay." They were going to love that.

"Give a shout when you're ready to go."

Jason nodded.

It didn't take long to gather his belongings. He washed the juice glasses, plate, and coffee cups he and Shipka had used, then sat down to wait for the washing machine to finish its rinse and spin cycle. When the buzzer went off, he tossed the linens in the dryer and hit the button. He picked up his bag and walked out to the front yard of the lodge.

Across the expanse of winter grass and rock, Kennedy was talking to the officer in charge. He spotted Jason, spoke a final word to the man in uniform, and started across the grass. He stopped, put his fingers to his mouth and gave a sharp, clear whistle like a cowboy trying to get the attention of a lost little dogie.

And sure enough, Bram stepped out from behind the dividing hedge and jogged over to join them as they walked down to the harbor.

"Can you believe it? They told me I couldn't watch them working the crime scene. They're marching around on my property too!"

Jason nodded vaguely. He wanted to hear what Kennedy had learned, but conscious of Bram's eager listening silence, restrained himself from asking the dozen questions on the tip of his tongue.

"They're doing a decent job processing the crime scene," Kennedy remarked, which was possibly code. If so, as usual when it came to Kennedy, one Jason didn't understand.

"Do they have the autopsy results yet?"

"No. But going by the evidence of blood loss and the bloodstain patterns, the theory is Shipka was whacked with something very large and sharp. A scythe. An ax. I'd concur with that."

"Eric Greenleaf," Jason said. "He's got an ax—and the attitude to go with it."

He'd spoken automatically and winced when Bram said, "*Eric?* Eric's a suspect?"

"No," Jason said quickly. "That was thinking out loud, not an actual suggestion. He's an interesting guy, though."

"Hey, I can see Eric killing someone before I could see Shep. Although if Eric was going to kill anyone, it would be his ex. No love lost there, I can tell you."

"Who's Eric Greenleaf?" Kennedy asked.

"The owner of *that*." Jason pointed to Camden Castle, a black silhouette against the sky.

Kennedy nodded thoughtfully. "Quaint," he observed after a moment.

That little drawl was so Kennedy. Jason laughed.

Kennedy's mouth curved in answer.

The adrenaline that had kept Jason moving at top speed while cleaning up the lodge and making sure he hadn't been framed, drained away on the short boat trip back to Cape Vincent. He had that weird hollow feeling again. He was cold and depressed and more confused than he liked to admit.

What now? He had no idea.

The wind had kicked up, and the water was choppy. He closed his eyes, concentrating on the feel of the sun and spray on his face.

"Seasick?" Kennedy asked suddenly.

Jason looked up in surprise. "Me? No."

Kennedy's brows drew together. "You're white as a sheet."

His voice was low, but Bram heard him. "Put your head over the side of the boat," he told Jason.

Jason said irritably, "I'm not going to get sick. I grew up on boats."

Bram looked skeptical.

Jason said to Kennedy, "I'm fine. Tired, that's all."

Kennedy didn't say anything, just continued to watch him in that steady, serious way.

Jason really wished he wouldn't. That kindness and evident concern just made it harder.

Bram, still apparently mulling over Jason's earlier comment, said, "Everyone on the island has an ax. There's an ax in the toolshed of the lodge."

If it wasn't already in the custody of the Jefferson County Sheriff's Department.

"That was a random remark," Jason said. "Greenleaf was rude and uncooperative, which was why he came to mind. I have no reason to suspect him of any crime. Seriously. Forget I said anything."

"No, but you got me thinking. Remembering."

"Got you thinking what?" Kennedy asked.

"Eric *is* a really weird guy. All the Greenleafs were crazy as hoot owls. If there's a homicidal maniac on the island, he'd be my first pick."

"Has Greenleaf ever threatened anyone? Attacked anyone?"

"He's always threatening people. Especially his ex. Maybe he finally snapped."

"Why would he kill a total stranger?" Jason objected. "Why wouldn't he kill his former girlfriend?"

Bram shrugged. "Maybe he wasn't a stranger. That reporter has been out here a couple of times asking questions about the Durrands and about what happened all those years ago. Maybe he asked one too many questions. Maybe he got on the wrong side of Eric. It's easy to do."

"Thanks for the tip," Kennedy said. "We'll look into it."

Bram offered his wide, cheerful smile. "Glad to help."

On the drive back to the hotel, Kennedy said, "If you're still worried about being a suspect in Shipka's homicide, don't be. I think you're off the hook."

"Why would that be?"

"I dropped a few hints as to the likelihood that Shipka's death will fall under the Bureau's purview, as part of my own interstate investigation."

Jason threw him a startled look. "*Do* you think Shipka was killed by your unsub? The MO is completely different."

"It's one hell of a coincidence if he wasn't." Kennedy's expression was bleak.

"It's one hell of a coincidence if he was, too."

"My point is you can stop worrying about being arrested for your boyfriend's murder."

Jason went very still. "My *boyfriend*?"

"Forget it."

"He wasn't my boyfriend. I knew him all of four days." How long had he and Kennedy been thrown together in Massachusetts? "If anyone was my boyfr—" Jason stopped. *That* was embarrassing. He said instead, striving to sound completely dispassionate, "That would mean your unsub followed Shipka to the island. *Or* he lives on the island. Isn't that kind of unlikely?"

"Yes."

"Well then?"

"Either way you look at it, there are one too many coincidences here. Unlikely or not, these cases do seem to intersect." Kennedy glanced at Jason. His mouth curved. "Which means it's very likely *our* cases intersect."

Jason had no response to that. The best he could manage was a weak, "Ha."

Kennedy said with a rare flash of humor, "Just what I said, Agent West."

A few minutes later they pulled into the mostly empty hotel parking lot, and Kennedy turned off the engine. For a moment or two, they sat gazing at the sparkling blue of the St. Lawrence.

Kennedy took his glasses off and pinched the bridge of his nose. "Christ, I'm tired," he muttered.

Jason looked at him in surprise. He couldn't remember if he'd ever heard Kennedy acknowledge any human frailty, including fatigue. At forty-six, he was still eleven years from mandatory retirement age, and he worked overtime to prove he was every bit as fit and energetic as agents half his age.

"Are we still flying out tonight?"

"Up to you. I think a good night's sleep won't do either of us any harm." He glanced briefly at Jason. "Have you called your office?"

"I wasn't able to speak to George. I had to leave a message. I'll try again when I get back to my room."

His unease must have shown because Kennedy's lip curled. "Don't worry, West. As far as anyone at the LA office knows, you were swept up as part of an interagency pissing match. Your rung on the ladder of success is still safe."

Kennedy's fluctuation between concern and those little aggressive digs was unsettling. Jason said, "You know, I didn't see you turning down promotion when it was offered."

"No. I couldn't afford to. I'd made too many enemies. I had to either move out of range or try to do my job the best I could as a moving target. I figured I'd be more effective if I took the promotion."

Jason had suspected something like that, but it was the first time Kennedy had come right out and said so.

Unwillingly, he asked, "Do you have any regrets?"

"Sure," Kennedy said. "I have plenty of regrets. About all kinds of things." He opened his car door. "If I had to do it all again, I'd make the same choices."

Chapter Eighteen

Of course, he didn't need to stay over just because Kennedy was choosing to. But the fact was, Jason was still worn out physically, mentally, and emotionally. The idea of eight hours of undisturbed sleep sounded like heaven. He needed to be sharp when he finally confronted his superiors back in LA.

At least he hoped that was what motivated his decision to stay. He hoped it was not the desire to spend additional time in Kennedy's company.

He booked his flight for the following morning and checked his messages—when he saw the state of his inbox, he wished he hadn't. Nothing from George, though. No phone call, no email, no text. His stomach knotted with anxiety.

Jesus. Was he going to be fired? Without warning? Without a hearing?

He glanced at the bedside clock. Four thirty. Which meant it was one thirty in Los Angeles. George might be at lunch. Or he might not. He might be sitting at his desk wondering why his errant ACT agent wasn't checking in.

If he was about to be canned, it would be better to know now. Jason phoned George—and ended up on hold where he spent the next eight minutes gnawing on his lip and staring out the window at the fishing boats.

George came on the line. "The prodigal son. I was just about to call you." He sounded... Actually, he sounded pretty much as usual. Cheerful, friendly, relaxed. "You okay?"

"Uh, yeah. I'm fine."

"I figured. I figured if anybody could get you out of the pokey fast, it would be Mr. Personality."

"You phoned Kennedy?" Jason couldn't hide his amazement.

George's laugh was more of a hoot. "*Me* phone *him*? That'd be the day."

"But how did Kennedy get stuck with bailing me out?"

"Uh, you're kidding about being out on bail, right? You weren't formally charged?"

"Yes. I'm kidding."

George was abruptly serious. "It was Kennedy's choice, believe me. He phoned me not long after you did. Said he was already on his way to New York. That since you were following up several lines of inquiry at his request, he felt it was his responsibility to see you didn't take the heat for a job that rightly should have fallen to his team."

"That was…"

A load of bullshit, frankly.

"Not what I'd have expected," George agreed. "I told you he likes you. Plus, there must be some reason agents fight tooth and nail to get into his unit."

"Do they?"

"Yeah. According to Jonnie, they do. Did you get your interview with Durrand?"

"Yep."

"Good. I look forward to reading your report."

"No, you don't."

George laughed. "You're flying back when?"

"Tomorrow morning. My plane leaves at seven."

"Travel safe. No more falling afoul of local law enforcement, okay?"

"I'll try. No promises."

George chuckled again and hung up.

Jason stared at his phone in disbelief.

What the hell had Kennedy told George? Because, far from getting ready to fire him, George had sounded almost jovial. Like Jason had done something particularly amusing by getting dragged in for questioning.

Had he taken this whole thing way too seriously?

No. Kennedy wouldn't have dropped his own investigation to fly to Jason's rescue if it hadn't been pretty damned serious. It seemed to Jason the most likely reason his running afoul of the Jefferson County Sheriff's Department was being treated like a boyish escapade and not an inter-agency FUBAR was whatever spin Kennedy had managed to put on the situation for Jason's superiors.

Kennedy might be a lousy boyfriend, but he sure as hell was a loyal friend.

When the alarm on his phone went off, Jason blinked up at the shadowy ceiling for a second or two, trying to figure out where he was.

Oh, right. The Buccaneer's Cove hotel in Cape Vincent. He was sup-posed to meet Sam—Kennedy—for dinner in…Jason peered at his phone screen…half an hour. He settled his head on the pillow, closed his eyes, and considered blowing off dinner. Every time he saw Kennedy, it just stirred up a lot of feelings he didn't want and didn't need.

But no. He couldn't do that. He owed Kennedy, so if Kennedy wanted to have dinner, the least Jason could do was make the same effort he would for any other colleague.

He sat up and reached for the lamp switch.

On the bright side, he had clean underwear, his own razor, and his job did not appear to be in imminent danger. A hot shower, a good meal, and he'd be his old self again.

The hot shower did work a minor miracle. Jason dressed in the jeans, white shirt, and navy blazer he'd originally planned on wearing for his interview with Barnaby.

He went next door and knocked. When nothing happened, he knocked again.

The door opened.

"Sorry. I got hung up on the phone." Kennedy was bare-chested, though he had gotten as far as putting on jeans and shoes. His blond hair was dark from the shower. He moved away from the door, and Jason stepped inside.

The room was the twin of his, right down to the rustic ship's wheel over the bed and vintage black and white boating photos. Kennedy's carryall sat open on the table. The navy-blue bedspread did not have a single wrinkle, so Kennedy had not been napping.

A brown leather travel frame on the bedside table caught Jason's eye.

Two photos. One was of a much younger and smiling Kennedy holding a dark-haired man in a playful headlock. The other was of the same dark-haired young man gazing solemnly out at the world.

It was kind of like getting gut-punched. Unexpected and paralyzing. For a second or two it was impossible for Jason to think past his immediate, visceral reaction.

One thing for sure, this frame and these photos had not been anywhere in sight in Massachusetts. But here they were prominently, pointedly on display in Kennedy's room now.

A reminder? For whom?

Kennedy was in the bathroom, hastily giving his chin a pass with his electric razor, and saying, "You look like you're feeling better."

Jason continued to study the photo. Shock had given way to a cold sinking feeling in the pit of his stomach. The guy in the photo with Kennedy looked superficially like himself. Dark hair, light eyes, *angular face, and thin build* as Crazy Kyser would have said.

Kennedy flicked off his razor and reached for the bottle of Escentric Molecules Molecule 03. The distinct scent of vetiver together with ginger, sandalwood, cedar, mellow balsams, and musk floated into the room where Jason stood.

Jason said, "Not your brother, I'm guessing?"

Kennedy's brows drew together, but he followed Jason's gaze, and his face went instantly expressionless. "No."

He had to ask. It had to be addressed. To ignore it would be the weirdest thing in an already weird situation. "Is he the reason you don't want to pursue anything else?"

"Yes." Kennedy's voice was oddly quiet.

After a moment, Jason said, "I see."

Maybe his anger wasn't reasonable, but it was real. *This* he had a right to be upset about. Sam had lied about not being involved with anyone, and that was not okay. Jason would never have slept with him—well, probably not, he hoped not—if he'd known Sam was involved. Committed.

Kennedy was watching him—warily, it seemed to Jason, but there was also a stoic line to his jaw. He expected Jason to be angry and hurt, and he was braced for an outburst.

Pride came to Jason's rescue. Pride and cold logic. *Did* he have a right to be angry? Sex, a few late-night phone calls, and the promise of a future dinner date where they would probably skip dinner. That was the extent of his "relationship" with Kennedy, if he wanted to get technical about it. There had been no commitment between them. If Kennedy had broken any vows, it was to the guy in the photo, and for all Jason knew, they had an open relationship. Or maybe they'd been separated at the time.

Who the hell knew?

Why the hell did it matter so much to him? It shouldn't.

The bottom line was Kennedy did not want to have a relationship with him, and really, it didn't matter why. *Why* didn't change anything.

"Ready?" Jason asked briskly, and had the satisfaction of seeing Kennedy's surprise.

It didn't stop Jason feeling that his still-beating heart had been ripped out of his chest, but it was a tiny comfort to be able to defy Kennedy's expectations.

"Yes." Kennedy grabbed his shirt off the hanger on the back of the bathroom door—steaming the wrinkles out of his shirt. Jason knew that trick too.

Kennedy buttoned up his shirt in record time and pulled on the black suit jacket he'd worn in LA. He hadn't packed much, but he'd been prepared for a variety of scenarios, it seemed. But then he was always prepared for a variety of scenarios.

They walked in deadly silence down the hall.

"Did you want to eat here or find another place?" Kennedy asked when they reached the hotel lobby.

"I don't care. I just want to eat and go to bed." Jason heard the echo of his words, mentally winced, and corrected, "Sleep."

Kennedy said nothing—not about to touch that with a ten-foot pole. He led the way to the empty dining room with its picturesque view of the nighttime harbor.

The girl behind the reception desk wore a nametag that read *Brandi*. Jason could only imagine how many times she'd heard variations on "you're a fine girl, what a good wife you would be" from the drunken fifty-plus fishing crowd.

Brandi glanced briefly away from her smartphone to tell them to seat themselves. Kennedy headed for a large round table by the window.

Jason smiled maliciously at the strategic placement of a safety zone of white linen and silver hurricane lanterns between them.

Brandi, the receptionist, who it seemed was also their waitress, delivered menus and took their drink orders. Kennedy ordered a ginger ale. Jason ordered a Kamikaze.

The drinks arrived right away. Kennedy ignored his, still frowning over the menu. He had donned his gold-rimmed reading glasses, which made him look academic and older. Jason set his menu aside and downed his drink before the waitress had time to depart.

Brandi's eyes widened as he indicated his glass.

"Again. Please."

She grinned. "Oh-KAY!"

Kennedy glanced over, and his brows rose. He made no comment, returning to his menu. Hiding behind it, Jason thought sourly.

"What's the situation in Oregon?" he asked, more because he wanted to force Kennedy to interact with him than from any desire to know.

Kennedy proceeded to tell him about a cold case bursting into flames: the hunt for a missing teenaged girl, crazed survivalists, a serial killer twisting ancient Indian rituals to his own macabre purposes, and an FBI agent abducted off his own doorstep.

Fifteen minutes later their meals arrived—Jason barely remembered ordering a seafood salad—and he was forced to say, "I had no idea. Given all that, I appreciate your flying out here to…"

And he did, but the memory of that bedside photo caused the words to stick in his throat. It didn't change the fact that with all hell breaking loose—okay, technically, it was the aftermath of all hell breaking loose, but still—Kennedy had made the decision to charge to Jason's rescue. That was more than kind, more than decent. It was the kind of thing you did for family—or people you felt very guilty about.

Kennedy didn't seem to hear Jason's gruff words. "I've got an opening in my unit. I'd like to bring Darling on board. I'm not sure he'll accept, but I think he's got the right instincts. In fact, I'd say he has a knack for our kind of work."

"Hunting monsters."

"They're human enough. That's what makes them frightening. Unfortunately, Darling's formed an attachment to one of the deputy sheriffs up there in the back of beyond."

Yes. How unfortunate to form an emotional attachment that might come before your fucking job.

"Oh, he'll take it," Jason said. "Even if he hadn't been stuck on morgue patrol for the past six months. He's ambitious, and it's an opportunity to work with the great Sam Kennedy. Who wouldn't jump at that?" That was hurt talking, though it came out sounding sarcastic.

Kennedy eyed him thoughtfully. "I seem to have…incurred your displeasure, West."

Incurred your displeasure. He was being ironic. Also maybe looking for a fight?

Or maybe Jason was the one looking for a fight. If so, that was the second Kamikaze.

He settled for a curt. "Nope."

He'd only had a quick look at the photo, but the image seemed to have imprinted itself in his memory. It was an old photo. Kennedy had been younger. Significantly younger. So it was a relationship of long standing, not a recent development. A recent development would have been painful, but…things happened. An ongoing committed relationship meant Kennedy had been involved when he and Jason first hooked up.

Either way you looked at it, he'd been cheating. Maybe not on Jason, but did that make it any better?

Except… Kennedy was no cheater. He was brutally honest and as direct as a blunt instrument. So what the hell?

If it was a current relationship, the photo would likely be contemporary.

That first night in Boston: *So are you married or involved or what?*

Kennedy was the one who'd asked.

In eight months, whether Kennedy was at home in Quantico or on the road, there had never been a hint of anyone else in his life. Okay, he'd referred to his mother in Wyoming a couple of times. But other than that, the closest thing he had to a relationship was Jason. Jason would have staked his life on it.

None of this made sense. Kennedy, of all people, traveling around with a couple of ancient photos like he was clinging to a lucky talisman in the face of temptation made the least sense of all.

Kennedy expelled a long breath. His eyes were a blaze of blue. The only real color in the candlelit room. He said carefully, "West—Jason—I want to stay friends. I think of you as a friend. I...care about you."

Jason stared at him. Why did that hurt so much? It really should help with the pain of rejection because he could see Kennedy meant every word. He could *feel* Kennedy meant every word. Why did it make it worse that Kennedy wanted to be his friend?

"I appreciate that. I appreciate—I'm grateful for everything you did for me today. But you said it yourself. It's not practical to..." He had to stop there because it felt like a self-inflicted wound to cut off all possibility of anything with Kennedy. Which...didn't that prove right there that amputation was necessary?

Kennedy's throat moved. He nodded. The lines in his face seemed more pronounced.

Another thing. Why did it make Jason's chest ache as much when he gave pain to Kennedy as when Kennedy hurt *him*?

"I don't understand," Jason said. It was the simple truth, straight from the heart. The way they had talked to each other for all those months. Although they had never talked about feelings. They had flirted plenty, but this...this was putting into words what he had imagined had been between the lines.

"I know."

And no explanation was going to be forthcoming.

But Jason persisted. It was too important not to try, even though it already felt like a doomed effort. "I...guess I don't have the right to ask, but it would help me understand..."

"Ask," Kennedy said.

"The guy in the photo—he's dead, isn't he?" Jason watched Kennedy's face.

Kennedy gave a crisp and uncompromising, "Yes."

"But he's the reason you're no longer interested in...me."

"Correct."

Ask and ye shall receive. But apparently, that was too cold even for Kennedy. He said, "It isn't a matter of my interest in you. I mean it when I say I care about you. What I told you in Kingsfield still goes."

Jason nodded. He did his best to match Sam's unemotional tone. "Right. But he's the reason you changed your mind about pursuing anything more than a work relationship. It's an old photo; you were both, what? College age? How did he die?"

It was one of the few times he saw Kennedy hesitate.

Jason decided to make it easy on him. "Was he murdered?"

Kennedy stared at Jason, his expression strange. As though this was a side of Jason he'd never seen, couldn't quite get a handle on. "Yes."

"His murder—"

Kennedy said harshly, "His name was Ethan."

"Ethan's murder is why you decided to join the FBI? To dedicate your life to hunting serial killers?"

Kennedy nodded slowly.

It made sense really. Personal motivation. Nothing unique about that. And yet the obvious explanation had never occurred to Jason.

"Okay. Ethan's death was the catalyst. What I don't understand is... that was how many years ago? I don't see what it has to do with today. I don't see why—"

Kennedy said quietly, fiercely, "Because I can't do my job the way I need to do it if I'm distracted by you."

"Distracted?" Jason repeated blankly. "Distracted how? It's not like I was taking up a lot of your time and energy."

Kennedy was still speaking with that startling, almost angry intensity. "Yeah, you were. Whether you know it or not. Take today for example. I've got an injured agent, two dead men, who knows how many other victims, and a media frenzy, but I drop everything to fly cross country because you need help."

They'd been talking softly, but Jason's voice rose at that. "I never asked for your help! I didn't—and don't—need your help."

"But here I am." Kennedy was acerbic. "Which is why it had to stop. Because I couldn't stop thinking about you. All the time. Wondering how you were, what you were doing, worrying if you were being careful, if you were still struggling."

"*Jesus.* I'm not struggling—" Jason tried to interrupt, but Kennedy kept right on talking.

"The best part of my day—any day—were the nights I got to talk to you for a couple of hours on the phone." He looked almost bewildered at the revelation. "I started feeling like I wanted time off, started thinking maybe I shouldn't take so many chances, like I should start planning for the future."

"There's nothing wrong with planning for the future."

"I'm not talking picking retirement investments. I wanted time with *you*, plain and simple. I was looking forward to that too much." Once again he seemed angry as he concluded, "I can't feel like that and still do my job the way I need to do it."

Jason burst out, "You keep saying that. What does it mean? Other people do their jobs and have lives outside of the Bureau."

"Not me. I don't get the results I get by having a life outside the Bureau." At Jason's open disbelief, he said, "When Ethan died, I swore it would not be for nothing. I swore I'd spend the rest of my life hunting the predators, stopping them from hurting other people, destroying other lives like our life had been destroyed. I made a vow. A commitment."

Married to murder. Fan-fucking-tastic. Jason hadn't missed that *our life* comment.

It didn't get clearer than that. Not something you really could argue with, nor did he want to try. He felt angry and sad and a little sick. Granted, he should have guessed at the bottom of Kennedy's phenomenal success lay obsession, but this wasn't normal workaholic stuff. This wasn't anything he could understand or deal with.

Nor was Kennedy asking for his understanding or anything else. As far as he was concerned, the possibility of a real relationship between them was effectively ended. It was friendship, take it or leave it.

And Jason was going to have to leave it because despite that masters in psychology, Kennedy was kidding himself about this. If he really did feel the way he described, there was no way they'd manage to keep it friendly and light and detached—if that was what he was picturing.

It was already a huge emotional mess—and the sexual frustration and tension between them was like a third presence at the table. Or maybe that was just Jason.

"Anything else I can get you gentlemen?" Brandi asked.

Kennedy looked inquiringly at Jason.

Jason shook his head.

"Just the bill," Kennedy said.

They sat in silence until Brandi brought the bill. Kennedy reached for it. Whatever. Let the BAU expense it.

They rose and walked into the lobby.

"What time is your flight tomorrow?" Kennedy asked as they crossed the parquet floor on the way to their rooms.

"Seven."

"I'm out at six. You're welcome to drive back to Watertown with me. I'll leave about five."

"Five. Ouch," Jason said.

In truth, he didn't give a damn about the time. He did not want to drive to the airport with Kennedy. He couldn't be around Kennedy right now. Maybe it should have comforted him to know that Kennedy did still care for him, that he hadn't done anything wrong, that this was Kennedy's problem and not his. But it wasn't comforting. It was…hopeless. How did it help knowing Kennedy still cared, if in the end, it all came to the same thing? If anything, the pointless, painful futility of Kennedy's choice just made it worse. They were not going to be together. Kennedy was committed to avenging his dead boyfriend or whatever the fuck his mission was supposed to be. Jason was collateral damage. He was expendable.

If he'd thought he was in pain before…

Maybe once he'd had time to think, to absorb, to process—a decade or two ought to do it—he'd be able to be pals with Kennedy. But right now? No could do.

"How about this," Jason said. "If I need a ride to the airport, I'll see you at five. Otherwise, you can assume I opted for shut-eye."

"Right." Kennedy hesitated. "I'll say good night now."

That was a tactful way of letting Jason know that feelings or no feelings, they would not be sharing a bed. Just in case Jason hadn't already got the message delivered by baseball bat?

"Good night," Jason said. "And again, thank you for everything. Including dinner."

He had stopped walking. Kennedy stopped too, looking at him in inquiry.

"I think I'll take a walk," Jason said. "Maybe get a drink somewhere."

He could see Kennedy didn't like that. He seemed undecided about what to do.

"Of course," he said finally, and Jason didn't think he imagined the reluctance. "I'll be in touch."

Jason nodded politely and headed for the front doors.

Kennedy was still standing in the lobby as Jason stepped out into the night.

Chapter Nineteen

A brisk walk in the chilly, damp night air helped.

A little.

Kennedy had once accused Jason of having a tendency toward dramatics.

No. "A flair for the dramatic." That's what he'd said. *You're curious, imaginative, and have a flair for the dramatic. You like to talk, you're a born smartass, and you get bored following a script.*

Was he going to spend the rest of his life remembering every damn thing Sam Kennedy had said to him?

Anyway, flair for the dramatic aside, he thought his emotional reaction to Kennedy's revelation was understandable. Knowledge didn't change anything, but at least he knew now what he had been up against. Nothing he did or didn't do would have changed the outcome. Kennedy had known in Massachusetts that he didn't want to get involved, and the fact that he'd gone against his own instincts was even flattering in a weird way.

Nor was it about lust. For eight months they'd simply talked. Long distance, for Christ's sake. Kennedy genuinely liked Jason. So there was another balm for Jason's ego. And everything he'd done since discovering Jason was in trouble reinforced the depth of his feelings for Jason, from bulldozing over the local cops to helping Jason dispose of evidence—er, not-evidence.

He was trying to be a good friend. Trying not to hurt Jason. He was trying, in his own fucked-up, obsessive, driven-by-demons way, to do the right thing.

On one level Jason could appreciate all of that. He really could. Did.

On another level…it just hurt.

Unbearably.

Why—*how*—had he let himself start caring so much? He'd known from the very first, from day one, certainly from that first night together in Boston, that getting involved with Sam Kennedy was a no go.

All these months. He'd kept assuring himself it was all under control, that he wasn't taking it that seriously. Who the hell was he kidding? Himself, apparently. And only himself. The truth was he'd been in way too deep from the beginning. Since Kingsfield. Since the night Sam had come to his hotel room after they'd said their goodbyes.

Before they'd ever left the village of Kingsfield, Jason was falling for Sam Kennedy.

Falling in love.

And nothing that had happened during the last eight months had changed that—although it sure as hell should have.

If he was mad at anyone, it was himself. For being such a fool. For going against his own better judgment. For choosing to fall in love with Sam Kennedy of all people.

Oh, hell yeah he wanted to meet this art teacher pal of Charlie's. Bring it on. Bring *him* on. Hell, have him jump out of the fucking birthday cake. If Jason had listened to his family and friends—hell, if he'd listened to George Potts—he'd have been busy dating normal people and that would have formed a natural defensive barrier against sad, fucked-up, freeze-dried Sam Kennedy, who wasn't just married to his job, he was married to his tragically dead lover. Who the hell could compete with that? Who would want to?

Especially when no one was asking him to.

The pub was called The Mermaid's Tale.

It sort of reminded Jason of Kingsfield's Blue Mermaid, with its dark, smoky taproom (though no one had smoked in there for decades) and jukebox playing golden oldies to a cast of regulars that seemed to include Gorton's Fisherman, Captain Crook, Cap'n Crunch and Charlie the Tuna. Kitschy fishing nets with sea shells covered the low ceiling, and a large oil painting of a very naked mermaid took up most of the wall behind the bar.

That mermaid fascinated Jason. She wore nothing but fish scales and a sly smile, and was impressively, anatomically correct down to the shading of her blue-green caudal fin.

He had walked himself to a standstill. Not physically. Emotionally. He was cold and tired and completely disheartened. He would have a beer and then walk back to the Buccaneer's Cove. Hopefully by then he'd be tired enough to sleep.

The bartender had just set a bottle of Stella Artois and a bowl of suspiciously dusty peanuts in front of Jason when the chair across from his own was dragged away from the table and Kennedy sat down.

And even after the last forty-five minutes of bitter reflection and self-recrimination, Jason's foolish heart still jumped around in his chest like an eager puppy when his master walked in the door. It was maddening.

Kennedy stared austerely across the table.

"Hey," Jason said. "Isn't this past your bedtime? Isn't staying up late liable to interfere with the way you catch bad guys?"

Kennedy was unamused. "What are you doing, Jason?"

Jason winked. "I'm having a beer, Sam. I've had a very stressful twenty-four hours, and I need a little time to process. What are *you* doing?"

"Following you."

Jason thought about his walk from the hotel and hoped he had not been muttering and mumbling to himself as he stalked along the moonlight streets. If he'd realized Kennedy was following him...

He said mockingly, "Just can't stay away from me, can you?"

It was hard to tell with the pirate's cave lighting in there, but he thought a tide of color rose in Kennedy's face. His eyes kindled with irritation. "You're not carrying. You're not armed. I noticed at dinner."

True. Jason had not worn his pistol to dinner. He had not planned on going anywhere afterwards but up to his room. "Bodyguard detail. That's below your paygrade."

Temper made Kennedy's eyes looked electric blue. "This is not smart. Wandering around unarmed and getting drunk is not useful."

"Probably not. But don't worry. I'm not going to get drunk. I'd still be drinking Kamikazes if I planned on getting drunk. Contrary to what you believe, I'm not careless or reckless."

"I didn't say you were."

"You think it, though."

Kennedy's voice dropped. "I don't think you're careless or reckless. I think you might feel you have something to prove, and we both know why that is."

"Here we go again. Our greatest hits. Because you think I froze eight months ago in Kingsfield."

Kennedy's gaze did not waver. "Yes. I think you froze in Kingsfield. But you didn't freeze the other night in Santa Monica. And it doesn't sound like you froze last night."

It was probably meant as some kind of concession, but Jason barely heard it. In Santa Monica and last night at Shipka's cottage, no one had been firing at him.

"That might be part of it too," he said thoughtfully.

Kennedy frowned. "What might be part of what?"

"Your belief that I'm going to get killed in the line of duty. Maybe that's part of your reluctance to get any more involved with me. You lost one boyfriend. Maybe you think it's contagious."

Again, it was probably the light—that gruesome shade of fish-scale green—but Kennedy seemed to lose color. He said softly, "Jesus *Christ*, Jason. I don't think you're going to get— Why the hell would you even say that?"

Jason shrugged. "I think it might be a factor."

"Yeah, well, it's not. Leave the psychoanalysis to the professionals."

Jason smiled. He'd had exactly the right amount to drink. He was still cognizant, still coherent, but his inhibitions were blowing in the wind. He felt a beautiful freedom from both his normal reticence and the restraints of his professional relationship with Kennedy.

He said casually, "Speaking of psychoanalysis, Dr. Jeremy Kyser has been writing me."

He'd had the childish wish to shock Kennedy out of his superhuman control, and his wish was granted.

"What?"

"What can I get you?" the bartender asked, appearing out of the gloom.

Kennedy said mechanically, "Whisky sour. Canadian Club, if you have it." His gaze never left Jason's face.

"You good?" the bartender asked Jason.

"I'll have another." And a headache chaser. But whatever. *In vino veritas.*

The bartender departed. Kennedy said, "Why in God's name wouldn't you tell me Kyser had contacted you? How long has that been going on?"

"Since October. He sent me a card for Halloween—"

"A card for—! Who the hell sends Halloween cards?"

"—which was fairly innocuous. And he sent me a birthday card. So he's not exactly stalking me."

"The hell he's not." Kennedy's face was tight with an emotion Jason couldn't quite categorize. Probably because it wasn't an expression Kennedy wore very often. Alarm? Anxiety? Aghastity?

Was there such a word? There was clearly such an emotion, and it was not reassuring. Especially as Jason had been trying to convince himself the communications from Kyser were nothing to be worried about. "Well, if he is, it's long distance. He's in Virginia now. That's your home turf."

"I don't understand why you waited until now to tell me this." Kennedy seemed genuinely troubled.

"I meant to tell you about the Halloween card the next time you called. But we didn't talk until Christmas. To be honest, I'd forgotten about it by then."

Kennedy's mouth opened, but the bartender arrived with their drinks.

"Jesus Christ," Kennedy muttered. He downed half his drink in one scowling swallow.

"I'm not thrilled either, but he's on the other side of the country— usually—and there's nothing threatening in the cards. You said yourself he wasn't part of our case in Massachusetts. It's not a crime to be strange."

"Tell me you kept the cards."

"Of course."

"I want to see them."

"I'm happy for you to see them. But honestly, I don't want to think about Kyser tonight." Jason leaned back in his chair and tilted the beer bottle to his lips.

Kennedy gave a little disbelieving shake of his head, sat back in his own chair, and shook the ice in his glass like he wondered where the rest of his drink had gone.

The jukebox was playing a duet between James Taylor and Mark Knopfler. "Sailing to Philadelphia."

It was my fate from birth

To make my mark upon the earth

That was Kennedy all right. A big man with big things to do. No room and no time for anything else. But if Jason gave in and looked across the table, he knew Kennedy would be watching him with that somber, brooding stare as though Jason had presented a problem Kennedy just couldn't quite solve.

Well, that made two of them. There were questions Jason would have liked to ask Kennedy too: Did they ever catch the guy who killed Ethan? Is it just me you won't sleep with, or are you still enjoying sex with non-friends? Do I just look sort of like Ethan, or do I remind you of him in other ways? Do you not see the Catch-22 of trying to hang on to a friend-ship with someone you're afraid you already care too much for?

But he kept his thoughts to himself. He didn't want Kennedy to walk out.

Maybe it was the alcohol. Maybe it was the subliminal messaging of several love songs in a row. The tension between them began to ease, the mood lightened.

Jason looked across at Kennedy and said, "All that's missing is a girl in a fish tank."

Kennedy smiled faintly, moved his head in assent.

For a minute or two they listened to the music and drank. Kennedy's mouth twisted in reluctant amusement. "Did you really tell O'Neill you wouldn't break out of that crypt because the window was so valuable?"

Jason sat up. "Hell, yes. That window is Tiffany glass. It's probably worth a quarter of a million dollars. It's irreplaceable."

Kennedy shook his head as though he thought Jason was a nut, but what he said was, "You're irreplaceable."

Was that what he'd said? Because he went back to looking at the mermaid painting and sipping his drink. He did not look remotely like a guy who would say, "You're irreplaceable."

Finally a song written in the last decade dropped on the jukebox. "Demons" by Imagine Dragons.

Jason said, "This song always reminds me of you."

Kennedy listened for a moment, shook his head. "I don't know it."

No, of course not, and maybe that second beer had been one too many.

Kennedy said suddenly, wryly, "I'm guessing you're very good at undercover work."

"I am. Why?"

Kennedy's smile was wry. "You lie very well. I watched you today. You don't try to oversell or elaborate."

Jason reddened. "I don't lie to you."

"No, I know." It didn't seem to make it any better for Kennedy.

The bartender made another pass. Kennedy ordered a second drink. Jason declined.

Kennedy seemed to be looking at Jason's hands. Jason couldn't see anything of interest there. Knowing Kennedy, he was probably thinking about something to do with fingerprints. But it reminded Jason of Santa Monica and searching Kerk's hotel room.

The night he'd discovered Kennedy had ended their relationship… how many months earlier? But forgot to tell Jason.

Maybe he was reaching the point of acceptance, because that hurt felt faraway now. Old. Maybe that was the beer. Maybe it was because Kennedy was sitting across from him, watching Jason even when he wasn't looking directly at him.

"I never did find that damned cufflink," Jason said.

Kennedy gave him a funny look.

"The one I lost at the Hotel Casa del Mar."

"Right."

"I know. It's just…my grandfather gave me those cufflinks. Which, come to think of it, was kind of an odd gift for a sixteen-year-old kid. But anyway, they had sentimental value."

"This was the grandfather who was the reason you joined the FBI?"

"Yeah. Sort of. My grandfather was the reason I wanted to fight to preserve our artistic and cultural heritage. Honey Corrigan is the reason I took that fight to the FBI." Jason's smile twisted at the recognition in Kennedy's eyes. "I'm not sure I realized that until Massachusetts. So I do understand, Sam. I do get your sense of mission. I just think you're wrong about the warrior-monk routine. I think you could still be effective in your job and have some kind of personal life. I don't mean with me. I mean with whoever. Someone who would be willing to take you on your terms."

Kennedy eyed him for a long moment. He set his glass down. "The problem is, I don't want *whoever*. I want you. All the time."

He did. It was right there, a fierce longing burning in his blue eyes. Jason didn't move a muscle. Didn't speak. He was afraid anything he said, anything he did would tip the scales the wrong way.

Kennedy said roughly, "Let's get out of here."

Chapter Twenty

It was that first night in Boston all over again.

Only this time when Kennedy unlocked his hotel door and let them both inside his room, they knocked over the lamp. That was because they were already half out of their clothes, complicating each other's efforts by trying to help.

Kennedy reached past Jason and the door slammed shut with a bang. Kennedy's arms closed around Jason once more. His hot mouth latched onto Jason, and he groaned as though kissing Jason was the sweetest thing in all the world.

He tasted like cheap whisky and himself, dark and dangerous. Jason forgot what he was doing and lost himself in the feel of Kennedy's lips moving hungrily on his own, Kennedy's tongue pushing into his mouth.

Kennedy reached down to unclip his holster, still trying to hang onto the kiss. Jason panted into Kennedy's mouth, struggling with Kennedy's suit jacket. Those shoulders were like a bulwark. Hell, Kennedy could probably just flex his chest, and the jacket as well as all the buttons of his shirt would fly off.

Kennedy got his holster off, and a couple of powerful shrugs dropped his suit jacket to the floor. Jason's own blazer was probably still out in the hallway—along with his shoes and socks. Kennedy's big hands locked on Jason's shoulders once more.

Jason laughed unsteadily into Kennedy's mouth. "Wait. Ouch…" He heard the seams of his shirt go and muttered, "You're saving me a fortune in dry cleaning bills."

He fumbled with Kennedy's belt buckle. Did he have a deadbolt on the damned thing? Combination lock? What the hell…

Ah. There.

"Christ, yes." Kennedy tore his mouth away to say in a rough voice. "Touch me, Jason."

Hard not to touch him with that hard, fierce erection poking through the softness of his taut cotton briefs and open jeans. Jesus, the wonder of it, of having this again, of being able to touch, and hold, and kiss. Jason had thought it was gone forever.

The light had gone out when the lamp fell. The room was pitch-black and had that damp, musty feel of all beach town cottages and hotels, though it still smelled of Kennedy's shower and his aftershave—and imminent sex.

Jason felt the edge of the mattress hit him behind the knees, and he grabbed for Kennedy who hiked him up—except this time there was no door or wall to support that move, and they lost their balance and went slamming down on the bed.

Speaking of how the FBI was portrayed in movies and TV, *that* was a move you never saw. They probably heard the crash all the way at the front desk. They probably heard that all the way to The Mermaid's Tale. Jason didn't care, he was laughing.

Kennedy said, "I'm too old for this. I think I put my back out," but he was laughing too—softly—and the sound went straight to Jason's heart. He'd never heard Kennedy laugh quite like that. He sounded…happy.

"Nobody's too old for this."

"Christ." Kennedy rested his hand against Jason's face as though he could see him in the dark. "I've wanted this—you—since I saw you walking across the beach in Santa Monica." Jason heard his smile. "In a goddamned tux, of all things."

"I've wanted you since we said goodbye that morning at Kingsfield."

"Yeah. Me too." Kennedy touched Jason's left nipple with his hot, wet tongue, and Jason gasped and jumped. His head hit the headboard with a thump.

"Ow. Déjà vu."

"I remember," Kennedy murmured. "I remember everything about that night. About you."

Jesus. God. Jason moaned and arched up. The rasp of Kennedy's tongue against the point of his nipple was making him crazy. Exquisite sensation crackled from the base of his spine to the base of his skull, short-circuiting all thought beyond needing, wanting more of Kennedy.

Kennedy turned his attentions to Jason's other nipple, and Jason moaned again.

"I like those sounds you make," Kennedy whispered. "The way you move."

Yeah, Jason was noisy during sex. And Kennedy was quieter than most. Focused. Intense. Attentive. Definitely attentive.

His hands closed on Kennedy's hips, and Kennedy leaned into him, offering easier access.

"Suck me?" Kennedy asked roughly. But despite the growl in his voice there was something almost diffident in the request.

"Yeah, of course. Whatever you want."

Kennedy kicked the rest of the way out of his jeans as Jason slid down the mattress, resituating himself. It wasn't the best position in the world, but it didn't matter once Jason took the head of Kennedy's cock into his mouth.

Kennedy made a sound of almost desperate relief and instinctively pushed forward. He murmured a quick apology, but Jason wasn't listening, wasn't worried. He'd have swallowed Kennedy whole if he could have. He sucked his cock with soft wet heat and then hard. Changing it up. Sweet and soft. Tight and hard. Using every bit of skill and expertise he had to make this good, the best Kennedy had ever had. To make himself unforgettable, irreplaceable.

"Good," Kennedy muttered. "So fucking good… Yeah, like that. Just like that."

Jason understood exactly what Chris Shipka had felt that night, trying to make his case through sex. Saying it all through body language, the vocabulary of sexual intimacy, because he wanted to make this the best Kennedy had ever had. His own neglected cock was thrusting up, straining hard, brushing Kennedy's ass cheeks. It didn't matter. This was about Kennedy. About giving him what he wanted—and even what he didn't yet know he wanted.

Kennedy's breathing was deep and harsh. He didn't say anything, but silence had never been so expressive. His fists punched the mattress above Jason's head, and Jason could see that his arms were trembling.

Jason relaxed his throat muscles and took still more of Kennedy. Kennedy made a small, broken sound. He tasted clean and sweet, a hint of soap and manly sweat and the salty cream of pre-cum.

"Going to come," Kennedy warned. Again Jason was reminded of Chris Shipka. The ghost at the banquet.

Sorry, Chris. Jason drew back, kissed the head of Kennedy's cock, tongued the cleft, took him back in and sucked hard.

Kennedy groaned and his back arched. He began to come in hard spurts of hot sticky wet release. Jason didn't swallow. He had said the truth when he told Kennedy he wasn't reckless or careless. Eight months apart and Kennedy considering himself a free agent? No, Jason was not going to lap down Kennedy's cream. He wiped semen from his chest and brow, wrapped his arms around Kennedy, encouraging Kennedy to let go, and Kennedy collapsed onto him.

Jason wrapped his arms around Kennedy's back, nuzzling his ear, his hair, his jaw. He tasted a salty trace of wetness on Kennedy's temple. Sweat? Semen? A tear? He had to grit his jaw against all the silly, emotional things he wanted to tell him.

Don't let this be the end. Don't let this be the last time. But Kennedy already knew how he felt. What he wanted. There was nothing he could say that Kennedy didn't already know.

They rested for a time, holding each other, breathing quietly. Not quite in unison, but not far from it.

Then Kennedy raised his head. "What about you? What would you like?" His breath was warm against Jason's face, surprisingly sweet despite the bite of whisky.

Jason licked his lips. "I want to be inside you."

"Yeah?" Kennedy sounded thoughtful. "I didn't really come prepared, but yeah. I think that can be arranged."

"Really?"

He must have sounded fairly astonished, because Sam's voice was amused. "Sure. Why not?"

"No reason. Well, I guess I thought you might have…" Conservative or old school ideas about who got to do what to whom? But really, recollecting how Kennedy operated in the rest of his life, he wasn't locked into roles or routine. On the job, he was about efficiency and expediency. He took the lead because he was always the expert, the guy with the most experience, and the job was too critical to waste a moment catering to other people's egos. But on his own time…he had never struck Jason as selfish or stingy.

"I think anything we do together would feel pretty damn good," Kennedy said, and Jason had to agree.

"Not to mention the fact, I'm not twenty anymore. My recovery time isn't what it used to be." Kennedy said it easily, matter of fact, but yeah. Of course.

Kennedy lifted off the bed in a limber move for a man who had been complaining about his back twenty minutes earlier. He disappeared into the bathroom, the light went on, followed by sounds of rummaging around. He exited the bathroom, the crack of light silhouetting his tall, powerful figure as returned to the bed.

Jason had yanked back the bedspread and blankets. Kennedy set something small on the nightstand and tossed him a foil packet. He stretched out on the sheet-covered mattress with easy, unselfconscious grace.

Jason donned the condom with the kind of speed demonstrated by superheroes out to stop speeding bullets and powerful locomotives, and leaned over Kennedy's back. He kissed the nape of his neck, and Kennedy gave a small, pleasurable shudder.

There was something unexpectedly vulnerable about the softness of Kennedy's hair and the curve where neck met shoulder.

Jason reached for the small plastic bottle on the nightstand. Complimentary lotion that smelled vaguely of cucumber and cocoanut and something beachy and fresh. It felt cool and slippery on Jason's fingers.

He parted the taut globes of Kennedy's buttocks with one hand, delicately probing the tight knot of his hole with the other. Jesus. The feel of that hot little pucker. It was all Jason could do to go slowly, carefully.

He pressed his fingertip against the clenched muscle, and Kennedy tensed, gave a soft, low groan.

That was pleasure, not pain, but Jason murmured, "Okay?"

"You've got a gentle touch."

How often did people make the effort to be gentle with Kennedy?

Jason leaned forward, pressed a row of small, velvety kisses down Kennedy's spine. He pushed his finger lightly in and out through the ring of muscle.

The fact that Kennedy was letting him do this felt crazy, unreal. But then it had felt crazy and unreal when Kennedy had done it to him too. His cock, already at attention, seemed to grow a couple of inches at the memory of being penetrated so deeply, so fully. He had loved that and he would love this. Kennedy was right. Anything they did together would feel great.

He took his time, and Kennedy preserved a thoughtful, listening silence throughout. When Jason pressed a second finger in, stretching him, seeking that nub of nerves and gland, Kennedy made an urgent sound and pushed back, drawing Jason's fingers in deeper.

Jason's heart was in his throat anticipating his cock sinking into that sweet hot grip.

"You're so quiet. I've never heard you so quiet during sex." There was a smile in Kennedy's voice, almost a note of teasing.

"I don't want to scare you."

Kennedy chuckled. "I don't scare easy."

No. True enough. It was hard to think of anything that might scare Kennedy.

Jason flexed his fingers and Kennedy's gasped, arching a little. "Jesus, yes. Do that again."

Jason did it again, leaning forward and trying to kiss Kennedy's mouth at that awkward angle, massaging the spongy bump with careful fingers. His own cock was rock hard, balls aching. He was afraid he was going to come the moment his dick touched Kennedy's hole.

Not that he wasn't willing to risk it. Jason lowered himself on top of Kennedy, relishing the feel of that powerful body beneath his own. "I can't believe we're here, together now," He whispered against Kennedy's hard shoulder. "This evening I thought…"

Kennedy wasn't in the mood for talk. His buttocks humped back against Jason's groin, and Jason obligingly withdrew his fingers out, replacing them in that moist heat with his dick.

So... good. He cried out as Kennedy's sphincter muscle contracted around him. "God. Yes. *Yes.*" He began to thrust and tug at that hot darkness. "Oh, God. Oh, Sam." He couldn't have shut up to save his life.

Sam let out a deep sound, something between a groan and a growl, and began to shove back hard against him. Jason's hands bit into his shoulders as he lunged into him, and for a few seconds it was a struggle to find the rhythm. Jason pushed aside all other thought, all other concerns, just concentrating on that moist satiny clutch, trying to drill deeper, needing to feel connection, coupled. Fire catching fire, blazing hotter. Sam's focused silence in contrast to Jason's desperate sounds as he pumped into him, reaching further and further for that yearned for release —

And finally...after exceptional and most enjoyable exertion...*Oh God...*there it was. Welling up like a hidden spring in the desert. Sudden and sweet, assuaging the terrible thirst that had come to feel like a lifetime of drought. Climax pulsed through him, refreshing and renewing him with every heartbeat.

"Sam...Sam..." Jason couldn't help it. Couldn't help clutching Sam like a life preserver, couldn't help the helpless noises as he began to come, pouring out stupid emotional things while his muscles melted and his cock spumed white hot release into the rubber safety net.

He collapsed on top of Sam, gasping for breath, quivering head to foot.

A long, long time later, Sam stirred, rolling over, holding Jason to him, and pulling the covers back up. Jason settled his head on Sam's chest, content when Sam's arms wrapped around him, holding him close. He kissed Jason's brow, said something that Jason didn't catch.

Jason smiled. Sometimes tone mattered more than words.

Shipka's remaining eye was fixed and blank, but his mouth moved.

"Ask Rodney Berguan," he whispered.

Another voice cut across Jason's rising horror. "Jason, you're okay." Calm, quiet, authoritative. "It's a dream. You're fine. It's not real."

Jason knew that voice.

He unstuck his eyelids, stopped gulping for air, stopped twitching. He began, confusedly, to take stock. Strong arms wrapped around him... his face buried in a broad, muscular chest... Sam.

He was in a hotel room with Sam. That was not a dream. The other...

His heart still thundered in his ears and his skin was slick with perspiration. He rasped, "I thought— I dreamed—"

Sam said, "I know. It's over. You're okay."

He probably did know too.

Jason nodded. He knew he should move away now, reassure Sam that he wasn't coming unglued. Not like he'd never seen a murder victim before. Never anyone he knew, but...still.

Sam's face was resting against Jason's hair, and Jason could hear the quiet, steady tenor of his breathing. The pulse beating against Sam's collarbone was rock steady. He thought maybe he was even getting to like that peculiar aftershave of Kennedy's.

Just a few moments more of this, of feeling safe and sheltered.

Not something anyone, man or woman, in their profession could admit to wanting, let alone needing, but the memory of Chris Shipka hacked to pieces...it had shaken him. The unnecessary, unhinged brutality of it. That wasn't sane. And yeah, you could argue that turning to murder was never a sane choice, but this was a different level of madness.

It scared him.

No lie.

After another minute, he pushed out of Sam's hold and turned onto his back. "Sorry. God. It's just...every time I go to sleep, I see him."

"It'll fade. The memory. You'll stop dreaming about it."

Sam spoke with the certainty of experience. Jason nodded, but what he was thinking was *maybe it shouldn't fade*. The horror of Shipka's murder, yes. He needed to stop seeing that every time he closed his eyes. But Shipka himself, he needed to remember. What Shipka had been trying to achieve—justice for Paris Havemeyer—that shouldn't be forgotten.

He realized he hadn't answered Sam. In the dark, every motion, every gesture was a rustling sound to be interpreted, but he thought Sam was pretty good at reading him at any time of day or night.

"It can't be your guy," Jason said. "The unsub. It can't be your unsub. That's not the same psyche at work. Is it?"

Kennedy said, "It's not the same kind of crime, no. That was a rage killing. But my unsub may not be working alone. He may have a partner."

"A partner."

He felt Kennedy's assent.

"Double the fun." His voice sounded off even to himself, and Kennedy reached over and traced a gentle hand down his chest.

"Listen. You're out of it now. This is my case, not yours."

Jason gave a disbelieving laugh. "It's *kind of* my case. Shipka came to me. He brought me information I can't just ignore. It's relevant to my case."

"And you'll keep working that angle. The larceny and fraud angle. From the safety of the LA office."

Jason raised his head, trying to read Sam's face in the dark. He didn't want to get into an argument over boundaries and authority, but if Sam thought Jason was okay with being relegated to the "safety of the LA office," he had another think coming.

He said, "Shipka knew about Donald Kerk, but he didn't mention interviewing Kerk. Or Berguan, for that matter."

"Who's Berguan?"

"Rodney Berguan was with Kerk the night Havemeyer disappeared. The three of them shared a taxi when they left the party at the gallery. Havemeyer said he wasn't ready to call it a night, so Kerk and Berguan continued home. They were the last people to see Havemeyer before he disappeared. Berguan went with Kerk to file the MPR when Havemeyer didn't turn up after a few days."

Sam made a noncommittal noise.

"It seems like Shipka would have started there, but he never mentioned interviewing Kerk or Berguan."

"Kerk was out of the country and maybe he couldn't locate Berguan. It was a long time ago."

"Maybe he's dead," Jason said. "Everyone else is."

"You're not," Sam said. "I'm not." He leaned over and kissed Jason.

Jason said, "I didn't think there was any chance of this again. Not after LA."

Sam shook his head. Not the most reassuring response.

Jason gave it a few seconds, but Sam still said nothing.

Jason's throat closed. But it would be better to know. He forced the words out.

"So is this it? Are we saying goodbye?"

The silence that followed seemed to last forever. Finally, Sam said, "I didn't think it would be this difficult."

"Which part?" Jason asked tersely.

"Is there a part that isn't difficult?" Sam said with bleak humor.

"Point."

Sam said slowly, "I thought I had this worked out, and I was prepared for you moving on. That had to happen. But."

"But?" Jason said quietly, "Oh. Shipka." From the point Sam learned that Jason had slept with Shipka, he had subtly changed, withdrawn. There had been those uncharacteristic flashes of aggression. Jason had noticed, but had trouble believing they came down to something as ordinary, as simple, as human as jealousy.

"Yeah. That was…not what I wanted. I wasn't prepared for that. For how much it would…"

Hurt.

Welcome to the club.

Jason said, "I take it you've been banging agents coast-to-coast for the past eight months?"

Sam inhaled sharply, started to cough, and had to clear his throat. "No," he said eventually. "In fact, that's when— No."

"That's when what?"

He shook his head.

"I see." Jason thought it over. What the hell. Was there really any mystery about this? Hadn't they been wrestling with it a week? "I'm going to say it then. I've had eight months—not to mention one hellish evening—to think about it. In a business like ours…well, I'd regret not saying it." He drew in a breath and dove. "I love you, Sam."

Sam raised his head.

"I know," Jason said. "Especially after your declaration of independence at dinner. But I do. I'm not sure how it happened because I wasn't looking for this. In particular, I wasn't looking for *this*. If that scares you…I can only tell you that I've heard everything you've said. I understand. Which isn't to say that I agree or I'm okay with it. I just know that this week was total hell. And that's not counting murder and getting locked in a crypt and being held by the police for questioning."

"I'm sorry," Sam said. "I didn't think it would matter that much to you."

Jason spluttered, "You didn't… *What?*"

Sam pulled him over, settling Jason's head on his chest. "And when I realized it did…there was still nothing I could do about it. I still feel the same about this. Being involved is not going to be good for either of us."

"But we are involved, Sam. You can call it what you want. Friends or fuck buddies. But if you're going to keep phoning me up—"

"We can call it what it is," Sam said. "It's not the word I'm afraid of. I love you. I've known for sure since Christmas when I couldn't stop myself from calling." He said self-mockingly, "I just had to hear your voice."

Jason remembered that phone call. Somehow it had been more painful than no call at all. Or maybe not.

Sam said, "But I meant what I said at dinner. I do want some kind of relationship with you. I want you in my life. Watching you walk away on Monday…I couldn't do it. I felt like I'd made a mistake there was no coming back from. And hearing you'd slept with Shipka. No." He was silent again. "I guess it depends on what you want."

Jason shook his head. How was he supposed to answer that? He said, "I want what we talked about in Massachusetts. I want to try."

Sam shook his head. "I know who I am. I *am* the job. Work will always come first for me. That means I'm not going to be there for dinner with the folks or Christmas or romantic getaways. I don't remember birthdays or anniversaries."

You would have been there for Ethan. You would have remembered for Ethan.

But Jason banished that thought. That way lay madness. It wasn't even necessarily true.

Instead, he said lightly, "Maybe you should wait until I propose before you start planning how you're going to leave me standing at the altar."

But Sam was not in a joking mood. "Whatever it is you need, Jason, I'm probably not that guy."

"Probably not," Jason conceded wearily. "And I can't promise that that doesn't matter or that I'll hang in there through thick and thin no matter how big an asshole you are. I don't know how high my tolerance for pain is. I just know I'm not ready to say goodbye."

Sam muttered, "It would kill me to say goodbye now."

It went a long way to assuaging the hurt of the past few days.

"We've still got—" Jason broke off to peer at the clock. "Hours till the next goodbye."

They kissed.

"See?" Jason murmured. "That didn't hurt so much, did it?"

"Not yet," Sam said quietly. "It will."

Chapter Twenty-One

Jason was still trying to track down Rabab Doody when his cell phone rang and Sam's ID flashed up.

Come to think of it, he needed to change that ID photo. In a mood of smart-assery, he'd attached a photo of Harry Callahan, AKA Dirty Harry, to Sam's contact info.

"Hi," Jason said. He couldn't help the note of warmth that crept into his voice. He thought of that quick, awkward goodbye kiss at Watertown International Airport that morning. Quick, awkward, but heartfelt.

Sam was brisk and businesslike. "I can't talk, but I wanted to remind you to send me those cards from Kyser. The actual cards. Not copies. Envelopes too, if you've still got them."

"The cards are at home. I'm at the office. I'll mail them out tomorrow."

"Good. Don't forget."

"No, sir!" Jason did his best marine corps recruit imitation. "I won't forget, sir."

Sam disconnected without comment. Or maybe that was his comment.

Jason shook his head and went back to the task of locating the elusive Mr. Doody. He was reluctant to tap Lux again so soon, though he was going to have to talk to the kid eventually.

Thanks to the time difference, he'd arrived in LA at ten thirty in the morning, and after a disconcertingly congenial meeting with George Potts and SAC Robert Wheat in Wheat's office, phoned Washington DC for a lengthy call with Karan Kapszukiewicz.

"So F-D is going to settle," Karan said, once he'd filled her in on the events of the last three days. "Damn."

"It sounds like they've decided to settle with the Ontarios. That doesn't mean the Ontarios will go for it."

"They'll go for it," Karan said gloomily. "From the first, they said they didn't want to go to court, if at all avoidable."

"Even so, the Durrands don't yet know about Ursula Martin. She's not going to settle."

"Martin still hasn't formally filed charges. That's the sticking point for a lot of victims. Actually going to court. I've got to tell you, Jason, my gut feeling is this one is starting to slip through our fingers."

Jason felt a flash of alarm. "I don't think it's as bad as all that. According to one of my sources, there are a number of other clients in similar circumstances to the Ontarios. They can't settle with everyone. If they had those kinds of financial resources, they wouldn't be secretly selling off clients' collections."

"Is this the source that's now deceased? The reporter?"

"Chris Shipka, yes."

"Who was unwilling to reveal *his* source to you."

Jason confirmed reluctantly.

"What about the forgery angle? Any progress there?"

"Nothing yet," Jason had to admit. "It's still early days."

Karan made a discontented "Mm," sound.

"I'm still pursuing leads. An informant gave up the name Rabab Doody. We don't have much on him, but what there is looks promising. In 2003 we arrested him for selling fake Joseph Zaritskys paintings privately and on eBay. He moved more than 60 pieces for almost $1.9 million. His story was in 1999 he'd discovered a cache of Zaritskys while cleaning out a Hancock Park man's basement. Doody did five years in federal prison."

"What's he been up to since he got out?"

"That's what I'm trying to find out."

Karan said, "That sounds promising, but."

But. There was always a but. Jason waited.

"I don't have to remind you, you've got a case load as tall as your desk. You want to think about how to prioritize your time and resources.

Just because we don't nail F-D this time around, doesn't mean they get away for good. We'll get them eventually."

"I know," Jason said. "I understand."

"I know it's disappointing." Karan's sympathy was genuine. "You've put a lot of time and effort into this one. But I've been doing this a long time, and I see all the signs of a case that's collapsing in on itself. Not for any lack of effort on your part. Sometimes the stars don't align."

"Right. Okay."

He toyed with the thought of bringing up the Paris Havemeyer missing person case, but he already knew what Karan's response would be. Too thin. Not enough to go on. Not when resources were so limited. Even if she did decide the Havemeyer case should be followed up on, she'd hand it off to Violent Crimes.

He *was* disappointed, but he understood her reservations. Despite the very dramatic events of the past days, he really wasn't one hell of a whole lot ahead of where he'd been on Monday when he'd first spotted that fake hanging in Shepherd Durrand's office. Nothing illegal there. It wasn't like Shepherd had tried to sell him the fake.

In fact, aside from the cursory interview with Barnaby, which had gone pretty much as he'd imagined, everything he had learned on Camden Island seemed to dovetail with the BAU's investigation rather than his own.

He spoke with Karan for a few minutes more then began to weed through his email. He hadn't missed that gentle hint about his caseload, and it was true that his other investigations had suffered this week. All the same, when he came to Shipka's email he stopped to read through his notes on the Havemeyer case.

Shipka had been a good reporter. He kept detailed records of his interviews, and his notes were thorough. It looked like he had tried on several occasions to talk to Donald Kerk, but Kerk had insisted there was no story to tell. He knew nothing about what had happened to Paris Havemeyer, and declined to speculate.

Not totally surprising, given that Kerk had remained friends with the Durrands.

Rodney Berguan had simply refused to talk to Shipka.

After doing a little digging, Jason suspected one reason Berguan might have chosen to keep quiet was that he now lived in Watertown, New York. Right in the Durrands' backyard, as it were.

Jason considered that piece of information.

Over twenty-seven thousand people lived in Watertown, so there was no reason Rodney Berguan shouldn't. Presumably, he wasn't living in fear of the Durrand brothers if he'd chosen to move within a stone's throw of their family estate. It was interesting—potentially—that Berguan had refused to speak to Shipka rather than simply do as Kerk had and insist he knew nothing. But not everyone loved the press. Maybe Shipka had rubbed him the wrong way. It was hard to know without talking to Berguan.

Talking to Berguan.

Well, why not? Maybe Berguan really didn't have anything to say, in which case he could say so to the FBI. Right?

Jason was searching for contact information on Berguan—his phone number was unlisted—when Jonnie rang.

"Hey! I heard about what happened in New York. How are you doing?" Jonnie Gould had the professional misfortune of being blessed with Malibu Barbie prettiness. When she had been partnered with Adam Darling, they had been nicknamed Barbie and Ken. But though Jonnie looked like a dumb beach bunny, she was a sharp and savvy agent—as well as being one of the nicest people Jason had ever met. He'd been sorry when she retired after her marriage to another agent—and sorrier when Sam had recruited her.

"I'm fine. How are you? How's Adam?"

"I'm tired. Looking forward to going home. I don't know how the hell Kennedy does it. He hasn't had a sick day in his entire career with the Bureau."

"He's a machine." Jason wasn't sure he was kidding.

"Adam's already on his way back to LA, I think. He'll be on sick leave for a few days, if he's got any sense. Kennedy's offered him a spot on the squad."

"You'll get to work together again."

"Yeah." Jonnie sounded doubtful. "I don't know. I'm not sure it's really what he wants."

"He sure as hell can't want to stay on morgue patrol."

"That's all over. He'll get a gold star out of this one." "Gold star" being Bu-ease for a formal commendation. The pathway to promotion. "He met a guy up here."

"*Adam* met a guy?" Jason was partly joking, partly not. No one was more focused on his career than Adam Darling. Dedication, or possibly ambition, had already cost him one long-term relationship. No wonder Kennedy thought he was the ideal candidate.

"I know. Anyway, I'm calling because Kennedy is requesting copies of your case notes on Fletcher-Durrand. Also, he'd like you to forward whatever information that reporter, Chris Shipka, sent you."

"*Why?*" Jason felt a flare of unease.

"I've been searching for connections between our victims and the Durrands, and it looks like we've got a couple of hits. Our first victim, the art critic Gemini Earnst, was both a long-time client and close friend of Barnaby Durrand."

"What about the second victim, the art teacher?"

"Wilson Lapham was also a painter *and* protégé of Shepherd Durrand."

"Protégé?"

"Exactly."

"Actually, I'm questioning what that means," Jason said. "I mean, I get that there was a personal and probably sexual relationship. Shepherd will reportedly slam anything with a pulse. Was there some kind of professional relationship?"

"The promise of an exhibition."

Jason said, "An exhibition of Lapham's works?"

"It sure sounds that way. You're the expert. What are the chances that exhibition would have ever materialized?"

"Zero to none." He amended, "In fairness, I haven't seen Lapham's work. Maybe he was a genius, but Fletcher-Durrand doesn't do one-man shows. Ever. They do themes, decades, schools. The idea of F-D hosting an exhibition of an unknown artist…I don't buy it."

"Interesting."

He braced himself to ask—suspecting this was why Kennedy had Jonnie phone rather than doing it himself, "Are you jerking my case out from under me?" He tried to make it sound like a joke, but Jonnie knew it was no laughing matter.

"Not at all. You're working your angle and we're working ours. We're all part of the same team."

"Sure." Sort of not really. They were all part of the same organization, yes. Same team? No.

Jonnie said with determined cheerfulness, "So long as the bad guys get taken down, does it matter who makes the tackle?"

"I want to say no," Jason said. "I'm pretty sure that's the right answer."

Jonnie's chuckle was sympathetic. "Hey, if it helps, so far Shepherd Durrand has an alibi for Earnst, Kerk and the reporter's death. Big Brother Barnaby has an alibi for Lapham and Kerk. So maybe they're both in the clear. Maybe the connection is coincidence. You've often said the art world is small and incestuous."

"I have?"

"Also that you believe Warhol is overrated and the best cure for a hangover is a McDonald's breakfast sandwich. Preferably sausage."

"Ah."

"I'll tell Kennedy you—"

"No," Jason said quickly. "Just...keep me in the loop."

"If it helps, he said to be tactful with you. I've never heard Kennedy show any concern for anyone's feelings before, so there's that."

"There's always that," Jason agreed.

Rodney Berguan did not have a landline, either listed or unlisted. If he had a cell phone number, Jason was unable to find it through the usual—and unusual—channels. He did have a current address, however, and it was still in Watertown.

He was weighing different possible excuses for a return trip to New York when Hickok phoned.

"What the hell, West. I read the *Valley Voice* story on that poor bastard Chris Shipka. He was murdered *next door* to you?"

Right. The *Valley Voice*. Reporters had called twice asking for an interview. Their calls were no longer being put through to Jason. Sometimes "official channels" were a lifesaver. Even so, how long before one of the national papers picked up the story? He'd be having reporters show up at his front door.

Again.

"Yes. I wasn't there when it happened. But yes. Someone broke in and stabbed him to death." Stabbed? Try hacked to death. Had Sam heard back from the Jefferson County Medical Examiner yet? Would he let Jason know if he did?

"What the fuck. What was he doing out there with you?"

"He wasn't with me. He was following a story. Our paths just happened to cross."

Hick sounded genuinely shocked. "I didn't like the guy, but... Maybe his crazy conspiracy stories weren't so crazy after all."

"Maybe not." Jason couldn't help remembering Shipka's claim that Hickok had brushed him off when he'd tried to get his help investigating Havemeyer's disappearance. No, more than that. Shipka had suspected, hinted anyway, that Hick might even be involved, at least peripherally. And, in fairness to Shipka, Hick was someone acquainted with all three concurrent investigations. Hick not only knew where the intersections were, he had a copy of the traffic map.

"Speaking of conspiracy theories. Hick, did Shipka ever come to you about a missing art student?"

Hickok made an exasperated sound. "The New York thing. Right? The German kid who disappeared after a party at Fletcher-Durrand New York. Yes, he approached me a couple of years back. Maybe two years ago. He wanted me to look into the case."

"What happened?"

"Let me guess," Hick said. "He told you I refused to investigate because I'm buddy-buddy with the Durrands. Is that about right?"

"I'm asking, that's all. The guy died pursuing this case—"

Hickok was generally such a relaxed and genial guy, it was startling to hear his angry, "Do you know that for a fact? He was a crime reporter.

He poked his nose into a lot of cases and a lot of investigations. Maybe one of those cases caught up with him."

Maybe Hick was feeling guilty he hadn't taken Shipka seriously. Or maybe something else was going on. Jason kept his own tone unemotional. "What happened when Shipka asked for your help?"

"I told him it was not only a cold case, it was a cold case in New York, which is not my jurisdiction. I told him what he needed was a private detective or a good investigative reporter." Hick sighed. "I didn't like the guy. I didn't like the stories he wrote about LAPD. We didn't get the kind of star-struck treatment you did, West. He rode our ass all the time. I admit, I could have been nicer, but what I told him was the truth. A missing person case in New York was out of my reach."

Fair enough. Shipka believed that the possible involvement of Shepherd Durrand put the case back in reach, but Jason understood Hickok's reasoning. LAPD was not the FBI.

"Did you believe him?" Jason asked.

Hickok made a dismissive sound, but said reluctantly, "I don't know. He believed he was onto something. I could see that. It doesn't mean he was right."

"You didn't seem to recognize him the night at the Hotel Casa del Mar."

"I didn't recognize him at first. Not until I saw his ID. He looked older. He'd put on weight. And, of course, he was dressed like a goddamned burglar."

There was that.

Hickok said reluctantly, "And then when I did recognize him, well, I didn't feel any obligation to rush to his aid. He had no business on that terrace. I didn't like the guy, but I didn't fly across the country to kill him, and that's easily verified."

"It's pretty hard to imagine," Jason agreed.

"Thanks for nothing." Hickok sounded a little disgruntled. "Anyway, the reason I called is to find out if you're still looking for Rabab Doody?"

Jason sat up. "You have a line on him?"

Hickok gave a sour laugh. "I do, yeah. In fact, I can take you to him."

Chapter Twenty-Two

The house was a yellow and white ranch style on a quiet street in Van Nuys. High concrete walls lined the property. A tall concrete block wall lined one side of the property, and tall hedges lined the other. The lawn was dead and the roses in the concrete planters were fading fast.

According to Hickok, Doody's girlfriend owned the house, but it did not look like anyone was home.

In fact, it did not look like anyone had been home for a long time.

Jason met Hickok on the curb in front of the house and they walked up the cement driveway together.

"He's been working as my informant for the past four years," Hick had said on the phone. "If he's playing me, I want to know."

After eight months' acquaintance with Sam Kennedy, it did go through Jason's brain that this might be some kind of elaborate trap, but Hickok seemed his normal self—possibly a little cooler than usual, but there was nothing like the insinuation you might be capable of murder to put a crimp in a friendship—and the street had Neighborhood Watch notices posted every few yards.

Not a likely place for an ambush.

Jason and Hickok reached the brick door stoop. The front door screen was plastered with real estate flyers, business cards, pizza delivery door hangers.

Hickok said wearily, "Goddamn it."

Jason turned back to study the dying yard. "If the grass is dead in February, they've been gone a while. At least a month."

"Here's a gas shut-off notice," Hickok muttered. "And here's another for the water."

"They're not planning on coming back."

Hickok swore again and led the way through the side gate and around to the back yard. The grass and roses were in the same state of neglect. A rusted patio set and a broken barbecue sat on a cement slab. Jason went to the sliding glass doors, cupped his hands and peered inside.

He could see a large empty room with a fireplace at one end. A single furry yellow slipper and a long cardboard tube, as used for wrapping paper, were the only signs anyone had ever lived there.

"Well, hell," Jason said.

That was putting it mildly. Not only was his grand larceny case on life support, it looked like his forgery case was DOA as well.

"They won't go far," Hickok said. "Not for long, anyway. All her family's here." He scratched his jaw thoughtfully. "I wonder what spooked him."

"At a guess? An FBI investigation."

"You don't know he's your forger," Hickok said. "Innocent until proven guilty."

"Sure."

"But I will say this, Doody's got the chops. He's the real deal. As good or better than your boy, Lux."

"Good enough to copy a Reuven Rubin?" Jason asked.

Hickok gave an acrid laugh. "Are you kidding me? He specialized in *Eretz-Yisrael* style. That's what got him into trouble on Ebay."

"What about Monet?"

Hickok shook his head. "Doody didn't paint that piece of crap. He may be a criminal, but he's not a monster."

Jason snorted. "Yeah. Well."

Hickok eyed him for a moment. "You win some, you lose some, Prince Charming. Cases like this can take years to wrap up. You know that. Or you should. Though you've been pretty damned lucky so far."

"I know." It wasn't just the thought of all those months of work going down the drain, it was the thought that Shipka's work on the Havemeyer case would go with them. Maybe not. Maybe Sam would solve that one too on his way to solving the Monet murders. It wasn't as comforting a thought as it should have been. Jason felt like he owed Shipka one.

That one, in particular.

* * * * *

Special Agent J.J. Russell barreled out of George's office as Jason was about to knock.

Russell glared at Jason, and swept past.

"What's his problem?" Jason asked, continuing into George's office.

George looked up, still rubbing his temples, and sighed. "Maybe I should have a revolving door put in."

"Is this a bad time?"

"Yes."

"I won't take long," Jason promised.

George shook his head in resignation, and pointed at one of the two chairs in front of his desk. "Let's hear it."

"I want to fly back to New York. If I fill out the travel request, could you sign it tonight?"

George cupped a hand to his right ear. "I think my hearing's going. I thought you said you wanted to fly *back* to New York."

"I do. Tomorrow morning, if I can't get a flight tonight."

"For the love of God, *why?*"

This was the tricky part. Jason did not want to lie to George, but no way in hell would telling the complete truth get him the permission he needed. "I discovered a short while ago that a witness crucial to my case is actually living in Watertown. He doesn't have a landline, and if he's got a cell phone number, I can't locate it. He doesn't seem to have an email address."

"Jason, you can't go flying back and forth across the country every time you want to interview someone. Send your questions to the New York office and let them handle the damned interview."

Jason resorted to entreaty. "My case is falling apart, George. This witness is my last shot at saving it. I can't trust this interview to anyone else."

"For God's sake, they've got *two* special agents on *their* ACT."

"I've got to look this guy in the eyes. Besides, you know how it is. Sometimes you don't even know what questions to ask until you've been talking to the witness for a while."

George looked doubtful as he studied Jason's face. He said in a fatherly tone, "Jason, you can't take every case this much to heart. I know you put a lot into Fletcher-Durrand, but if we don't get them this time around, we'll get them the next."

"One last shot," Jason pressed. "If the interview doesn't pan out, okay. But at least I know I gave it everything."

George studied him. He studied the file on his desk. He studied the framed photos of his wife and kids. He studied Jason again—and groaned. "I know I'm going to regret this. I can feel it in my bones. *Okay.*"

Jason just managed not to fist pump. "*Yes.* Thank you, George."

"*But.* This time you're taking a partner."

Jason's relief changed to wariness. "What? A partner? Who?"

George smiled an evil smile. "J.J. Russell."

"*Russell?*"

"Take it or leave it."

"Yeah, but *Russell?*"

"If you'd had a partner the last time, none of what happened to you would have happened. Correct?"

There was no arguing with that, and though George was too kind to say it aloud, they both knew that had Jason had a partner with him on Camden Island, Chris Shipka might still be alive.

Jason subsided. "Okay, you're right. But does it have to be Russell?"

"Yes, it has to be Russell. We're understaffed and you're both short a partner. Besides, I want him out of the office until he cools off." George's normally pleasant features were adamantine. "We'll call it a trade-off."

Jason grimaced. "If that's what it takes. Will you break the news to Russell or do I?"

"As tempting as the thought is, I'll tell him," George said. "Get the travel request form on my desk *before* five. I'm leaving on time tonight."

"…your sisters permission to throw you a party at Capo Restaurant? Because that seems to be the plan for your birthday, and I distinctly remember you saying you didn't want a fuss this year."

Jason could hear the cool, patrician tones of his mother's voice as he let himself in his front door. He set down his carryall, stepped over the pile of mail in front of the door, and grabbed for the phone.

"Hi, Mom."

"Jason dear. You're there. Good. Charlotte said you were out of town again." Ariadne Harley-West was known for three things: her impeccable breeding, her exquisite sense of style, and her superhuman ability to tune-out that which did not please her. The only time her superpowers had failed her was when she had found herself pregnant at forty-seven, having already raised—and successfully married off—two daughters.

She viewed Jason with slightly bemused, detached affection and had supervised his rearing with scrupulous attention to detail. Jason viewed her in much the same light, and tried to live up to familial expectation as the only son and heir.

"I just got in," Jason said. "I'm flying out again tomorrow morning. Yes, I did tell Sophie a very small, private party would maybe be okay."

"Ah." There was a volume of subtext in that contemplative syllable. "I haven't been consulted, but 'small and private' doesn't seem to have registered."

"Great."

"If you'd like me to have your father put the, er, *kibosh* on the whole affair—"

"No, that's okay. If it means that much to them. It's just a couple of hours."

"Very well, dear. How was your trip?"

Jason had no idea how to answer that. His mother considered all newspapers "tabloid," and rarely watched television. Even so, he was a little surprised she hadn't heard about his recent misadventures, if only because his father and sisters did pay close attention to world events. He had the increasingly concerned voice mails to prove it. But maybe Jason held for questioning in a murder investigation was one of the things his mother preferred to tune-out.

"Interesting," he answered.

They chatted briefly, which was typical of their conversations. Only when his mother was reminiscing about her father, Emerson Harley, did Jason feel like they really, truly communicated. Ariadne had idolized her father and believed he was the finest role model a boy could have.

"Please remember to be careful, dear," she said in parting.

"Always," Jason replied.

He hung up, gathered the mail from the floor and sorted it quickly. Happily, there were no additional communications from Dr. Jeremy Kyser. Everything else could wait. He made a mental note to find Kyser's previous cards to send Sam, but that could wait too.

He went to the fridge to see if there was anything still edible, and glumly considered a dozen eggs, a carton of half-and-half (soured), and a jar of tapas someone had sent him in a Christmas gift basket.

He was pouring the spoiled half-and-half down the sink when his cell phone rang.

The image of Harry Callahan glaring down his .44 Magnum popped up, and Jason answered. "Hey. I was just thinking about you."

"I figured. Jonnie tells me you're afraid we're going to yank your case out from under you." Sam sounded resigned.

Jason mentally consigned Jonnie to hell. "No. I know you're not interested in the fraud, larceny and forgery aspects of my case—which is falling apart anyway."

"Is it?"

"Yep," Jason tried to be stoic. "Pretty much. The Durrands are making noises like they're going to settle with the complainants. I have another victim, but she's been dragging her feet about actually filing charges, and now she's not answering my phone calls. Shipka told me there were other victims out there, but he wouldn't give me his source, so that avenue is also closed. At least for now."

"I'm sorry." Sam sounded sincere. "I know you worked your ass off on this one."

"Yeah, well. I know even solid cases can crumble. And I know that building a case like this can take years, and just because we couldn't nail Fletcher-Durrand this time doesn't mean we won't get them the next."

Sam said, "That's all true. It still hurts like hell when you have to shelve a case you've put your heart and soul into."

"Yeah." Sympathy from Sam somehow made it worse. "Have you heard from Detective O'Neill? He's not taking my calls."

Sam said gravely, "No? And you two hit it off so well. Yes, I've heard from O'Neill. What is it you want to know? The ME determined that Shipka was killed with an ax."

"An *ax*."

"Yes. Wielded by a right-handed assailant who was taller and considerably stronger than Shipka. Time of death was likely between one and four-thirty."

"Taller and considerably stronger than Shipka wouldn't be Shepherd or Barnaby. Is O'Neill still—"

"Looking at you? No. He's convinced you're hiding something, but he suspects it has to do with your investigation. Which irritates him all the more." Kennedy hesitated. "Look, if we do uncover anything that relates to your case, you'll have that evidence."

"Thanks. I know. Did they determine whether Shipka ever interviewed the Patricks? That might narrow down time of death."

"No. He did not interview the neighbors. It sounds like he never left the cottage after the two of you parted ways."

Jason opened his mouth to say something that might move the conversation into more personal channels, but Kennedy spoke first.

"That's not the only reason I called. I want to pick your brain about those paintings."

"Which paintings? The fake Monets?"

"That's right. What do you think of them?"

"It's funny you ask. I was looking at the photos of them right before I left the office. They're *really* bad."

"Which means what?" Kennedy sounded alert.

"Well, they're almost too bad to be real. What I mean is, they're bad, but they're still an accurate representation of Monet's technique. It's hard to explain. It takes a certain amount of skill—as well as knowledge—to be able to copy someone else's style. But then the execution is terrible. Almost too terrible."

How do you mean?

"Deliberately terrible," Jason said. "Like a caricature. Like someone painted them as a joke. Except for the fact that they represent murder scenes."

"Yeah." There was satisfaction in Kennedy's tone. "That's what I hoped you'd say. That's what I hoped you'd see."

"There's a sense of humor at work, but it's…malevolent."

"A malevolent sense of humor." Kennedy seemed to be turning the words over in his mind. "Yes. That syncs."

Did it?

Jason said slowly, "You think these paintings were intended to throw you off the trail."

"That's good, West. Yes. Something like that. I think we're meant to interpret those paintings as the outward expression of a violently deranged mind—the signature of a classic serial killer. But, in fact, I believe they're a distraction devised by a cold, calculating and absolutely methodical brain. The paintings are intended to obscure what's really going on."

"What's really going on?" Jason considered. "The victims were all connected to Fletcher-Durrand, so…you're saying there is no serial killer? The Monets were painted to disguise the real motive behind these murders?"

"Oh, there's a serial killer. He's pretending to be a different kind of serial killer, that's all. And that's pretty fucking clever, even for your average sociopath."

Jason said, "That's why you think Shipka was killed by your unsub. It doesn't matter that the MO doesn't match. The MO was always stagecraft."

"Exactly. That's exactly right."

Which was kind of terrifying, really. Because the murderous rage expended on Shipka had been the real thing, the real face of this unsub. Ruthless, reckless, relentless.

"Who are you looking at?" Jason asked.

Sam did not answer directly. "Do you think Barnaby or Shepherd Durrand could have painted those Monets?"

"Barnaby attended Cooper Union. I'm not aware he ever did any real painting. He may be a closet artist. Shepherd did not attend art school. He went to USC and majored in business. I've never heard anyone mention he painted."

"I see."

"It might be Shepherd's sense of humor," Jason said slowly. "Not Barnaby's."

Sam made another of those noncommittal noises.

Jason waited.

Sure enough, after a moment or two Sam asked, "What did you make of Bramwell Stockton?"

"Who?"

"The owner of the boat rental place. Seaport Sloops."

That seemed straight out of left field. "Bram? I didn't really think much about him."

"No? I felt like he was making an effort to insert himself into the investigation. He was just a little too interested. A little too interested in serial killers, in general. Also, he went out of his way to throw suspicion on his neighbor, Eric Greenleaf."

Jason said, "Maybe he thinks Greenleaf is the most likely candidate. By all accounts—including my own—Greenleaf's a strange guy."

"Maybe," Sam agreed. "I had Jonnie do some checking on Stockton. He travels around the country quite a bit to do repairs on antique and classic boats."

Okay, that was starting to sound like maybe the beginning of a case against Mr. Seaport Sloops. Still. *Bram*? Jason was willing to bow to Sam's experience, but personally, he hadn't picked up any particularly hinky vibes. On the other hand, if he'd learned anything from Kennedy, it was that the image of a serial killer as a weird and isolated loner was a myth propagated by the media. An alarming number of serial offenders were completely integrated into their community, even pillars of that community.

Jason asked, "Is he an amateur painter as well?"

"Unknown. We're still fine-combing Stockton's background. Anyway," Sam's tone changed, grew brisk. "They're calling my flight."

Was he ever *not* flying somewhere?

"Right," Jason said. He wanted to ask, well, a lot of things—none of them relevant to what was on Sam's mind. He was very conscious of everything Sam had said in Cape Vincent about being a distraction and always having to come second, so he said with equal briskness, "Safe travels."

There was a funny hesitation, while both of them waited for the other to hang-up.

Sam said, "I'll call you tomorrow," and disconnected.

Chapter Twenty-Three

If planes came equipped with ejector seats, Jason would have pressed the button on Special Agent J.J. Russell somewhere over Nevada.

Russell was smart and ambitious. Also, tall, dark and good-looking. Just the way Sam liked them, though he had not liked Russell.

Jason had never liked the guy either, and he was pretty sure that by the time they reached Watertown, he would actively hate him. Russell probably felt the same, but he had to vent to someone, and Jason was the only one around.

Some of it, Jason sympathized with. Having to catch a six-a.m. flight on a Saturday morning was not anyone's idea of a good time. Russell had had a rough week. He needed a day off. Clearly. The rest of it…Jason knew Sam was not universally beloved, but listening to Russell bitch about what an arrogant, smug, pompous prick he was tested his patience.

He said finally, mildly, "Really? I kind of enjoyed working with him." Was eight-thirty in the morning too early to order a Kamikaze? It was eleven-thirty New York time. True, they were still five hours away from New York.

"Why not? You got a commendation out of it," Russell said bitterly. "And so will Darling although he's the biggest screw-up I ever worked with." He was off and running once more.

Jason checked his messages and did his best to ignore the diatribe next door. He'd have preferred the screaming baby four rows back as a traveling companion.

Lux was still not returning his phone calls. Jason sighed. Something was up with the kid. Meanwhile, he and Stripes were still playing phone tag. Did it matter now? It seemed like Sam would be wrapping up his case any minute. He was not asking for any additional info or follow-up from Jason.

In fact, this trip to interview Rodney Berguan was probably unnecessary. A waste of taxpayer time and money as Jason tried to expunge his guilt over what had happened to Shipka? Jonnie had phoned to let him know Sam had arranged for an Evidence Response Team to examine the three graveyards on Camden Island.

"If your missing art student is there, we'll find him," she promised.

If Paris Havemeyer belonged to anyone, it was Chris Shipka, but Jason understood from Jonnie's conciliatory tone that this was another gesture from Sam. Reassurance that he was not forgetting the work Jason had already put in. Not that Jason had thought he would. Sam had his own reasons for wanting Havemeyer's body found on that island.

"I'm a team player," Russell was saying. "What's good for the team is good for all the players. But what's good for all the players is not necessarily good for the team..."

Yeah, whatever. Blah, blah, blah. Russell was still so green, he had moss between his ears.

There were several returned calls relating to various other cases, a couple of texts from his sisters regarding birthday party details he did not want to know about, and a message from Hickok.

"Just giving you a heads-up." Hickok's normally jovial tone was flat. "No word yet on where Doody might have disappeared to, but I just learned Shepherd Durrand left for Paris last night. One way ticket."

* * * * *

Though it was three forty-five in the afternoon by the time they landed on his doorstep, Rodney Berguan was not dressed for receiving visitors. He answered the door in a silky green paisley dressing gown, sagging white briefs, and tennis socks.

Berguan looked Jason and Russell up and down, propped a freckled hand on his hip, and drawled, "Whatever church you're selling, sign me up, boys. Hallelujah!"

He was older than Jason expected. Closer to sixty than forty, and he looked like he'd had a tough life, though it didn't seem to have dampened his spirits any.

Jason and Russell showed their creds and Berguan seemed astonished and flattered that it was no mistake. They were, in fact, there to see him.

He led the way through a hoarder's paradise to a small, surprisingly cozy kitchen. A giant white Persian cat crouched on the table lapping liquid from a pink teacup. Berguan did not seem to notice, gesturing Jason and Russell to sit down.

After declining offers of coffee, tea, and, finally, gin and tonic, Jason was finally able to turn Berguan's attention to the night Paris Havemeyer had disappeared.

Berguan propped his chin in his palm and gazed dreamily into space. "Sure, I remember. Klaus and I were ready to call it a night, but the kid still wanted to party."

"Klaus?" Jason asked quickly. Was this a new player?

"Don." Berguan winked at him. "I used to call him Klaus. He liked it."

Jason didn't dare look at Russell, but he could hear what he was thinking. "Why did Havemeyer leave the party at the gallery, if he wasn't ready to go home?"

"Who knows." Berguan thought it over. "I think Klaus dragged him out. The kid was, well, a little the worse for wear. If you know what I mean. We all were, but he was a goer. And...sometimes those after-party parties could get a little rough."

"A little rough how?"

Berguan made an AC/DC gesture.

"I'm not sure what that means," Jason said.

Berguan's brows shot up. "You really *are* a choir boy!"

"No, I mean in this particular context."

"Have you ever met Shepherd Durrand?"

"Yes."

"Then you should understand. Shep could be very charming. And he could be the cruelest motherfucker you ever wanted to avoid meeting. He liked his boys bruised and bloody, and that's not an exaggeration. There were the things we saw and rumors of things nobody was meant to see. Klaus was crazy about Shepherd, but I think he felt a little loyalty to a fellow countryman." Berguan laughed and shook his head. "But you can't protect someone who doesn't want to be protected."

"You think Havemeyer went back to the gallery after you and Kerk let him off at his apartment?"

"No."

"No?"

Berguan shook his head. He picked his teacup up and sipped. Jason glanced at Russell. He was holding the white Persian. The front of his suit-coat was covered in white fur. His expression was that of one suffering the tortures of the damned. He glared at Jason.

Berguan said finally, "I can't see that it matters now. Especially if Klaus is dead." He set his teacup down. "No. It wouldn't have happened at the gallery. I know the police searched the gallery, but that was a waste of time. He'd have sent the car."

"The car? Which car?" Jason asked. "Who would have sent the car?"

"Back then, he had a 1950s maroon Daimler," Berguan said. "He loved that car. Loved swanning around in it. He had—"

"*Who?*" Jason demanded.

Berguan looked taken aback. "Shepherd. That's who we're talking about, isn't it? He used to send that car for his conquests. Send the car and his driver to pick them up. They'd go back to his apartment, or, if they were someone he considered really special, he'd take them out to the island. Have you been to that island?"

"Yes."

"Back then we used to call it Fantasy Island." Berguan shuddered. "It's like one giant graveyard." He leaned over to the cat and said, "Would you like more tea, sweetie?"

The cat closed its eyes and began to purr.

Jason said, "You think Shepherd took the Havemeyer kid to Camden Island?"

"Yep."

"Why didn't you report that to the police?"

Berguan sat up straight. "Klaus. He was adamant it couldn't be true. And I didn't have any proof. It would have been my word against theirs—and against Klaus's. The Durrands were important people. Still are. And I'm…me."

"Did Havemeyer say anything to indicate he believed Shepherd was coming for him?"

"I don't know. I don't remember that. He was giggling, silly, stoned. He was acting like someone with a special secret. You know how it is."

Jason remembered being nineteen. He thought about the police report Berguan had filed with Kerk. "The last time you saw Havemeyer, was he going into his apartment or headed toward the street?"

"He was just standing on the front steps, waving goodbye to us."

So really…nothing tangible. No actual proof of anything.

Watching him, Berguan said suddenly, "I'll tell you why I thought Shepherd must have done it. As our taxi was turning the corner, I glanced back and I thought I saw that big maroon Daimler gliding up the street toward Havemeyer's place. I even told Klaus. It seemed kind of funny at the time." Berguan shrugged. "Not so funny later. But I couldn't have sworn to it, you see. I wasn't sure what I saw. Not sure enough to get up in court."

Jason nodded.

"Suspecting what you did, can I ask why you moved here, sir? So close to the Durrands?"

Berguan frowned. "They're not the *mafia*, for God's sake. They're not the *CIA*. My *mother* lives next door. She's lived in this town her entire life. I grew up here."

Sometimes it really was that simple.

Russell put the cat down and gave him a pointed look. Jason nodded, and rose. But memory niggled at him. There had been something, a point he meant to follow up on. What?

It came to him. "The driver. You said Shepherd would send the car and a driver for his conquests?"

Berguan was tying his robe shut in a belated attempt at modesty. "Yep. He had a chauffeur. Well, really, it was only that cousin of his. What a weirdo *he* was. Another art student, of course. We were all art students back then. He had that Peter Frampton Botticelli angel hair. Twenty years too late, I might add."

"His *cousin?*" Jason asked sharply. "What was the cousin's name?"

"The cousin? Let me think. They had a love-hate relationship, those two. Of course, the Durrands were the ones with all the money. Not the recipe for domestic bliss, let me tell you. Aaron, was it? No. *Eric.* That's it. I remember because his family lived on that island too, and I thought the name was appropriate. Greenleaf. Eric Greenleaf."

* * * * *

Sam's calls were going straight to message.

Jesus Christ. He was always on the phone, why the hell was he not picking up?

Jason tried again, and this time left a terse message. "Call me. It's urgent. *Please* call me."

"What the hell are we supposed to do in Cape Vincent?" Russell was asking, over the prim voice of the GPS.

"Just drive."

The rental car swerved. "You're not my boss, West. You don't get to give me sweeping commands like you're goddamned Sam Kennedy."

Jason barely heard, busy phoning Jonnie.

Please pick up. God. God. Please. Pick up the fucking phone, Jonnie.

"Hey," Jonnie said cheerfully. "What's up?"

"Where are you? Are you with Sam?"

"Um, no. I'm back in Virginia. I'm having lunch with my darling husband on my day off."

"That Evidence Response Team. Are they on the island now? Is Sam with them?"

"Yes. They should be on the island by now. Why?" Jonnie's voice grew concerned. "What's wrong?"

"Eric Greenleaf is the unsub."

"Who?"

"Sam's not answering my calls. Can you try to get hold of him? Can you tell him, his unsub is Eric Greenleaf. He's a neighbor and cousin of the Durrands. Sam will know who I mean."

"Jason." Jonnie made a faint sound of exasperation. "Our guy is Bram Stockton. He owns a boat rental and repair service. Sam and I—"

"*No*. I'm telling you, it's *not* Stockton. It's Greenleaf. You've got to take my word for it. I worked this too, and *this* is where our cases intersect. The unsub is Greenleaf, and he's a raving psychopath. He's probably got an arsenal of weapons in that castle of his, and he's crazy enough to try to take out the entire ERT."

Jonnie was silent for a moment. "Okay. I'll see if I can get hold of Sam. He said cell phone reception is sketchy out there."

The relief was huge. And fleeting. Even with Jonnie's buy-in, there was no guarantee of reinforcements reaching the island in time. Jason said, "It *is* sketchy. I'm calling the Jefferson County Sheriff's Department now."

"Where are you?"

"Russell and I are on our way to Cape Vincent. We'll try to get a boat out to the island."

"We'll *what*?" Russell threw alarmed looks Jason's way. "What did you say?"

"All right. I'm on it. I'll get hold of somebody on that island," Jonnie said. "Be careful out there."

Jason clicked off and tried ringing the Jefferson County Sheriff's Department.

"We're going out to that island?" Russell asked. "Are you kidding?"

Pick up. Will you please pick up?

"Are you listening to me, West?"

Detective O'Neill was also not taking Jason's phone calls.

"Look, Agent West, he's in the middle of an interrogation right now. He'll call you back," the desk sergeant told Jason. He sounded defensive. Jason had made quite an impression on the Jefferson County SD.

"It can't wait," Jason insisted. "This is a matter of life or death. And by the way, if he's interviewing Bram Stockton, that interview can wait. He's got the wrong guy."

"Not according to your boss, he doesn't. Your boss is why we brought Stockton in."

"Look, please. I'm not exaggerating. This is life or death. I've got to talk to O'Neill. There is the very real threat of an active shooter incident on that island."

Russell said, "Goddamn, West. If you're wrong about this, it's your job. And maybe mine too."

After some background commotion, Detective O'Neill came on the line.

"Special Agent, West? What do you mean we've got an active shooter on Camden Island?"

Jason drew in a breath. This had to be concise and to the point because he could feel O'Neill dying for an excuse to hang-up on him. "Eric Greenleaf is your unsub. Your perp. He helped Shepherd Durrand abduct and murder a German art student in 1998. And I doubt if that art student was the only victim. In fact, I know he wasn't. A young man by the name of Marco Poveda filed charges against Durrand the year before the Havemeyer kid disappeared. I believe Greenleaf has been part of some kind of ongoing art forgery scam with Durrand, and when it looked like Chris Shipka was getting close to uncovering their operation, he murdered him."

"What the hell…" O'Neill sounded winded. "You've got proof of all this?"

No way was there time for *that* explanation. Jason rushed on. "There's an FBI Evidence Recovery Team on that island right now searching for Havemeyer's body."

"I know that. *They've* gone through the proper channels, and we've been cooper—"

"If you know anything about Greenleaf at all, and I'm guessing you must, you have to know that's going to create an extremely volatile situation. If Greenleaf was willing to attack Chris Shipka, possibly in broad daylight, I believe he's crazy enough to open fire on that team. If he feels he's got nothing left to lose…"

There was a short, sharp silence on the other end of the phone.

"You know what," Detective O'Neill said. "This is one time I think you could be right."

Chapter Twenty-Four

"Are you sure this is a good idea," Daisy was saying uneasily, as they rounded the point and headed toward the old dock and ruined boat houses behind Camden Castle.

"No." Russell soberly checked his weapon. He swore as spray shot up, hitting him in the face. The bow of the boat crashed down in the gray-blue water. The water was rough. A storm was blowing in from Canada. And probably not the only one.

Jason had already checked his weapon three times. It was compulsive. A tic he had developed after the shooting in Miami. Even though his being shot had absolutely nothing to do with the state of his own weapon.

"He may not recognize the ERT for what it is," Jason said. He was trying to convince himself of this scenario. "He may mistake them for crime scene personnel following up on Shipka's murder. He may still be holed up in his lair. That would be the best-case scenario. In that case, we can just hold him in place and wait for reinforcements."

Russell shot him a look of disbelief. "With FBI initials plastered all over their jackets and gear?"

Oh yeah. That.

"Patrol boats coming in from the west," Daisy reported, shading her eyes. "The island will be crawling with cops before long."

"Thank God for that," Russell muttered, and Jason silently agreed.

He had still received no response from Sam. No word from Jonnie either. It worried him, even though he knew reception could be tricky on the island. There was no sound of gunfire drifting from the interior, so that was a good sign. Shots would carry on a day like this.

In fact, the silence was almost eerie.

"Greenleaf must have a boat?" Jason asked Daisy, to distract himself.

She nodded. "He keeps it in the skiff house." She pointed at the large, green and white building coming up on their port side.

As the wind-scoured shoreline grew closer, Daisy said, "I don't know if that dock is safe. It's liable to collapse under you."

"Bring us in as close as you can," Jason said. "We'll swim the rest of the way."

Russell gaped at him. "Uh no, Rambo. I'll take my chances with the dock, if you don't mind."

In the end, with some skilled seamanship on Daisy's part, they managed to dock and disembark safely.

"Should I wait for you?" Daisy called, as Jason and Russell pulled their weapons and jogged down the splintered wooded walkway.

"No," Jason called back. "Stay safe. Get back to the marina."

She waved acknowledgment, and gunned the motor.

It took Jason and Russell four nerve-wracking minutes to cross the rocky beach of the small harbor and scramble up the winter-bare hillside to the back of the ruined mansion. They stuck to cover where they could, but there was not much of it. A few boulders, the occasional evergreen. It was more a test of nerve than endurance. Every minute Jason expected to hear a shot ring out.

The absolute silence was equally unnerving.

They reached the back of the castle, breathing hard but apparently undetected.

"Are you sure someone lives here?" Russell whispered, wiping his forehead.

Today no smoke drifted from any of the chimneys. No laundry hung in the side courtyard. There was no sign of life at all.

Maybe Shepherd wasn't the only one who had suddenly decided a vacation might be just the thing. Maybe Greenleaf had also come to the conclusion things at home were getting a little too hot.

"He did four days ago."

Russell tiptoed across a small patio and signed he would circle around the west wing of the house.

Jason nodded.

Russell began to move along the rear of the building, dropping down when he came to the first set of windows. Jason turned and started down the stone walkway, past the double tier of the garden's retaining walls, until he came to the wide flight of steps leading to the terrace and the clock tower.

He glanced back, but Russell was now out of sight.

Back to the wall, pistol at high ready, Jason sidled up the steps, freezing when he heard the whispered crunch of dead leaves. Someone was quietly making their way across the terrace toward him. It couldn't be Russell. Not that fast.

Jason's heart rocketed in his chest, but that was adrenaline, not fear. Okay, maybe a little fear. He had a healthy respect for Greenleaf and his trusty ax.

He made it to the top of the stairs, listening hard.

The footsteps had stopped. Was this other listening as well?

Sweat prickled his hairline, trickled down his spine. He bent down, felt for a pebble, and pitched it into the dead brush over the wall. For a small stone, it created a satisfying crash as it went down through the dead branches and leaves.

He heard the scrape of footsteps moving toward the end of the terrace, and came around the side of the clock tower, pistol leveled—only to find himself staring down the barrel of a Glock 19.

For a split second, his brain straight-lined, though the hand holding his own weapon, never wavered. *Squeeze trigger... don't squeeze trigger...* He was processing, deciding, recognizing that he had already taken too long. Suddenly the face in front of him came into sharp focus.

Sam.

"*Jason?*" Sam exclaimed in disbelief, lowering his pistol. His eyes looked black in his white face.

"*Sam?*" Until he saw Sam in front of him, alive and perfectly unharmed, Jason hadn't realized how worried he'd been. Relief left him almost shaky.

"What the hell are you doing here?" Sam demanded. He glanced around as though expecting to see reinforcements—or maybe a magic carpet. "How did you get here?"

"Didn't Jonnie get hold of you?"

Sam shook his head. "The cell phone reception is shit out here. I haven't been able to call out since we arrived. What's going on? Why are you here?"

"Eric Greenleaf is your unsub."

An odd expression crossed Sam's face. He did not look as surprised as he should have. In fact, he almost looked like Jason's words had just confirmed something for him. "Is he?" he said softly.

He moved toward Jason, hustling him back toward the cover of the stairs. "Good to know, because that asshole's around here somewhere. I spotted him scoping us while we were processing the tribal burial grounds. And by scoping, I mean he had a rifle. I thought it might be a good idea to see what he was up to, and tracked him back here. He disappeared before he reached the house."

Jason's heart dropped. "Disappeared?"

Sam nodded somberly.

"The sheriffs were landing about the time we arrived," Jason said. "They're using the dock by the lodge as a staging point."

"We?"

"J.J. Russell is with me."

Sam's brows shot up. He opened his mouth, but then staggered back. Jason only then registered that loud, terrifying bang, which seemed to echo around the stone turrets and towers. Blindly, Sam reached for the wall behind him, dropping his weapon. His other hand went to his forehead, coming away covered in blood. He sat down heavily on the low wall and slowly, slowly sagged backwards.

Jason's heart stopped. He couldn't seem to make sense of what he was seeing. He wheeled, bringing his weapon up and firing, as Eric Greenleaf strode down the terrace toward him, also firing. His shot went wide.

Jason's shot grazed Greenleaf across the ribs, but didn't seem to stop him at all. Greenleaf shot again, and for the second time missed Jason.

Everything was happening so fast. Too fast to process. And yet, weirdly, it felt like slow motion. It was like an alternate reality. There was no conscious thought. Jason could only rely on training and instinct.

"*FBI, halt.*" Russell was coming up on Greenleaf from behind. He fired, and he *must* have hit Greenleaf, because Greenleaf jerked and stopped. But maybe it was a glancing shot, or maybe Greenleaf was pumped up on adrenaline and chemical substances. He whirled, firing at Russell, who dived for cover.

There were more voices. More shots. More people. It was chaos. The air was sharp with the smell of gun smoke and approaching rain. Birds darted in and out of the clock tower, crying their alarm.

Jason spared a quick look back at Sam, and saw to his horror that Sam had gone over the wall. Over the wall and into the water.

All thought seemed to stop there. Jason leveled his pistol and this time shot Greenleaf squarely in the chest. It didn't faze him.

He's wearing a goddamned vest.

Greenleaf pointed his rifle at Jason again. Jason had two options. He went over the wall after Sam. Greenleaf's shot just missed his ear. He heard it whine past, felt the burn of it against his cheek, and then he was tumbling through the sky, falling through the skeleton fingertips of dead trees. He saw blue water rushing toward him.

How the hell far? More than twenty feet? Shit. Jason did his best to straighten into vertical position, closed his eyes, squeezed his feet together, clenched his buttocks and crossed his hands across his crotch. He hit the water like an arrow slicing through, remembering belatedly to breathe out. The cold was a shock, and seemed to freeze his lungs for an instant. He spread his arms and legs wide to slow his descent. His bulky jacket made his movements difficult, slow.

Thank God for his lifeguard training. Thank God for a lifetime spent in the water.

He opened his eyes and saw a streak of silver carve a trail through the water in front of him—and then another.

Greenleaf was firing into the water.

That bastard just didn't give up.

Where the hell was Sam? Had he ended up in the trees or landed in the water? Jason peered through the murky water and another stream of silver bubbled past his nose.

Russell, will you please *kill that bastard?*

His lungs were starting to burn with the need to breathe. He looked this way and that, feeling something close to panic with each passing second.

Where is he?

His heart thudded in his ears. There. A few yards ahead of him. Something pale and bulky drifting slowly down through the layers of water. Jason's heart jumped in hopeful recognition. With a burst of renewed energy, he kicked toward the object, and saw with relief that it was Sam.

He couldn't see Sam's face. His pale hair drifted slowly, languidly like sea grass. His fingers were lax, motionless.

Jason wrapped an arm across Sam's chest—these jackets were going to drown them both—and began a clumsy sidestroke to the surface. Sam was a heavy and helpless weight, and Jason knew there was a very good chance they were both going to drown.

He hung on with all his strength and kept swimming, refusing to breathe. Every cell in his body was screaming for oxygen. His vision darkened on the outer edges. No more bullets churning past, so that was the good news.

Jason looked up, saw daylight overhead and clawed for it with his free hand. He kicked hard, scooped water, stretched... His head broke surface and he gulped in enormous sweet lungfuls of air.

Gasping, treading water, he looked around to see how far they had drifted from the point. Not that far, but getting ashore would be tricky.

No more gunshots. He looked toward the castle, but couldn't see what was happening behind the terrace walls.

Keeping Sam locked in a cross-chest hold, Jason tried to see if he was breathing. Sam's eyes were closed. His lashes looked dark against the pallor of his face. The water had washed the blood away, but scarlet continued to well from the crease across Sam's scalp. A crease, not a hole. The wound didn't look that deep, in the opinion of someone who'd been shot three times, but head wounds were tricky.

A wave sloshed over them, and Jason kicked to keep them both afloat. The sound of a boat's motor was like the answer to a prayer.

Jason turned, still treading water, and spotted Daisy on slow approach. He waved to her—he didn't have the breath left to yell--and she waved vigorously back.

The boat put-putted toward them. "I thought I better hang around," Daisy called, after killing the boat's engine. "I saw you go off that terrace."

"Thank God you did."

"Yeah, it's my lot in life to rescue handsome men from this island." She was grinning as she threw Jason an orange ring buoy.

Together they managed to haul Sam's sodden body onto the boat.

"Is he breathing?" Daisy asked, as Jason rolled Sam onto his side, and bent over him.

Jason listened tensely, but he didn't need to. Sam's chest was rising and falling in perfect relaxed rhythm, like he fell into rivers every day.

He sat back on his heels, wiping his face. It wasn't all river water, though he was about as cold and wet as he could ever remember being in his life.

"Oops," Daisy said. "Look at that. That lucky bastard's still alive."

Jason looked down, and Sam's eyes were open. So blue. Bluer than the St. Lawrence. Bluer than the sky. Bluer than once-in-a-blue-moon. He frowned at Jason and then a funny smile crossed his face.

"Don't I know you?" Sam whispered.

Jason bent down, and Daisy murmured, "Oh my. You will by the end of *that* kiss."

* * * * *

"Hey," George was saying, "I'm his supervisor, and I *still* don't know what the hell was going on out there."

Everyone within earshot at the table laughed. That was more about the quantity and quality of the alcohol being served. One thing about Sophie and Charlie. They knew how to throw a birthday party.

George raised his glass in a semi-toast to Jason. Five days earlier he had not been so amused.

You told me you were interviewing a witness in your forgery case. You never said a damned thing about a witness to a homicide cold case!

True, the cases had turned out to be one in the same, and saving the life of a BAU Chief did go some way to mitigating Jason's transgressions. He would play hell getting permission to travel anytime soon, though.

Russell, who had been the one to finally nail Greenleaf, had come out of the incident on Camden Island with a commendation, which Jason found funny. Less funny was the news he and Russell were to be permanently partnered.

Anyway. Though Jason's case had flatlined, the BAU had their man. When Eric Greenleaf had learned Shepherd Durrand was on the run, he had started talking, and as far as Jason understood, had not shut up yet.

Greenleaf admitted to killing Earnst, Lapham, and Kerk, but claimed it was under duress from Shepherd, who had feared their multi-million-dollar forgery scheme was about to come crashing down on them. He adamantly denied killing Havemeyer, whose body had been discovered in the Native American burial ground on Camden Island. That, he insisted, was all Shepherd's doing. Yes, he had been working as a chauffeur for his cousin at the time, but had not been present when Havemeyer—a willing victim, by his account—had met his accidental death at the hands of Shepherd during some rough sex play.

Greenleaf had admitted to killing Shipka, but claimed it had happened during a mental blackout. He had no recollection of the crime itself. He stated that after learning Shipka was back on the island and re-interviewing neighbors, he had snapped. He had gone to see Shipka in a panic, just to talk. After realizing Shipka was dead, he had taken his laptop and thrown it in the river.

"It's all bullshit," Sam had told Jason. "This guy is nobody's puppet. Besides, who goes for a chat while carrying an ax? The Havemeyer kid died from a bullet to the back of his skull. Greenleaf killed them all, and he enjoyed killing them. But this is where we start. We work from here, negotiating for each piece of the truth."

Greenleaf admitted to painting the fake Monets—had seemed proud of them—but again insisted the paintings had been Shepherd's idea, an attempt—as Sam had speculated—to trick law enforcement into believing they were dealing with a deranged serial killer.

"Which we were—and are," Sam had commented.

Sam had been meticulous about keeping Jason informed on everything they learned from Greenleaf, but very little of it helped Jason's investigation. Greenleaf insisted he had not painted the forgeries sold by the Durrands, insisted he did not know who *had* painted them, and—this had been the real death blow to Jason's investigation—insisted Barnaby had nothing to do with any of it. His animosity was all directed at Shepherd, his partner, sometimes pal, and co-conspirator. The fact that Shepherd had fled the country, hadn't endeared him either. Greenleaf was eagerly cooperating with the Bureau's attempts to locate the fugitive.

"Barnaby had to suspect," Jason protested. "How could he not know what was going on?"

"Maybe he did suspect," Sam said. "Maybe he didn't want to know."

Yes. That, Jason could believe. He remembered Barnaby's shock at learning Kerk was dead.

"Why did Greenleaf kill Kerk?" Jason asked Sam. "Why now?"

"It sounds like enough time had passed that even Kerk, loyal friend that he was, started to question what did happen to Paris Havemeyer. Probably thanks to Chris Shipka, who kept trying to interview him. He brought the subject up at lunch with Barnaby and Shepherd, and it sounds like Shepherd phoned Greenleaf to tell him they had a problem."

"Greenleaf met Kerk for lunch on the Friday that Kerk died?" Jason guessed.

"Yep. That's how it sounds. He followed Kerk back to his hotel, maybe even arranged to meet him later near the pier."

"But the painting of the body in the water. That was already cured. He'd have had to finish that before he ever knew Kerk was in the country."

Sam said, "I think that painting was originally intended for someone else. I'm guessing your investigation was getting a little too hot for comfort, and Durrand and Greenleaf had decided to fold up their operation, which necessitated getting rid of a couple of loose ends."

"Rabab Doody," Jason said. "That's why he took off so suddenly."

"We won't know until we talk to Mr. Doody, but that would be my guess."

To be continued.

That was the way it went sometimes. Jason's investigation was at a standstill, at least temporarily, and Sam was busy preparing his case for eventual trial.

They'd had a nice, but all too brief, evening together in Cape Vincent while Sam rested and recovered from his ordeal, but by noon the next day they were both catching planes to opposite sides of the country.

Until the next time.

It was tough, no question. But Jason had signed on with eyes wide open. He missed Sam. He missed him every day. And he would have to get used to missing him. Because Sam had made no promises, and did not appear to have plans to be on Jason's side of the world anytime soon.

In the meantime, Charlotte was right. Alexander, the newly-single art professor from UCLA, was a keeper. Not for Jason, but for someone. Alex was smart, funny, personable and very cute. He had curly blond hair, blue eyes, and a wicked grin.

"Would you like to go out sometime?" he asked Jason, when they happened to meet up at the bar for the third time.

"I'm kind of seeing someone," Jason had said regretfully. And he did regret it, because if not for Sam, he'd have definitely been interested in getting to know Alexander better.

Alexander looked surprised to hear it, and slightly disappointed. He'd smiled nicely, a good sport. A nice guy.

Jason was on his way back to his table when his cell phone rang.

Harry Callahan flashed up, and Jason answered.

"Hi!"

Sam said, "I'm out in the lobby. They're telling me this is an invitation only event."

"You're...where?" Jason held the phone closer to his ear. It was noisy in the room, and he was pretty sure he had not heard correctly.

"The lobby. The reception area." Sam was curt. "Capo Restaurant. Right?"

"Uh, yeah." Jason was already making his way through the crowded banquet room, heading swiftly for the lobby. "You're here?"

Yes. Sam was there. Taller than everyone else in the room. In his black power suit and gray tie, he looked a little forbidding for someone on his way to a birthday party. But he spotted Jason, and his face relaxed. Though he still looked ever so slightly self-conscious.

"Hey," Jason said, reaching him at last. "You're here." He was thrilled, but also amazed.

"Yes."

"I thought you didn't do birthdays."

Sam's mouth twisted. "It seems I do *occasionally* do birthdays."

Jason laughed. "I'm flattered. But before you walk in there, you should know half the LA field office is here. So, if you want to keep our friendship under wraps maybe we could meet up later."

Sam snorted. "I can take a little office gossip, if you can."

Jason stared at him. Sam met his gaze calmly. "It's not a problem for me," he said, and being Sam, that was probably true.

"Okay. Well, then. Let me introduce you to my—"

Sam put a hand on his arm. "Wait a minute."

Jason looked at him inquiry.

"I didn't have time to buy you a present."

"Your being here is the best present you could give me." That was the truth, and Jason wanted Sam to know it.

Sam's mouth gave another of those self-mocking quirks. "I do have something for you, though." He reached into his pocket and handed Jason something small and gold.

Jason stared down at Grandpa Harley's Tiffany cufflink. He looked at Sam. "It's mine. It's the one I lost."

"Yeah."

"Where did you find it?"

"In the hall outside Kerk's hotel room. I went back that night after the rest of you left."

"You've had it all this time?"

Sam shook his head, acknowledging the oddness of his behavior. "I know. I kept meaning to give it back to you, but…"

Jason was smiling, but puzzled. "But what?"

Sam hesitated. Said quietly, "I figured if I hung onto it, I'd always have an excuse to see you."

Jason's hands closed on the piece of metal, still warm from Sam's fingers. He could feel that glow all the way to his heart. He stared into Sam's blue gaze. "And now?"

Sam's hand tightened on Jason's arm. He drew Jason in and kissed him right there in the restaurant lobby. It was a surprisingly sweet brush of lips.

Sam said, "I don't need any more excuses."

The End

Watch for the return
of Jason West and Sam Kennedy in

THE MAGICIAN MURDERS
(THE ART OF MURDER BOOK II)

Coming Winter/Spring 2018

Author Notes

Thank you to the following people: L.B. Gregg, Keren Reed, Dianne Thies, Nicole Kimberling, and Ginn Hale. Your help was invaluable.

Those of you paying close attention will recognize that the events of *Winter Kill* quickly overtake Jason and Sam in *The Monet Murders*. Despite my best effort, the timeline did not *exactly* line-up—everything is off by one day. I realize this is a cruel and unusual punishment to inflict on my OCD readers, but I gently remind you that this is just a made-up story. (Or did that just make it worse?)

Two famous real life art world crimes inspired elements of this story: the M. Knoedler & Company art fraud scandal and the 1985 murder of Norwegian art student Eigil Dag Vesti.

About the Author

Bestselling author of over sixty titles of classic Male/Male fiction featuring twisty mystery, kickass adventure, and unapologetic man-on-man romance, JOSH LANYON has been called "arguably the single most influential voice in m/m romance today."

Her work has been translated into nine languages. The FBI thriller *Fair Game* was the first Male/Male title to be published by Harlequin Mondadori, the largest romance publisher in Italy. The Adrien English series was awarded the All Time Favorite Couple by the Goodreads M/M Romance Group. Josh is an Eppie Award winner, a four-time Lambda Literary Award finalist (twice for Gay Mystery), and the first ever recipient of the Goodreads All Time Favorite M/M Author award.

Josh is married and lives in Southern California.

Find other Josh Lanyon titles at www.joshlanyon.com
Follow Josh on Twitter, Facebook, and Goodreads.

Also by the Author

NOVELS

The ADRIEN ENGLISH Mysteries

Fatal Shadows

A Dangerous Thing

The Hell You Say

Death of a Pirate King

The Dark Tide

Stranger Things Have Happened

So This is Christmas

The HOLMES & MORIARITY Mysteries

Somebody Killed His Editor

All She Wrote

The Boy with the Painful Tattoo

The ALL'S FAIR Series

Fair Game

Fair Play

Fair Chance

The ART OF MURDER Series

The Mermaid Murders

The Monet Murders

OTHER NOVELS

The Ghost Wore Yellow Socks

Mexican Heat (with Laura Baumbach)

Strange Fortune

Come Unto These Yellow Sands

Stranger on the Shore

Winter Kill

Jefferson Blythe, Esquire

Murder in Pastel

The Curse of the Blue Scarab

NOVELLAS

The DANGEROUS GROUND Series

Dangerous Ground

Old Poison

Blood Heat

Dead Run

Kick Start

The I SPY Series

I Spy Something Bloody

I Spy Something Wicked

I Spy Something Christmas

The IN A DARK WOOD Series

In a Dark Wood

The Parting Glass

THE DARK HORSE SERIES

The Dark Horse

The White Knight

THE DOYLE & SPAIN SERIES

Snowball in Hell

THE HAUNTED HEART SERIES

Haunted Heart: Winter

THE XOXO FILES SERIES

Mummy Dearest

OTHER NOVELLAS

Cards on the Table

The Dark Farewell

The Darkling Thrush

This Rough Magic

The Dickens with Love

Don't Look Back

A Ghost of a Chance

Lovers and Other Strangers

Out of the Blue

A Vintage Affair

Lone Star (in *Men Under the Mistletoe*)

Green Glass Beads (in *Irregulars*)

Blood Red Butterfly

Everything I Know

Baby, It's Cold (in *Comfort and Joy*)

A Case of Christmas

Murder Between the Pages

SHORT STORIES

A Limited Engagement

The French Have a Word for It

In Sunshine or In Shadow

Until We Meet Once More

Icecapade (in His for the Holidays)

Perfect Day

Heart Trouble

In Plain Sight

Wedding Favors

Wizard's Moon

Night Watch

Fade to Black

Plenty of Fish

PETIT MORTS
(SWEET SPOT COLLECTION)

Other People's Weddings

Slings and Arrows

Sort of Stranger Than Fiction

Critic's Choice

Just Desserts

COLLECTIONS

Short Stories (Vol. 1)

Sweet Spot (the Petit Morts)

Merry Christmas, Darling
(Holiday Codas)

Christmas Waltz (Holiday Codas 2)

I Spy…Three Novellas

Point Blank (Five Dangerous
Ground Novellas)

Dark Horse, White Knight
(Two Novellas)